The Emerald Amulet

A novel

J.P. Cunningham

ISBN-10: 1466392789
ISBN-13: 9781466392786
Library of Congress Control Number: 2011918557
CreateSpace, North Charleston, South Carolina

This book is dedicated to María de los Angeles Villaseca—to Maja...best friend and wife now for more than three decades. Without Maja's patience, love and assistance, this book would not have been possible. Here's to at least thirty-five more years together.

J.P. Cunningham

I.

Young Eduardo grew accustomed to playing with Sean, a blond and blue-eyed, pale-skinned boy. The blond boy's father, Edwin O'Connor, had lived in his spacious, lavishly appointed home for decades. O'Connor owned mines nearby, where precious gems emerged from the rich mountains, after a great deal of coaxing from workers employed by his company. The blond boy's mother—Edwin's wife—had died giving birth to Sean. Edwin buried his wife and then proceeded to spoil young Sean terribly, feeling sorry for a boy growing up without a mother's love. Edwin showered his son with presents and fine clothes, often imported from the United States. He would have to travel north to the U.S. from time to time in order to maintain contact with bankers and equipment suppliers; to see about other investments in the States; to deal with importers of his emeralds; and then in turn to come home heavy-laden with lavish gifts for young master Sean. At first, the child was fascinated by each load of goodies accompanying his father. Eventually, Edwin began to realize that he might have overdone the gift-giving and the extravagant amount of attention paid to the child.

Eduardo, two years younger than Sean, was the son of one of the maids long-employed by Señor O'Connor. The maid's son had always been accepted by Don Edwin as a playmate for Sean. Eduardo's mother— a widow, raven-haired, brown-eyed, and with skin more deeply dark than she wanted it to be—was quiet, shy, hard-working and completely focused on loving and caring for her only child. Tall and dignified, she took great pride not only in her son's handsome appearance but also in his intelligence and good nature. As soon as Eduardo was old enough to understand, she explained to him why she seemed to be his only parent...explaining to the boy that his father, an Englishman, had died in a tragic accident before Eduardo's birth. She never delved into the subject of why the boy did not have an English surname and dreaded the day when she would have to explain never having been married by the Church. Eduardo had always been equally proud of his mother, proud of her beauty and of the confident way she carried herself even as she finished each day exhausted by the heavy work she always had to endure.

This one morning, as she began washing clothes, was not a school day, and so Eduardo and Sean joined forces after breakfast to go on "an expedition" into the jungle. Eduardo's mother bent over to give her nine-year-old little man a hug and warned him to take care while out in the forest. Without hugging the eleven-year-old Sean, she cautioned him warmly to be careful and to watch after the younger boy. Then she straightened the small backpack Sean had draped over his right shoulder. Duly dispatched, the two young adventurers took off down the path away from the large estate and into the forest.

The path narrowed and the incline increased as they continued. The sun shone brightly and heated up the morning. A dense canopy of treetops overhead filtered the sunlight, creating an intermittent pattern of shadow and flickering light as the boys hiked along the path. The undergrowth, too thick to penetrate in ages past, had long since been cleared away. It was a path to an abandoned mining site: a site left unattended now for generations. Edwin O'Connor knew how much boys liked to venture out, and kept the path cleared enough for anyone to be able to walk through the forest to enjoy it. He himself enjoyed wandering along the trail from time to time. Understanding the danger in allowing small boys to go out alone and unarmed, he generally sent an armed employee to follow them—skilled enough as a hunter to be able to follow without being noticed and yet close enough to be able to protect them with a rifle if needed. This one morning, this precaution was not taken.

Pretending that they were on a hunt for wild game, Sean carried a toy rifle and Eduardo carried a stick as his pretended weapon. Monkeys high in the trees raucously mocked the boys and their imagined skills as experienced hunters down on the ground below.

Early afternoon arrived. The boys felt hunger and stopped to sit and eat. They pulled out of the backpack the small rolls and cold meat and fruit packed for them by Eduardo's mother. They shared water from Sean's canteen and sat and talked about the size of the lion they had almost bagged along the way. In their minds, it was just as real as if the massive feline's foul breath had been close enough to feel and to smell. But, frightened by them, the lion had discreetly run away, escaping the threat of each boy's weapon and skill... or so they imagined.

The boys, having finished their snack, took off again along the path, climbing a steeper incline. Within an hour, having gone uphill and then downhill, they came to a cave that each had known about before. O'Connor had sternly advised them to avoid this cave, which had been the site of the original mining operation, begun by the earliest Spanish invaders of Colombia. Don Edwin had gone to great length to encourage them to fear this place, or at least to respect it, and with good reason. Many a grown man had ventured into it without managing to come out alive. Approaching the mouth of the cave and the small clearing in front of it, Sean slipped off his pack and sat on a rock. Eduardo, coming up close behind him, kneeled on one knee.

"Tired?" he asked.

"A little. It is a shame that we can't go into that cave, isn't it?"

"Not so much. It's big, old, dark and ugly. And you know your father has strictly forbidden us from going into it."

Sean glanced over wistfully. "He isn't here. Are you *afraid* to go in?"

"Yes! Of course. And you should be too. Now let's go. We should start walking back now so that we can be home before dark."

Sean sat looking into the darkness of the mouth of the cave. He got up and began tentatively to walk toward and then into it. "Sean! Come on. Don't be foolish. Let's go now. Let's go home."

Sean stood in the entrance to the ancient cavern, noting even there at its outer limits a distinctively stale musty odor. He looked inside and saw absolutely nothing, except for the black abyss glaring back at him. He turned toward Eduardo. "We have good flashlights and matches. Let's go only a little way into it to see what's inside."

"You're crazy. And I'm not. I'm going home."

"Coward! Come on. We have a candle for each of us for emergencies in my sack. And the flashlights are good. Let's see just a little."

Without waiting, Sean turned and pulled out his light and began surveying the walls and ceiling of the entrance of the cave. He looked and listened, confident that any perceived danger was nothing more than that...more imagined than real. Then he turned back toward Eduardo and beckoned him to follow. "Stop being so timid. Let's go."

Eduardo, knowing better and having far more common sense than the older Sean, nevertheless gave in and walked toward the cave entrance.

The two of them stood for a moment, looking at each other for reassurance, and then tentatively stepped forward.

Each, equally concerned about the ceiling, knew that at some point they would find bats hanging upside down, probably in great numbers. Each tread gently and did the best he could to study as much as possible of the inside of the cave.

The entranceway was surprisingly wide and inviting. Each boy had assumed that it would be narrow and cramped for a very long way, but it was not. The floor was level and relatively smooth and dry near the entrance. As they walked farther—careful to glance back in order to reassure themselves that some semblance of the light of day could still be seen from the entrance—they took short steps venturing forward.

Within four or five meters inside, the sound began to change. Stopping to listen carefully, the boys could hear water dripping somewhere in the distance and began to hear the astonishing absence of sound...a hollow emptiness deep within the cave.

Emboldened by the success of walking into a strictly forbidden and ominously forbidding place, the boys stopped again after walking a bit farther.

"Now are you happy?" Eduardo asked.

"Shh. Be still. We're fine so far. Come on."

Eduardo rolled his eyes in disgust and muttered to himself, "What an idiot." Not entirely sure who was the bigger fool, he followed Sean farther as the path beneath them began ever so slowly to slope downward, taking them deeper and lower into this long-ignored space.

As Eduardo looked back, he realized the traces of daylight from outside were now too far behind them to be seen. A large spider scampered across the floor ahead of them. Gradually the tunnel narrowed and began to curve to the right. He grabbed Sean's arm and pleaded, "Friend, we have to turn around and go home. It will be dark soon, before we can get home."

Ignoring his partner, Sean continued until they came to a "Y" with one path leading gently to the left and the second one leading more sharply to the right. Sean stopped, considering whether this was becoming more of an adventure than he had expected it to be. He stood and listened carefully. "You hear that?"

Eduardo, frightened by now, whispered back, "Hear what?"

"Shhhh. Listen."

Together each remained perfectly still and strained to hear any sound down either corridor. Eduardo thought he had noticed a sound coming from down the path to the right. "Hear it? There," said Sean pointing in that direction.

"Yes. I do. Now let's get out of here. It will not be difficult to turn back and to find our way out. I want to go home now."

Sean, still ignoring him, began walking slowly again. Eduardo, too afraid at this point to turn back, gave up and followed Sean. Several meters farther, the boys began hearing the sound of a human voice—a person humming some unfamiliar tune. And then as they stepped softly, trying not to be heard, the boys realized that there was a gentle glow up ahead. Eduardo, unable to restrain himself, whispered aggressively in Sean's ear, "How can you think it safe for us to surprise someone here in this place so far away from anyone we know?"

Sean considered that question for a second and finally answered, "Maybe you're right. Let's go." He turned quietly and followed Eduardo as they began heading back. Before they could have gone ten steps, a woman's voice called out to them from behind. Both boys froze, each young heart beating so frantically that it seemed as if each heart would be heard throughout the cavern. The voice persisted. "Boys. Boys, you're not going to leave without joining me, are you?"

Wanting to run as quickly as possible toward the entrance, each boy felt compelled to turn and look. There was something soothing about the sound of this woman's voice. Nothing at all seemed threatening in her tone or manner. Standing in the corridor and only partially illuminated, she looked white-haired and shriveled. She gestured for them to come toward her and toward the light. Without stopping to discuss it, and without hesitating to consider the advisability of what they were doing, each boy stepped nearer. She walked back down the corridor and turned into what appeared to be a side room or chamber.

As they followed her and approached the entrance to the room, the glow of the light became brighter. A pleasant aroma of something cooking scented the stale air of the cave, and they could hear the sound of an animal breathing. As they stepped into the entrance to the large chamber, lit by torchlight, with a fire in the center of the room and a bubbling and steaming pot suspended over it, they noticed a cage at the side of the room with a small wild cat inside, golden-colored with small black spots, and noticed the cat nervously pacing back and forth within the confines of the cage.

"Come in. And good welcome. There's nothing to be afraid of. I was expecting you," the old woman said as she shuffled awkwardly toward a small table on the side of the room. There were three bowls and spoons set up and ready to use. She took one of the bowls and walked toward the cooking pot and ladled steaming hot soup into each bowl. Then she sat, smiling, ready to eat with the two stunned boys.

For some strange reason, neither boy felt intimidated by the woman. Of course, if they had been older and wiser, they would not have followed her into her chamber in the first place, or for that matter, would not have first ventured into the forbidden cavern at all.

They watched the small wild cat pacing within its cage. The soup smelled enticing. She sat quietly, hands folded in front of her. Eduardo asked her, "Are you not going to eat?"

Looking surprised, she reached for her spoon and said, "Of course, I'm sorry. It's quite all right you know. Nothing to worry about." With that, she slipped her spoon into the broth and eagerly slurped it down. "It's very good. Try it."

By this time—completely convinced that this whole escapade was the most ridiculous situation he had ever gotten himself into and that it was almost certainly the silliest situation he would ever stumble into in the future—Eduardo reluctantly, albeit hungrily, ate his soup. Sean, seeing his younger friend brave enough to sample the steaming concoction, decided he might as well try it too.

Looking briefly at the old woman, who was seated, watchfully waiting for a verdict on the quality of her meal, Eduardo commented cheerfully, "It *is* good. Thank you."

Sean concurred. "It's delicious."

The old woman, obviously pleased by the compliments, began to enjoy her own serving.

Eduardo looked at her and stopped eating for a moment, asking, "You said you had been expecting us. How could that be?"

She continued eating but did say, "Were you not inside my cave?"

Eduardo said, "But we were so silent as we came inside."

Picking up her own bowl as she rose from her seat, she brushed aside his concern, saying now with her back to them as she walked back to the cauldron to serve herself more, "That's neither here nor there. I'm glad to have you with me. But you must go back outside and home now quickly before night falls. I do have one thing to do, though, before you leave."

Sean, hungrier than he had realized, remained entirely focused on his soup and the small piece of bread she had given him. Thinking better of it, instead of serving herself (or them) more soup, she walked over to her bed and picked up something. Sitting down, she held out on the small dining table a silver necklace with a startlingly beautiful emerald at its base. She held the masculine-looking chain gently draped over her left hand as she fondled the sparkling green stone with her right.

"Lovely, isn't it?"

As she turned the stone slightly from side to side, the candlelight and light from the torches reflected flashes of fire from its multiple facets. The small wild cat paced back and forth even more anxiously inside its cage.

"Oh, calm down, my pet. Everything's all right" she said soothingly aside.

Sean, mesmerized by the stone, asked eagerly, "What is it? Why do you have it?"

Largely ignoring his second question, she addressed his first with, "It's a perfect emerald, set in the form of an amulet."

Eduardo asked, "What is an amulet?"

"Something meant to offer protection to the person who wears it."

"How can it protect?" Sean asked.

"I don't know, really. I only know that it has worked for centuries, and that it's intended now for you. It is yours."

Eduardo asked, completely perplexed, "For which of us? We are two separate boys, not one."

"It is meant for the son of Edwin O'Connor."

Eduardo, clearly disappointed that the beautiful stone was not intended for him, said disgustedly, "Oh, come on. You cannot be serious."

"Oh, I am. I am. I am quite serious indeed."

Sean, so stunned that he could scarcely speak, managed to say, "I don't understand at all."

"Take it. Wear it and then, as I said earlier, you must go." With that, she held it out over the table without turning it over to either boy. Sean took it into his hands and admired it, turning it over and over, fascinated by its sparkle, color and clarity. Eduardo sat and smiled, still dazed by the whole experience. They rose to leave and Sean put the necklace around his neck to wear it proudly.

"Now be careful as you leave. Keep in mind how you came into the cave and retrace your steps. Oh, and I almost forgot. This amulet has protected particular persons both in Ireland and here beginning long, long ago. There is a saying in English that governs its use and prevents its misuse. And it goes like this:

> *"He who wears this,*
> *less malice or vice,*
> *is protected completely,*
> *but so only thrice."*

Eduardo, with a clearer head than Sean, asked the old woman to repeat the saying, which she did, allowing him to commit it to memory. And then they departed, the mysterious old woman waving warmly to them as they left, and with Eduardo surefootedly leading the way, meticulously retracing steps to the front of the cavern. Walking briskly, the boys hurried back along the forest path toward home, arriving only slightly after dark.

As they approached the house, Señor O'Connor, pacing on his front porch, first heard them approach and then saw the flickering lights of their flashlights bouncing in the dark. Clearly visible in the light of the yard surrounding the large house, they walked up close enough to see him waiting, arms sternly crossed, and then heard his booming voice, "Boys! How dare you stay away so long and into the night! Get in here this minute!"

Eduardo, aware that the entire side trip had not been his idea in the first place, also knew that he would suffer the same punishment as would O'Connor's son. Sean, well accustomed by now to his father's wrath at moments like these, could not avoid trembling with fear at what he knew he was about to endure.

"Eduardo, I'll deal with you in the morning. For now, go to your house. Your mother is nearly sick with concern for you. Sean O'Connor! Come here."

Eduardo, deeply dreading the punishment that he knew he would receive in the morning and overcome by shame and fear, shuffled along to the small cabin where his mother and he shared two tiny rooms. Sean, not wanting to make his father aware of the amulet, had removed the chain from around his neck and had slipped the entire piece of jewelry into his sack. Eduardo, arriving back at his cabin, encountered not anger but overwhelming love and relief displayed by his mother, who smothered him with an all-consuming hug and covered him with kisses. "I could not survive without you, my love. Please don't do anything like this ever again," she pleaded. Then putting him to bed, she lovingly tucked him in.

Eduardo lay in bed, somewhat relieved by the reception he had gotten from his mother, although too nervous to sleep at the prospect of what he feared might lie ahead. As he struggled to sleep, he could hear from the estate owner's home the resounding echo of a belt hitting loudly across the backside of young Sean. Although there were only three such sounds of impact and insult, the noise seemed wildly magnified. The sound echoed repeatedly in his mind, as the now drowsy Eduardo finally drifted off to sleep.

The next morning at daybreak Eduardo, awakened by his mother with a kiss, got out of bed and dressed. The sun was up and shining brightly, its light beaming through the one window in Eduardo's tiny room, sending long, bright streaks of light across his bed. Squinting against the effect of its glare, he dressed and went into the one other room to have warm milk and a roll with his mother.

"You must never do anything like that again, my child. I need you with me, and you are too young to understand how dangerous the mountains can be, especially in the dark."

"I'm sorry, Mother. I'll remember." He didn't bother blaming the infraction on his playmate. There would be no point. Besides, there was no anger or resentment in her voice; only forgiveness with undertones of desperately unconditional love toward him. "Now Don Edwin wants to see you. You must go."

"This man is not my father. I shouldn't have to go to him about this."

"Go, Son. He is a good man, a fair man. He's been very good to me through the years, and to you as well. Now go."

Eduardo, as often before, displaying maturity far beyond his years, nodded in agreement and gave her a kiss on the cheek when she bent down to receive it. He left the small cabin to walk to the owner's house. As he stepped onto the porch and up to the front door, he hesitated for a moment, gathering up courage to knock bravely on the facing of the ornately decorated wooden door. He knocked, more timidly than he intended. And he stood back a step or two when the door opened and Edwin O'Connor appeared in the doorway, seeming to tower over him.

Instead of shouting and moving against young Eduardo as violently as the child feared, Edwin O'Connor stood perfectly still, glaring calmly at the boy. Sensing the child's fear, he took the boy's hand and said very gently, "Come with me."

Taking the grown man's hand and following him to the end of the porch, Eduardo sat in one of the chairs suggested by Señor O'Connor. The man remained standing and spoke to the boy while looking out into the forest. "Eduardo, you are a fine young boy. You had our permission to go with Sean on an outing into the forest. You did not have permission to stay out so late. What did the two of you do?"

Eduardo at that point realized that Sean had said nothing about the cave and wondered if it would be wise to mention it at all. Things seemed to be going reasonably well so far. And Eduardo certainly did not want to bring down the wrath of this man on himself too easily. Thinking quickly, he said, "We lost our way after wandering from the path, and it cost us much time in the afternoon."

O'Connor, experienced enough to know that the boy at best was probably only speaking half-truth, chose not to challenge his integrity for now. There was something admirable about this child. O'Connor had always seen more character in this child than he had sensed in his own son. He decided only to discover more about what had truly happened the day before. "Whose idea was it to wander off the path?"

Eduardo looking down at the floor, embarrassed and afraid, thought better than to implicate the son of the man standing over him. "It was my idea," he said almost inaudibly.

Instead of growing angry, O'Connor stood looking at the child, realizing he was almost certainly lying. But this only made him prouder of the boy's strength. He knew his son Sean was exactly the type to lead someone astray. Even so, he had hoped young Eduardo would have the strength of character not to betray his friend. Don Edwin had been right.

"It was wrong, what you did. But I'm not going to punish you this time. You seem penitent enough to me. I punished my boy last night partly out of anger and partly out of frustration and concern. You two must not do anything like this again. Your mother worries about you. And I worry a great deal about both of you."

Eduardo was not sure whom the man meant by "both of you," but remained silent since things were going so smoothly so far. He did not want to provoke anger in Don Edwin. "Now go. You and Sean are to remain away from each other for the rest of this week. That is your punishment. Go and behave ."

Eduardo nodded and walked back to his mother's cabin. He had fully expected to be beaten and to return to his cabin bruised and battered. Instead, he returned chastised but untouched, embarrassed but unharmed.

O'Connor walked back into his house, back into the office he maintained at home, and considered how disappointed he was once again with his son Sean and with the fact that Sean had so quickly and easily mentioned his friend Eduardo as the person responsible for the decision to go astray. O'Connor knew at that moment that Sean was lying. He had seen him lie before in situations like this. He was surprised to hear Eduardo lie, even though the motivation was to protect Sean.

The evening before, Sean, beaten and shouted at by his father, threw a tantrum insisting how unfair his treatment was, provoking even more anger from Edwin until the father caught himself and held back realizing that the boy had had enough. Sean's insolence and lack of respect for authority were ever-present. They brought out the worst in Edwin O'Connor, which in turn seemed to provoke tremendous hostility within the boy toward his father. It was a cycle that Edwin had long since grown tired of. Sick of the conflicts, he often ignored his boy's behavior and bad attitude, and that in turn only made the boy bolder and worse.

Edwin sat at his desk trying to concentrate on his paperwork and yet unable to focus. He wondered if Sean would ever mature into the young man it appeared that little Eduardo was already becoming or perhaps had already become.

☆ ☆ ☆

The rest of the week passed slowly. Sean spent his days alone inside the big house. Eduardo helped his mother with her work whenever he could. She allowed him to play alone outside their cabin. The weekend passed and then on Monday morning Eduardo's mother—when asked by him if he could play with Sean that day—answered, "yes." O'Connor also told Sean that he was free to play again with Eduardo, warning both to behave. O'Connor left the house on business. From time to time, he had to travel to the port city of Puerto Lindo in connection with the export from Colombia of his company's production of precious stones.

The two boys played well together throughout the week. On the fourth day though, knowing that his father would be returning within a day and a half or so, Sean suggested to Eduardo that they quietly venture into the forest once again to the site of the cave, to see if they could visit one more time with the old woman. Eduardo adamantly refused. "How can you even think of such a thing? Did you not hear at all what your father told you—what he told both of us?"

"I'll carry the amulet with me. Maybe it will protect both of us against any harm. Come on. We can't wait to think about it. Your mother is down by the river washing clothes. We should go now."

"Forget it! I won't. Go by yourself if you want."

Sean, stiffening in defiance, said, "All right, I will. I will go alone." And with that he began walking down the same path as before.

Eduardo at first ignored him until he realized that Sean was serious and was quickly disappearing along the path. Finally, Eduardo spat on the ground in disgust, got up and followed Sean, running to catch up with him.

Eduardo said breathlessly, "We have to make this very brief."

"All right. We can't run the whole way. But we'll walk quickly. Let's go."

Being so determined to get to the cave and back quickly, they made very good time, arriving at the mouth of the cave before the sun was in its highest point in the sky. Sean had only brought one flashlight. Less intimidated by the darkness of the cavern now, they proceeded into the cave and followed the same path inside it. Arriving at the spot near where they had originally found the old woman, they realized there was absolutely nothing there. They could not find the chamber where she had seemed to make her home.

Frustrated, they gave up and returned exactly the same way back and sat down in front of the cave's opening. "I know we didn't both imagine it. She was there!" Sean said, disbelieving more the fact that she had vanished than the fact that he and Eduardo had met with her.

"It doesn't matter. We have to go home now. Let's go back before my mother even misses us."

They left, walking almost as quickly on the return as they had walked coming to the cave. They stopped briefly along the way to rest. Sean sat on a log and Eduardo on a rock facing Sean.

"Where could she have gone?" Sean asked, irritated as much as perplexed.

"How would I know? It almost makes me wonder if she was real."

Sean says impatiently, "How could she *not* have been real? Was the soup not hot and good? Could you not smell the place around us and then the woman herself—the mustiness of her aged self? She was there. And isn't *this* real enough?" He held up the emerald amulet, admiring it as he showed it to Eduardo again, wondering to himself from where it had actually come.

"We need to go. I can't get in trouble again so soon, even if you can."

Sean, knowing that Eduardo was right, nodded in agreement and rose. Suddenly screaming, he jerked in pain and grabbed his lower leg. He looked back behind him and saw the snake slithering away--revolting coward that it was—trying desperately to escape rather than to risk danger for itself.

Eduardo, by the time Sean realized what had happened, pursued the snake and beat it to death with a large stick. Even as a nine-year-old, he had experience with snakes and knew to avoid panic and to kill the snake as quickly as possible. He also understood that Sean was going to need help immediately, but he did not have his knife with him since they had left so quickly that morning. Instead, he persuaded Sean to sit back. Eduardo bent down and bit the area where the two-holed bite was. He bit hard enough to break skin and sucked whatever blood he could and spat several times to keep from swallowing the powerful venom himself, then washing out his mouth with water from his canteen. Gasping for breath, he went through that process a second time. His lips went numb. He rinsed his mouth again, hoping to regain the feeling in his lips.

Sean, crying hysterically, was already in shock from the bite. The snake had bitten deeply and its venom would work quickly. Eduardo, sensing immediately the vile taste—a concoction of venom and blood and skin and dirt—felt nauseated himself, but remained the strong man he needed to be at this moment instead of the very small boy he actually was.

"We have to get you back quickly. We must get you to a doctor. Can you walk?"

Through his tears, Sean cried, "It hurts! My God, it hurts."

"Get up. We need to try at least for you to walk. Here, lean on me. Put your arm around my shoulder and hold on." Eduardo struggled to brace the slightly larger boy and they began haltingly to walk. After several meters, Sean, already beginning to feel light-headed, slowed down and spoke. "I can't do it. I have to rest."

"Come on! Please! I can't carry you. You're too heavy for me."

Sean let go and sat on the path, putting his head down between his knees. "You go on back and get help. Run." Sean, by this time exhausted from trying to walk that distance and at the same time already affected by the poison, was struggling to catch his breath. Eduardo, with the stinging effect of diluted venom in his own mouth, could imagine what effect the full poison must be having on his friend.

After starting out, Eduardo stopped and then turned back. He ran back to Sean and reminded him about the amulet. "The amulet can protect you. Try it." Sean, having completely forgotten about the amulet, and not seriously believing that it could accomplish anything, began to wonder if perhaps it might be of some help. He took it in his hands and , having no idea what to do, held it tightly and concentrated, asking it to help him survive.

The amulet did not change color. It did not become warmer or larger or smaller. There was no change at all. Sean decided that it was a hoax, a waste of time. "Go on. Run. But, take this and hide it for me." He handed the amulet to Eduardo and then lay down on the ground, trying to rest and recover.

Eduardo slipped the necklace and its amulet around his own neck, under his shirt and ran as quickly as he could, arriving back at his mother's cabin only to find it empty. He hid the amulet and ran to the larger house and found her in the back of the building. "Mother! We must go quickly to get Sean. He's been bitten by a poisonous snake." He turned toward another maid working beside his mother and said authoritatively, "Get Emilio quickly. He'll need to carry the boy back. And send someone for the doctor quickly. Run!"

"Sean bitten by a snake?"

"We have to hurry. Please."

Speaking as she ran with the boy back into the forest, she asked him with a scolding tone, "So you and he disobeyed us and so soon. You see what happens?"

"I know. I'm sorry. I'm so very sorry."

They ran until both were exhausted, but his mother's legs gave out more quickly than did the boy's. "Slow down. I'll walk quickly. But I can't run anymore," she said panting as she spoke.

He took her hand and tugged her forward. "Mother, hurry."

They kept going until they saw Sean lying in the distance on the ground, by now unconscious. She had also forgotten to grab a knife to make the cut needed to allow the venom to bleed out. But by now it was too late for that approach to be of much use, since the venom had already begun to wend its way through Sean's bloodstream, throughout his small body. With time, it would cause his heart and his breathing to cease. "I hope Emilio comes right behind us," she said, in a tone that indicated that even this might be too late.

Then Emilio, one of Don Edwin's trusted servants, arrived. Big and strong and out of breath from having run too hard, Emilio cared deeply for both of these boys, even though he had often gossiped with the maids about how spoiled Sean had always been. "Take him up, and let's hurry back," the mother said, trying to help the man pick up the eleven-year-old Sean; already as heavy as a small man even though still very much a boy.

With Sean loaded up on his shoulders, Emilio began to walk as quickly as possible. He was strong, but nowhere nearly strong enough to run with this much weight on his shoulders. They arrived back at the large house. Emilio took the boy to the room and laid him on his own bed. Eduardo's mother began to clean Sean with a wet cloth. There was little to do until the doctor arrived. Sean was already running a high fever and was clearly in shock. The woman stood over the boy, feeling within herself a swelling up of guilt…guilt for thinking at this moment how grateful she was that this was someone else's son and not her own lying on the bed unconscious and full of deadly venom.

Eduardo stood by the bed, praying for Sean to recover. Eduardo's mother filled with pity and concern about the bad-mannered boy who had been her son's only playmate for so long. She also knew how desperately O'Connor cared for his son and hoped that they could have the boy in good shape in time for the father's return at the end of the week.

They stood as patiently as possible, waiting for the doctor to arrive. Then tired of standing, they sat and waited. Hours passed. Sean lay peacefully, still breathing but unconscious. Late in the afternoon the doctor arrived, hurrying into the house and into the boy's bedroom, taking out his stethoscope and checking the boy's temperature and blood pressure. He asked when it had happened and asked Eduardo to describe what sort of snake had bitten Sean. As Eduardo described the appearance of the snake, the doctor could no longer conceal his concern.

He had arrived full of hope and determination to cure whatever ailed the boy. Gradually, he came to grips with reality and became silent and subdued, not wanting to say out loud what he knew to be the case: that the venom was already throughout the boy's system. There is never uncertainty about any person's death to come. There is always shock at the realization that the death of one so young is to come on one particular day, without time for those around him to comprehend the impact. The doctor finally sat quietly and waited along with the others, by now as helpless a bystander as anyone in the room.

After a bit, he put his tools back into his bag and stood, adjusting the covers around the boy, as if he were merely tucking him in for a night's rest. He turned toward the woman and to young Eduardo and shook his head gently. "There's nothing to do now but to wait. I have to go."

Eduardo, who had struggled throughout the ordeal to remain strong and to help in any way that he might, felt tears welling up and then running down his cheeks. He could not believe this had happened. He had not wanted to go into the forest the second time. He had almost begged Sean to obey O'Connor and to remain on the estate. But then he had gone along with Sean anyway. And so Eduardo as he saw it was as guilty as Sean had been of disobeying the authority of Edwin O'Connor. Don Edwin's orders had been intended to punish... yes...but also to protect. To protect the boys against their own immaturity and foolishness; to protect them against their enormous lack of respect for the danger of the jungle and for the world outside. And now Sean was paying for disobedience. How was Eduardo to pay? Nothing that could be done to him could approach the punishment of having to witness the slow death of his young friend, of having to realize how ineffective he had been in preventing disaster, of how complicit he had been in the unpermitted activities.

Eduardo's mother brought a simple dinner into the room: fresh bread, cold chicken and raw onion. They balanced plates on their laps and ate quietly, almost reverently, each minute hoping that Sean would awaken; that he would sit up and ask to have something to eat. They finished and she took the plates back to the kitchen and then brought hot chocolate back for Eduardo. She stood leaning against the door while he drank it all.

As Eduardo finished his last sip and placed the mug aside, he turned to his mother and watched her. Suddenly she tensed up and stood up straight, looking intently at Sean, and walked toward the bed to pick up his wrist and hold it. She placed her fingers at the side of the boy's throat and seemed to press against it gently. Holding it there for what seemed an eternity, she then dropped her hand, picking up a mirror on the night table. She held the mirror just at the base of Sean's nose as if wanting to look inside.

But it was not any part of the boy that she needed to see in that instant. She was looking for any sign, however slight, of vaporized breath on the glass of the mirror. And yet no sign of life appeared. She put down the mirror and turned toward Eduardo, tears streaming down both her cheeks.

"Son, he's gone. Sean has gone to be with God."

Eduardo began to cry, trying to hold back but unable to do it. She stepped toward him and embraced him tightly, soaking up the warmth of his skin, the movement of his breathing...holding him and listening to and feeling his sobs. At that moment, she felt more appreciation for the life of her own child than she could remember having felt at any point in her life. She stood holding him, rocking gently, saying over and over to herself, "Oh, my child, my child" and " How I love you."

Each reassured by the continued existence of the other, mother and child felt free to separate. Eduardo sat back down and his mother stepped to the bed to pull the covers over the face of what remained of Sean. She took her son and they walked back together to her cabin. It was late.

She placed Eduardo in his bed, tucked him in carefully and gave him a kiss on the forehead. "Sleep well, my baby," she said softly before slipping out of his room to go to her own bed where she began to cry softly to herself, overwhelmed by thoughts of how closely disaster had come to her son and how closely it had come to her.

Eduardo, his mind racing with images of events and the emotions of the day, felt exhausted and yet could not go to sleep no matter how he tried. He thought of the amulet, which he had shoved beneath his mattress. He reached under to pull it out carefully. He held it in his hands, admiring its beauty—a beauty he could clearly appreciate even in the pale glow of moonlight through his window. He could not believe that the amulet was worthless. As he held it, he realized it felt warmer in his hand than it had before. Ever so slightly, it began to give off a soft glow in his hands before fading back to its normal luster.

The woman in the cave had not been imagined by both boys together. She had been real. The amulet was real. He could not help believing that whatever power it might have was genuine. He returned it to its place underneath the mattress and repeated the saying that described the amulet's power...the saying that he had memorized from the old woman. As he heard that message reverberating through confused thoughts, he finally slipped away into a tormented, restless sleep.

✲ ✲ ✲

Eduardo's mother succeeded in sending a telegram to Edwin O'Connor: a message that his son had tragically died and that the father must return immediately from Puerto Lindo. O'Connor arrived back the following morning after receiving the sad news. As he entered the house, she happened to be walking through the hallway toward the front door, passing by Edwin's study and saw him. She noticed the redness of his eyes and how swollen they were from hours of weeping. She reached out to take his hand and said only, "I'm so very sorry."

Don Edwin, struggling not to cry, replied as if he were not actually living inside his own body but was instead aloft, "I know. Thank you." He let go her hand and walked upstairs toward the boy's room.

"Wait. If you're looking for where we placed him, we set the coffin in the parlor."

"I see."

And he stepped back down the few stairs he had already ascended and walked toward the open door to the room where then he saw the bier holding the simple wooden casket. Overcome by emotion at the sight of his son's body now still and silent, Edwin approached the coffin and knelt before it, placing one hand on the side. He began to sob. The woman, horribly in pain herself to see any father suffer so, stood back, knowing that nothing she could possibly say or do could comfort him at this moment; knowing that distracting him from the necessary outpouring of grief, from the catharsis of profound mourning, would only leave horribly poisonous grief bottled up inside the poor man, leaving him distracted and unable to deal with life. It was best to let it all out and to let him give vent to as much of it as possible. There could be no moment when absolute privacy was more needed.

She knew firsthand how intensely felt love could be at the moment of first holding a newborn infant. She could only imagine the horror of first having to accept the reality of death of that same young person. She hoped never to experience the pain of surviving as a parent. She could not bear the sight of Don Edwin's suffering and so left him to himself and went back to her work elsewhere in the house, trying to avoid him for the remainder of the morning.

Eventually, the father, having endured as much as he could at one time, sought out the maid and approached her when he found her in the kitchen. "Now, please tell me what happened." He patiently waited for her reply.

Putting down the silver she was polishing, she wiped her hands carefully on a separate cloth—giving herself a moment to collect her thoughts—and tried to decide what to say and how to convey it. Grief often converts itself quickly into other emotions, such as anger or impatience or even into aggression. She did not want to misspeak, inadvertently provoking her employer's fury. She had seen him suddenly grow angry before and had learned how diplomatically to avoid provoking such anger.

"Sean and Eduardo could not resist one more outing into the forest. They were trying to go quickly back to the abandoned mine, to the cave entrance and then back home again before we noticed they were gone. On their way back, Sean was bitten by a snake. Eduardo ran home to get help. Then we had the doctor come from the village as soon as possible here to the house. But there was nothing that could be done...nothing at all."

Surprisingly, his first remark was that, "At least they weren't both bitten. Is Eduardo all right?"

She had been staring at the floor as she spoke. At this point, she looked up, gazing into Edwin's wet, red eyes, and replied, with tears forming in her own eyes, "Yes. And thank you for asking."

"He was not a well-behaved boy... Sean wasn't. I had spoiled him badly after his mother's death. I know that. He was an insolent child. He seemed very deeply to resent the few times that I managed to discipline him. There may have been times when he even hated me, especially this past week."

"You were a good father. Loving, attentive. You must not feel guilty. Bad things happen. He did not deserve this, and neither did you."

Edwin looked at her and smiled as if to express his deepest appreciation. He turned and left the kitchen and went to his office, which had always been his refuge. Just before stepping through the door, he said with his back to her, "We'll notify the priest. We'll have a small funeral at the village chapel and will bury him near the house." With that, he continued to his office.

She picked up her work again and, polishing each piece of silver that had been in Edwin's family for at least two generations, found herself picturing these fine heirlooms intended to be passed along to Sean upon his marriage at some young age. She imagined what a fine young man the child might have become with such a father as example. Ignoring the naughtiness of Sean's temperament, she imagined how that energy could have matured into useful, admirable traits centered upon resisting evil and upon defending people and ideas worth defending.

And then she caught herself and realized that there was no point to imagining such things. It might well have been pre-ordained that Sean would not live to maturity, and that he would forever be remembered as a petulant child, never given an opportunity to redeem himself as an adult.

Her thoughts turned instead to her own small boy Eduardo and to what he might someday become: not wealthy, not inheriting the fortune of a great man like O'Connor, but a good man in his own right—dependable , hard-working, a man of integrity, caring for a family and for others around him. She could dream. Living from day to day, gaining only glimpses of what it might be like to be associated not only with wealth but with people, free to think about grander things than mere survival. She was aware that she had been fortunate. Living comfortably and well with a roof over her own head as well as a separate room for her one and only child. Much more importantly, she had been granted the gift of the life of that child: her wonderful boy Eduardo. And, unable to consider anything this morning other than the fragility of, the precious nature of life itself, she felt a rush of memories of life about her child—of his beautiful face, his smile and laugh, the musty smell of boyish sweat on his skin after a day of playing happily and worry-free. She hoped that the good person within this child's skin would mature someday into a fine young man, never losing his best qualities and never acquiring bad habits. She daydreamed about the possibility of his growing into the same sort of man she wished had remained in her own life as partner for her and as father to Eduardo. She dreamed. She wept, surviving as always by concentrating above all else upon her work.

The funeral Mass drew to a close. Eduardo and his mother sat in the simple pew behind Edwin O'Connor. O'Connor sat alone, calmly listening, taking whatever solace he could from the brief homily offered by the poorly educated but devout and dedicated priest. Edwin had long ago lost most of his own faith, although clinging to its remnants desperately at this moment, hoping that if he at least appeared to believe in God, and that this would somehow pave the way for his son to have a place in Heaven, knowing full well that his son had done nothing to deserve such a reward. On the other hand, the child had never done anything evil.

Edwin felt comfortable assuming that people either deserved heavenly reward or did not. He had great difficulty accepting the notion of a God not only omnipotent and omniscient but also all-forgiving, full of grace with forgetful disregard for sins sincerely regretted. Edwin felt more comfortable assuming that bad people deserved and might actually receive just punishment. He believed in the righteousness of retribution more than in limitless capacity to forgive and forget. He could not see that his own inability to forgive, even himself, was sadly out of touch with the image of a God who, when confronted with a penitent sinner newly arrived at the pearly gates, might simply turn absentmindedly aside, smiling and saying: "Really? When did that happen?"

And this was exactly the concept inarticulately but passionately promoted by this particular priest this morning, an approach unlike that which Edwin had ever witnessed from any representative of the church. It was a much-needed message at a moment such as this: a message more heartfelt than persuasive in terms of connecting with Edwin O'Connor— the person who most needed the benefit of any comfort that it might offer.

Leaving, Edwin turned slightly and gestured to young Eduardo to step forward. The boy moved around to stand beside O'Connor. The tall and well-dressed gentleman took the hand of the little boy, and they walked out together. Although he had not consciously thought it out in advance, as they exited the small chapel, it occurred to Edwin how desperately he needed the balance afforded by that small hand and by the touch of this little boy. It lessened the pain somehow of realizing that his own son would never again be there to walk alongside him. At this time, the burden of that realization was more than Edwin could bear.

Eduardo felt very much at ease holding the hand of the lord of the manor. O'Connor had always treated him and his mother very well, keeping distance while treating them with respect and seeing that they had whatever they needed. Although not father to Eduardo, Don Edwin had been the principal provider and protector for as long as the boy could remember; and Eduardo felt a deep sense of appreciation for that connection as he escorted the deeply wounded man.

Once outside the chapel, O'Connor let go of the boy's hand and bent down ever so slightly toward him and said, "I know that it was not your fault, Eduardo. Don't worry about that. Go. Be with your mother."

Eduardo went to his mother, and she reached down, picked him up, kissed him hard on the cheek, hugged him tightly, and let him down to take his hand. They walked toward the wagon where O'Connor sat, hands loosely grasping the reins of the two horses resting idly by. They climbed into the back of the wagon along with Emilio and one other maid, and O'Connor jerked the reins, startling the horses into action for the ride back home. A separate wagon, ahead of them, carried the small coffin.

Seated beside the boy, and jostled about by the rough ride, his mother held Eduardo tightly up against her. The four of them sat, struggling to remember pleasant moments involving Sean. No one wanted to speak. So they sat in silence and watched the road fall behind them as they moved forward.

After burying Sean, O'Connor retreated to his study without speaking. No longer tearful, he seemed resigned to continuing life alone. Eduardo's mother knew the patrón well enough to know that he was beginning the process of putting memories of the boy behind him. He was focusing on as many other thoughts as possible, separating himself from pain, building a sturdy wall between himself and what had already slipped into the past. He was struggling to set aside his dead son as nothing more than a distant memory, something entirely apart from whatever life might remain.

The day passed slowly. Eduardo—uninterested in play, wanting not to think too much about the fact that he now had no playmate—had the unfamiliar feeling of wishing that school would begin. He sat in the yard outside the cabin and drew pictures in the dirt with a short stick. The afternoon dragged on, seemingly forever. His mother, noticing his melancholy, asked him to help with her chores, which he did gladly, thrilled to have something to occupy time and thoughts and happy to be close to his mother.

That night he slipped into bed, and she came to tuck him in. As she sat on the bed not knowing exactly what to say, she smiled at him. He at first wondered whether to discuss it with her or not, but then decided to pull out the emerald amulet.

"Isn't it beautiful?"

He laid it in her hand, grinning broadly, proud of his only valuable possession.

Stunned, she said, "Yes, it is! But where did you get it? Eduardo, you didn't steal this, did you?"

"Of course not. Someone gave it to us."

"To us?"

"To Sean and me." He hesitated for a second and then added, "Well... it was given to Sean, but I was with him when he got it. And now he's gone."

"I don't understand. Who would give you such a thing?"

"Well, you know the first day we went into the jungle and were late getting back? It was that day. We found the cave Señor O'Connor had told us never to enter. Sean insisted that we go in to see what was inside. I didn't want to go in." He looked down as he said, "But I went with him anyway. I was scared, but we went much deeper inside than he said he would. And we found something."

"You found this lying on the ground?"

"No. We saw a light and found a chamber where an old woman lives... or lived. She let us in. She was very nice and fed us delicious soup."

"Oh, Eduardo!" his mother said, disappointed at the boy's far-fetched tale, but at the same time impressed by the clarity and vividness of his imagination.

"I'm serious, Mother. The chamber was lighted by torches and was warmer and dryer than the rest of the cave. She had a small table and chairs for eating and a fire in the center of the room with a cooking pot hung over it. It was late in the day, and we had not eaten enough. I was hungry, and the soup smelled wonderful. She tasted it first to show us that it was all right. We ate and talked. Before we left, she gave us this and called it an emerald amulet, meant to protect the person who wears it. She said it came from far away and that there was a spell on it. There are rules about who it will help. She taught us a saying in English... I suppose because it comes from a place where English is spoken. The saying went like this:

> *"He who wears this,*
> *Less malice or vice,*
> *Is protected completely*
> *But so only thrice."*

By this time, his mother was so astonished by how elaborately and well her son could tell an untruth that she scarcely knew what to say. But she did recover enough to scold him, "Eduardo, I'm very disappointed in you. You must not tell such extravagant lies. Now where did this come from? Tell me the truth!"

Deeply offended and hurt by his mother's refusal to believe him, and regretting his decision to share something so important with her, he sat upright in bed and insisted, his green eyes blazing, "Mother, I am not lying. This did happen exactly as I've told you. I don't understand it myself. But it did happen. And there's more." He decided to get out from under the covers entirely and sat beside her on the bed. "We went back later, to see if the chamber was still there with the old woman inside it. Sean insisted that we go and was going to go by himself. I could not let him go into the jungle alone. So I followed. We went back into the cave but could not find any sign of the lighted chamber or the woman. We knew where the chamber had been. But now there was not even an opening in the side of the tunnel. There was nothing. We gave up and tried to hurry home. As we stopped to rest, that was when the snake bit Sean."

He stopped for a minute and his mother remained silent, having noticed that there was something in the boy's voice that sounded too sincere to be ignored. Then he added, "Sean knew the snakebite was serious. He remembered the old woman's saying and he grabbed hold of the amulet and tried to get its help. But it stayed cold in his hand. Nothing happened. But after Sean died and I sat that night in this bed and held the amulet in my hand studying it, it grew warm and glowed gently in the night. There *is* something special about it, Mother. I know the old woman was real. I know she gave us this. And I think there may be magic in this emerald. I believe it, Mother."

Staring at the stone, she gave it back to him, considering what to say next. She rose from the bed. If it was given to Sean, then you must turn it over to Señor O'Connor. It should be his now."

"I don't think so. It did nothing for Sean. As I tried to talk him into staying around the house and not to go back into the jungle, he mentioned to me how much he hated his father for punishing him for nothing. Sean had much resentment inside him. And when I held it and studied it seriously for the first time, it was as if...as if it tried to tell me that it was rightfully mine. I think, Mother, that it is meant to be mine."

She sighed deeply. "Well, it does seem as if it was never meant to be O'Connor's in the first place. I cannot believe this fantastic story, but at the same time you seem to be telling the truth. We'll keep it. But I will put it away safely for you." Then she pulled back the covers and encouraged him to slip back under them. She went once again through the process of tucking him in, kissed him goodnight and left with the amulet and its chain in her apron pocket.

Once back in her own room, she knelt down by her bed and pulled out the small strongbox that had been given to her years before, found the key and opened it, gingerly placing the emerald amulet inside it and then locking the box, placing it securely out of sight. Before going to sleep, she remembered not so much the details of Eduardo's story as the boy's confidence in the telling of the tale. It did in fact appear that Eduardo believed it all to be true, just as sincerely as if he had experienced every bit of it. What if it were true? He was certainly not a child who had a habit of lying.

What if the amulet did in fact have the power to protect her son's life and well-being, not only once but possibly three times throughout his life? She had never heard of anything as strange as this before. If there were only the slightest chance of its being true, she would have to safeguard the amulet very carefully. She vowed to herself that she owed it not only to the boy but to herself to keep the amulet available for him as long as possible. She owed it to him because of her love for him. She owed it to herself out of pure selfishness, since she wanted more than anything to ensure that no harm would come to her one and only son. Sean O'Connor's early death served as a reminder to her of how fragile life can be.

II.

As Eduardo sat at his desk in the modest schoolroom looking out the window, he completed the last short essay of his final exam. He considered how to conclude the final paragraph and became distracted by the beautiful greenery of the jungle outside. He basked in the glow of sunshine flooding through the window pane, defining one long parallelogram of light on the floor beside him. With plenty of time to review his work, he finished before all the others. He cared greatly today, as always, about the quality of his work. He reviewed each of his well-composed brief answers to the questions about his country. He, as required, wrote in his best Spanish—the language of the Conquerors. He also understood the language of the Motilone tribe and loved the sound of it—the Motilone tribe being his mother's heritage.

Proficient as well in English, as a result of having lived his young life on the property of (and with his mother in the employ of) Señor Edwin O'Connor, Eduardo could have taken this history exam in English. With raven-black hair and with skin somewhat lighter than the golden tones of his mother's, Eduardo had a face that stood out among his fellow students largely due to the striking effect of his green eyes.

He had always been a good student with an enormous appetite for learning. He had a questioning mind... receiving information, registering and retaining whatever seemed most important and discarding immediately anything that sounded like mere opinion. He enjoyed all academic subjects equally well, but he had a special place in his heart for the study of the history of his country and continent.

There had been times, especially within his final two years, when he wondered what it might be like to continue his education, to go to another school somewhere and to have even more opportunities to acquire knowledge. He had no great ambition. At the same time, he basked in the warmth of his mother's love and care throughout all these years, and felt sorrow at her having lived all these many years without a husband. He felt that concern for her and for what he assumed must have been a great emptiness within her much more than he felt sorrow for his own lack of a father.

He watched his mother work diligently and patiently, never questioning whether her situation was just or not. She simply endured—loving and providing for her one and only son. Eduardo's going away to school would mean her being left completely alone. She still lived and worked on the property and under the protection of Señor O'Connor, the great Patrón or lord of the estate, who had provided a home for her and her child, always ensuring that she and her boy never lacked for clothing or food. The patrón always provided a safe and secure place for them to live comfortably if not to prosper. Eduardo was still extremely young and yet aware of what he had received. But he was mature enough to know how important it is to work hard at something that matters, even if that which matters most is as specific as the provision of basics for someone you love.

At this moment, he felt especially full of a sense of accomplishment and at the same time full of a sense of a life filled with infinite possibilities. He had come very far already. On the other hand, he knew that he had far yet to go. And there was something slightly confusing about all of this at once. Gratifying…terrifying…completing high school was a moment calling for feelings of pride and yet at the same time felt intimidating.

With all of these thoughts tumbling clumsily over efforts to concentrate on essay answers, he still managed to improve several sentences and to add facts at first omitted. Then at last he laid down his pen. He was finished and smiled.

The young woman who taught this class approached him and asked quietly, "Ready?"

"Yes," he said as he folded his test booklet and handed it to her.

She smiled, knowing without looking at it the fine quality of the work that would be inside. She had taken great pride in the work of this young student, in his eager questions, his quickness to offer not only answers during class but also original ideas. This young man was the exceptionally bright, naturally inquisitive, dedicated soul that every teacher hopes to see at least once during a career. She hoped to see him continue with his studies, but dared not say much, for she knew that opportunities might be extremely limited and that family responsibilities and cultural tradition would probably keep him too near home to accomplish all that his mind might allow him to achieve in the years ahead.

"You may go, Eduardo. It has truly been a pleasure," she said, lightly touching his shoulder and smiling broadly as she dismissed him.

He rose after reaching down to pick up his small book sack and left the classroom, wondering as he walked out the door if this would be the last classroom he would ever live and work within. But he did not dwell on this concern for long. The warmth of the sun, the fresh rich smell of the mountain air refreshed him after the stuffiness of the classroom. The trees were filled with the sounds of birds, the sounds of life. He had completed high school, and was ready to begin life. For now, that seemed like sufficient cause to celebrate.

He entered the large house through the front door and headed directly for the kitchen. It had never occurred to Eduardo or to any of the servants or servants' kin to come and go through the back door. Señor O'Connor never entertained guests and seldom if ever had visitors. He had always been a solitary man, wholly dedicated to his business. Despite the presence of wife and child, he always preferred solitude. He was an unpretentious person, never exhibiting a need to separate himself physically from the people who helped him to live comfortably. He wanted them to live decently and to be content. He understood, as they did, that differences existed between them—differences of heritage, distinctions of degree in terms of education and of manners. But, at the same time, he appreciated—as the servants who had remained with him the longest also understood—that to a great extent they were all involved in making the estate a success: a safe, clean environment for passing free hours, a refuge for all those involved in living here in the world of this estate.

O'Connor understood his place; he expected the servants to remember theirs. But he had nothing to prove. For those workers who took their work seriously, who understood their place in life and who respected him as employer and protector, he extended respect and fair treatment. Eduardo had been raised to understand that he was welcome to come and go as he pleased in the large house and did so respectfully and yet only as often as needed. This morning, he had arrived back from school to give his mother a tremendous embrace and to spend at least one moment of simple celebration of what he had just accomplished. He knew that he had done well on his exams. He accomplished what she had wanted desperately for him to achieve: to obtain as much formal education as possible.

He entered the kitchen and noticed his mother standing over the cabinet. She looked up, noticed him and wiped her hands on her apron. He thought to himself how lovely she always had been and still was. Working, smiling, proud. She raised up both arms in welcome, inviting him in for that warm, comforting maternal hug that had always meant so much to him for as long as he could remember. "I'm through. It's done."

"I know. And I'm so proud! Look at you", she said while holding him back at arm's length, admiring him, then looking him straight in the eye instead of looking down, as in years past, to the little boy. He was now a young man, prepared, mature enough to begin. She knew that there must be much going through his mind and she tried to avoid being too demanding. A young man must be left free to decide which way to go. She knew that she could offer advice if asked, but also that she must be careful not to press him into what she really desired. After all, what she desired most was for him to grow and to mature into full manhood, to marry and to remain nearby, at home in some role allowing him to contribute to a community, to be husband and father to someone but still (and always) her son. He was still very young, yes...but already a man. "You did well, I know."

"I think I did, Mamá. I know I did. And the graduation is tomorrow morning."

"It is. And that's a big day for us. For you it will be a big day. But today you work. I need you to split wood this afternoon. Let me feed you and then you must begin." She put together a plate of roast pork, rice, plantain, beans, and corn cake. He sat and ate well and then walked back to their cabin to take off his shirt, to put on his simpler trousers and to head out for work; glad to have something physical to do, to use his back, his shoulders, to set up a rhythm he could sustain throughout the remainder of the day. To sweat freely, to see a clearly tangible pile of accomplishment beside him, to know what he had done, and to have time to relish some sense of finality that he had worried might never come.

All afternoon, he took breaks only briefly. As sunset approached, he completed his work, trying not to leave anything undone for the following day. With the last piece split and put aside, he stretched his arms above his head and then out to his sides and relaxed. Sweat rolling off each arm and off his brow, he felt refreshed and more alert...if possible, more complete. With both mind and body exhausted from the day, he set aside the small axe and ambled back toward home.

Eduardo sat and read by candlelight that evening in the cabin. His mother was expected to work until O'Connor's dinner was finished. She contributed to the work involved in cleaning up and putting things away. The other maid was away visiting her family. Eduardo had already eaten earlier in the evening in the kitchen.

Tired from an afternoon of physical labor, he knew that his mother must be tired as well, as she always was by the end of a long day. He sensed that there might be something more than fatique contributing to this silence and to the concerned look in her expression. He wondered what the reason might be but lacked the energy to ask. He grew drowsy as he read and ended up falling asleep on his bed. He was by now shirtless, wearing only his work pants; his book fell awkwardly to the floor without disturbing him.

The next day was to be even more substantial...a turning point in his life. He would graduate and would also receive recognition for his accomplishments. He would become the first in his mother's family to complete a formal education. As he ended the last day of exams, he struggled to concentrate on the book in front of him, unable to put aside his uncertainty as to whether this turning point was to be more a conclusion or a beginning. Sound asleep at last, he failed to hear his mother walking into the cabin. She looked in and, seeing him so, and not wanting to disturb him, went to bed herself... filling with pride as she considered what she had accomplished by being so patient and working for Edwin O'Connor for so many years. Above all, she considered what her fine young son had made of the opportunity given him.

The few chairs in place were sufficient for the tiny crowd. It was a very small class of nine students, and the graduation ceremony would be short and simple. There were no speeches, except from the schoolmistress of this rural public school. The students were children of modest families nearby, and a few family members who could escape work were in attendance to acknowledge what their children had done. Few had hopes of anything further being accomplished by these children.

As he sat waiting, Eduardo understood that it was unreasonable to think of his someday being allowed to spend more time in a classroom.

What he had already achieved was to be greatly appreciated. This moment of graduation from high school needed to be savored.

With diplomas handed out, and with Eduardo acknowledged as the top student; and with kind words expressed, the ceremony drew to a close. Near its conclusion, as Eduardo stepped up to accept his certificate, he saw in the back Edwin O'Connor standing tall, a smile beaming across his face. Eduardo felt astonished that such a distinguished man would bother to attend such an insignificant event. The patrón truly honored Eduardo by his presence. Eduardo felt proud to know that someone he admired greatly would consider this small event worth time and attention.

Eduardo had always admired and respected the patrón. He often thought how wonderful it might be to stand so tall, so well-dressed and so fair-skinned. Richly textured clothing, blue eyes, pallid complexion, all combined to create the impression that here stood someone important, someone above those around him: a fine gentleman. Yet the patrón never seemed the peacock or the snob. Far from it. He kept distant. But no one who worked for him would ever go hungry or be abused or could ever ask for a benefactor more respectful of the dignity of each employee. Yes, Don Edwin was a wealthy man but also a compassionate man. So thought the boy as he walked back to his seat, diploma in hand and prepared for whatever might lie ahead. He could face anything now.

By the time Eduardo had sat back down, Don Edwin had left. But Don Edwin had in fact come that fine morning and had smiled, acknowledging something significant about this boy, in his hard work and achievements; and so in turn acknowledging the boy's mother and her importance. Eduardo felt enormously proud.

That evening, as Eduardo supped in the kitchen with his mother, Señor O'Connor surprised them, offering greetings and saying, "Young man, come with me to my study."

Eduardo glanced at his mother and, looking bewildered, got up from the table to follow. His mother took his plate, sounding nervous and said, "Son, hurry. It must be important. He never comes in here like this."

Eduardo felt his heart beating faster as he walked down the hallway to the glass door slightly shut. He knocked gently and heard "Come in" and ventured into the one room he had never seen—O'Connor's inner sanctum, his office, his retreat. "Please, boy, sit down. I have something to say to you."

Eduardo sat, trying not to show outwardly the concern he felt about why he might have been called in. Assuming it was to be criticized for something he had either done or failed to do, his mind raced through what could possibly have precipitated this unfortunate development.

Not completely recovered from the ecstatic feeling of accomplishment associated with the ceremony this morning, Eduardo suffered from a mixture of confusion and fear. "Yes sir," he said respectfully and then sat in the hard-backed chair in front of and slightly to the side of the large wooden desk.

Señor O'Connor, sensing the boy's apprehension, tried to relax himself and leaned back in his office chair. "You have nothing to fear. I'm not going to say or do anything that would harm you." Edwin smiled kindly as he spoke. The boy had always envied the intense blueness of O'Connor's foreign eyes and could not help being distracted by their color as the man spoke. "I wanted to give you something to mark this day. And I also wanted to discuss a proposition with you."

The patrón's quiet, soothing manner of speaking and his relaxed way of rocking gently in his chair should have calmed young Eduardo. It did not. Until Eduardo knew precisely what this was about, he would not be able to avoid concern.

O'Connor reached down and opened one of his desk drawers and pulled something out. He held it up against the backdrop of his right hand. It was a beautifully shiny new gold pocketwatch with a gold chain and brown leather fob attached. He held it up so that it could be seen clearly. "This is what I want to give you, Eduardo." He flipped open the lid and explained, "It has your name engraved on the inside. Here, take it." He held it forward, extending it so that the boy could get up and hold it in his own hands. "It's a gift in honor of the fine work you've done in school through the years and also in appreciation for all the work you have done around here throughout your childhood, helping your mother and in turn helping me. You've been a fine boy, Eduardo. You deserve recognition."

Completely stunned, Eduardo did not know what to say. Even so, he did manage to say "Thank you. Thank you so very much, Señor O'Connor. I appreciate it."

"That's quite all right. I've watched you grow and begin to mature. The teacher has told me that you are an especially bright young fellow and that she thinks you should be enabled to continue your education."

Eduardo sat silently, not wanting to admit that continuing his education was, for obvious reasons, completely out of the question. His mother would not be able to afford sending him away. No one should understand this fact better than the man who had employed her for so long. Eduardo sat, thinking about how insensitive and even hurtful it was of O'Connor to mention this. Meanwhile, he admired the beautiful watch.

O'Connor had not been looking at the boy. He had been looking at his own hands as he turned his wedding ring around on his finger. He had always continued to wear that ring ever since his wife's death and had a habit of nervously toying with it especially when struggling to decide how to say something important to someone. Eduardo had heard his mother comment about this nervous habit before. He looked up and saw the perplexed expression on the boy's face, and also noticed the boy admiring the watch. "You like it?"

"Oh, yes, I like it very much."

"It is recognition in more than one sense, at least in my mind. The fine gold is a symbol of success… of material wealth, something worth striving toward. The timepiece itself serves as a reminder of how important it is not to waste a minute in doing whatever is most important. Always remember these points."

"I will, of course."

"Eduardo, one thing that is also very important is never to waste a resource. And I have the impression that your mind and spirit are resources worth developing. I want to help you to continue your education, and I'm prepared to pay the entire cost of sending you to a particular university if you can gain admission to the program…something I think that you'll be able to do."

At this point, Eduardo, already overcome by his master's generosity in the extravagant gift of the watch, was too overwhelmed to have the slightest idea as to how to respond, and so could not get anything out other than, "Sir?"

"I mean it. It's difficult to find the words to express how much I miss Sean. It hurts every day to think about my son not having had the chance to grow and to mature into manhood. I would have gladly supported him in whatever he needed in order to get him established. But I never had that opportunity. I do though have that opportunity with you. And you to my mind are at least as deserving of such support as Sean would have been. It would be my pleasure to give you the same chance in life that I would have given him."

Tears began to well up in Eduardo's eyes. Clearly perplexed by all of this at once, he wiped his eyes, struggling not to cry.

O'Connor meanwhile had gotten up and walked toward the window, looking out and speaking with his back turned to Eduardo. Having finished his offer, he turned and realized that he had laid out too much on the simple boy all at once and spoke more affectionately as he returned to his seat and looked at the boy/man who sat before him. "I'm sorry. Maybe I've handled this badly. You don't have to comment of course on the offer of a university education. That's something you and your mother should consider together. And there's time to consider it. So say nothing now. Just know that I am proud of you, young Eduardo. Extremely proud. And it would be an honor to give you the start in life that I think you deserve." With that, he smiled and extended his right hand.

Eduardo, realizing he was being politely dismissed, rose to shake hands with Don Edwin. "Thank you so much for the watch. And also for your offer to help."

"You may go," said the patrón.

Eduardo took the watch and slipped it into his pants pocket. He realized it was too fine a watch for him to carry at all times. But for now he wanted very much to assure himself that it was his own to keep. And so, with it securely placed in his pocket, he strode out of the office, out the front door, carrying his head and shoulders more proudly than ever as he strode across the porch and the yard back to the cabin, imagining for a moment what it might be like to be a gentleman like Señor O'Connor someday—an educated, successful man with a large home, an estate and servants. My God. It was too much even to imagine. Or was it?

By the time he entered the small cabin, he realized it was a wonderful thought... the idea of becoming something more than what he had always clearly been destined to be. But it could only be that—a dream and nothing more. It was too much to assume that this was real. And so he must not allow himself to think about it too much. He must put it aside for now. His mother had to work the remainder of the day. But he knew she would be free in the evening on this particular day. He would be able to visit with her without her being so exhausted.

The following day would be Sunday. Eduardo and his mother would attend Mass together. Although O'Connor had been born a Catholic in Ireland and had for many years remained reasonably devout, he had through the years lost most of his faith and had lost all of the discipline required of a good Catholic. He did not attend Mass regularly anymore, but he was sympathetic enough to allow his servants the entire morning off on Sundays and, after dinner had been taken care of in early afternoon, leaving most of the rest of the day free for the servants. There would be time for Eduardo to visit with his mother on Sunday. But this was not something that could wait overnight. After all, this was still his graduation day; a very special day, and he must savor it while it lasted.

He had been asked by his mother to help in cleaning the cabin and had not done it. So he occupied his hands and his mind with work, helping him pass the time for the remainder of the afternoon. Finally, earlier than expected, his mother walked in, giving him a tremendous hug. "Oh, my fine young man, I'm proud of you!" she said rocking him side to side while still hugging him. Then she let go and went in to sit in her favorite chair. "I'm tired. Let me sit and rest for a few minutes and listen about your visit with O'Connor."

Eduardo followed her across the room and sat on the floor, cross-legged at her feet. Easing gradually into his story, "He said he was very proud of my accomplishment and of me and that he wanted to give me something as a gift." Then he pulled the watch with its chain and fob out of his pocket and showed it to her. "This. Isn't it beautiful?"

She gently took the fine watch in her hand and held it carefully, afraid of dropping it, and enormously confused by the generosity of the gift. She knew O'Connor well enough to know that it was something freely given.

"He spoke awkwardly of why he was doing it. But I think he misses Sean terribly, even more now as he sees me completing school."

Still admiring the watch, she looked up at the boy, never surprised by how much insight the youngster could bring to situations. "You're right," she said. "But even so, it is too much. Should you keep it?"

Eduardo, offended and shocked by the question, quickly replied, "It's mine! He wanted to give it to me. I'll treasure it always and will protect it." With this, he gently reached forward and took it from her hand.

Relinquishing it, she sat back and sighed. 'What more did he say?"

Accepting that the watch was safe, Eduardo answered, "He said that it should remind me of the importance of trying to be successful and that its use as a keeper of time should serve as a reminder of the importance of not wasting a minute in the pursuit of success. He also said the gold is a symbol of wealth, a symbol of success."

Letting her head back slightly, she closed her eyes briefly and clarified, "Wealth would be wonderful. But success can mean many things, Son, and does not always involve money."

"I know. You've always said that. But, still, it does seem nice... the idea of being able to have a big house and a big, beautiful black car from the United States like Señor O'Connor has. He lives well."

"So have we. We have been blessed with all that we need."

"Yes, we have. But most of it because of his wealth."

She laughed slightly. "That's only partly true." She knew there was no point in arguing with this boy, so full of himself, especially today of all days, and so clearly filling with ambition as any young man might be and should be at this age. So she simply went along. Then she opened her eyes and sat up. "I have good news for you."

He turned his head slightly, wondering to himself how this day could possibly get any better, and asked, "What?"

In the village, there is a gem cutter by the name of Alberto. He is an older man and very skilled in preparing rough emeralds for sale as finely cut stones. I have approached him, and he has told me that he needs an apprentice. He has no sons and would like to have a bright young person willing to work hard and to learn. There is no one to compare with Alberto in terms of skill and knowledge about emeralds. He makes a comfortable living. And there is no way to learn his craft without apprenticing under a skilled workman."

"And you'd like me to be his apprentice. Am I not old for that now?"

"I asked him. He said not at all. He said that he would not want to begin apprenticing too young a boy anyway. He pays a small percentage of his work to you as a living and meanwhile you help him with the work as you become able. Eventually you would take over his trade. Isn't this wonderful?!" Her eyes glistened with excitement as she shared this good news with her son. She felt terribly proud of young Eduardo. She had given birth to him, had raised him, and felt especially pleased to see him now turning into the young man she had hoped he might become.

Eduardo looked down at the watch and thought about his conversation with Señor O'Connor. Then he looked up again and saw his mother's eyes shining and the eager look in her expression. He simply asked, "You'd like very much for me to do this, wouldn't you?"

Sensing hesitation in his voice and manner, she asked, "Of course, but wouldn't you be excited to be able to do it?"

Not wanting to disappoint her and realizing that working in this way so close to home would allow him to be closer to her, close enough to see about her as time went by and as she became older...his mind racing, one thought tumbling clumsily over another... he struggled not to show on his face all that was going through his mind. "Of course. When should I speak to him?"

Releasing a great sigh of relief, she said, "We can enjoy Sunday tomorrow and then you could go Monday morning. Now let's eat. I'm hungry." She headed back to the small table in her room, where she and her son would sit together to eat what she had brought on two covered plates carried from the kitchen.

Eduardo ate quietly with his mother. He had had enough excitement for one day. He tried not to feel disappointed. After all, to be apprenticed to an expert craftsman would be a fine opportunity. If he were to be patient and to learn well, he could grow into a tradesman and respected member of the community. Not so bad, after all, to aspire toward that. It was not difficult to pass time quietly in the evening this way, considering this sort of future. His mother was clearly exhausted. After they had finished their supper, he offered to take the plates back to the house. By the time he returned, his mother had fallen asleep in the rocking chair by her bed. He read for a short time, not knowing whether to wake her or to let her sleep.

Finally, he walked to her chair and gently awakened her. "Mother, you need to go to bed so that you can sleep all night."

"Oh, I guess I slipped away," she laughed. " Goodnight, son."

And he left her room and retired to his own, along with his book about the history of South America. He read for only a while before realizing that he would not be able to stretch out any longer this splendid , albeit confusing day. There was much to think about. But he was too exhausted to deal with all of it now. As he got into bed, he took the gold watch from his small night table, turning it over in his hand and holding it up to his ear to hear the clearly discernible ticking sound. It was a fine watch. He considered Señor O'Connor's comment about the timepiece serving as a reminder of the idea that time marches on, quickly and that life does not last forever. It would be difficult to decide what to do with the years that lay ahead. But this was too much to consider now.

✢ ✢ ✢

The chapel had been built to hold a much smaller congregation than the church now held. The priest added another mass during the morning and so addressed the problem. Eduardo and his mother went to early mass together. She led the way down the center aisle, crossing herself before entering a pew to the right. Eduardo followed her, as he had for as long as he could recall. It wasn't that he intended to be such a good boy all that time. He simply was good without trying, and his mother was so proud of him that she often bragged to the priest, who sometimes would admonish her against the sin of pride. Even so, the priest was also proud of this boy.

The chapel was full; people stood in the back. The mass lasted just over an hour. The uninspiring homily was blessedly brief and simple but sharply focused on the gospel lesson for that day. Even if the priest had been extremely well educated, he would have needed to keep his language and his message simple and to the point. After all, these were uneducated people…devout, hard-working people. The priest was prepared to do his job and cared about his flock. And his flock cared deeply about him, even though he was still a young man, much younger than the prior priest who had died two years earlier. The older cleric never demonstrated any passion for his calling and had little empathy for the challenges his parishioners faced. He only performed the basic functions of his job. This younger man approached the challenge differently and as a result found himself much loved by parishioners.

The service completed, Eduardo and his mother exited, standing in line to greet the father at the door as they left. "Congratulations, Eduardo," said the priest. We are all proud of you for doing so well. What will you do next?"

Eduardo hesitated only briefly, and said smiling, "I have to think about that."

"Of course. I understand. Well, we all wish you a good life and hope you will find a way to remain nearby. Good day."

The mother stood slightly to one side, smiling and nodding in agreement. She took Eduardo's arm and gently guided him to the side. "Come here for a second. You need to meet someone."

All he saw in the direction they were headed was an older man, slightly stooped, wearing glasses and apparently waiting for them. Eduardo had seen the man before but had never met him. Even though the village was small, the separateness of O'Connor's house and the estate did not allow children the opportunity to get to know everyone around the village. Eduardo and his mother approached the old man. He seemed to straighten his stance and began to smile as they came near.

"Eduardo, I want you to meet Maestro Alberto Gonzalez, master emerald cutter."

The old man held out his hand. His expression suggested not only greeting but genuine warmth. Eduardo noticed the old hand, wrinkled, not unusually large, but strong with long slender fingers, hands only slightly calloused, worn, used, durable, adept.

"Good morning, Don Alberto. It's a pleasure to meet you."

Señor Gonzalez replied warmly, "The same here. I understand you may be interested in learning a trade."

Eduardo, trying to support his mother, did not hesitate but answered with a qualified "Yes, perhaps."

The old man, not surprised by the boy's hesitance added, "Well, we can talk about it more seriously tomorrow morning. I wanted to meet you."

The boy asked, 'I have not seen you here before, have I?"

"Eduardo!" his mother scolded.

"I'm sorry. But I haven't, have I?"

"It's true. It has been a long time since I've attended Mass. Your mother invited me to come, and I thought I would, if only to meet you."

Trying to sound more respectful, the boy reached out to shake hands, "Well, it's good to meet you and I'll be there bright and early tomorrow to talk."

Surprised by how much confidence the boy showed, the old man shook hands with him firmly and smiled, "Until tomorrow."

Eduardo walked home with his mother. As they walked, she asked "You know, you did not sound excited by the prospect of being an apprentice. It's a marvelous opportunity. You do realize that, don't you?"

He hesitated, wondering how to open the subject and finally decided to say what was on his mind. "I'm a little unsure, Mamá."

"What about?"

"Well, Señor O'Connor took me aside yesterday and offered to pay for me to attend a university in Puerto Lindo, if I could gain acceptance there."

Her face clouded. She was unable to hide her disappointment. If her son left the estate and the village, he would be very far away for years and would probably end up settling someplace far away. Who would take care of her as the years passed? She could not help herself. "Puerto Lindo is far away. And it takes so long to get a university degree."

"That's true. The teacher says it takes four years."

"So you've talked about this with the teacher as well?"

"She was answering my question a year ago or so when she commented that I would be a good student in a university. I asked her how long it takes and she told me."

His mother stopped walking and considered how to say it but could not find a better way than just to say right out what was in her heart. "I don't want you to go, my son. I want you close to me through the years. If you go there to study, you'll stay there. I know it."

Not wanting to argue, he simply gave up for now and added, "It is just a thought. It was very kind of the patrón to make the offer."

Somewhat more relaxed, she continued walking, "That's true. He is a very good man. He has always been good to both of us."

Eduardo walked the rest of the way quietly beside her. She said nothing more. Each lost in thought: she thinking about how desperately she wanted her son near her, wanting him to marry and to settle nearby so that he could take care of her some day and he thinking not about how attractive it would be to be away but about how much more interesting it might be to be able to study seriously rather than to become a tradesman. Although he was pulled toward leaving, he felt a tremendous desire to be around the place—and person—whom he had always loved. Maybe it would be enough to have a trade and to live in the only place he'd ever known. There was no reason to assume that things would be better on the outside...none at all. Neither mother nor son was completely at ease that evening. Neither slept well. Each struggled not to say exactly what was thought.

The distance from O'Connor's estate to the village was only a mile or so. Although the road was wide enough for vehicles, it was seldom traveled by anyone. O'Connor had a big beautiful black sedan that had impressed Eduardo to no end. Although he never pictured himself in a position of having one—he never even imagined himself driving—he did admire it greatly.

Most of the meager traffic on this dirt road was on foot. Eduardo, awakened early by his mother, and after joining her for a quiet breakfast in the large house's kitchen, set out on his own walking to the village that Monday morning. He had not slept well but was young enough to feel rested and ready for the day.

As he trudged along, he heard the sound of O'Connor's car coming behind him. He stopped and turned to look. A plume of dust flew up behind it, fanning out like a bleached peacock's tail, with only the color-less shape. The sedan approached but slowed as it came nearer, carrying its dust cloud toward Eduardo, choking him for a moment until it dissipated. The car window lowered on the driver's side.

"Get in?", O'Connor half-said and half-asked.

"Thank you," Eduardo answered politely as he stepped around the car to open the back door.

"No, you can ride up here with me. Get in."

He did as suggested and sat uncomfortably in the seat up front with the patrón.

"You seem to be going into the village. To see anyone in particular?"

"I'm going to a small shop where the gem cutter works."

"You mean Don Alberto? Alberto Gonzalez?"

"Yes."

"He's a good man. And why are you going to see him, if I might ask?"

"He is willing to take an apprentice. I'm going to visit with him about that."

O'Connor looked surprised and slowed the car, turning to look at the boy's face. "What about the offer I made?"

Eduardo, by this time extremely uncomfortable, almost afraid of how O'Connor might react, said hesitantly, "I appreciate very much your generous offer, and I'm still considering it. But I also need to consider this as one option. I hope you're not offended."

O'Connor always impressed by the boy's honesty and openness, seemed to relax and focused again on his driving. "Makes sense to me. A young man needs to consider alternatives. And Sr. Gonzalez is a fine man and would be an excellent teacher of a distinguished trade."

Not really knowing what to say, and caught off-guard by the sudden degree of attention by the owner, Eduardo said again awkwardly, "Thank you."

O'Connor arrived quickly at the edge of the village, needing to head on through it and beyond, and stopped briefly to let the boy out. Before he pulled away, O'Connor told Eduardo, "Listen to all he has to say. Consider it carefully. But keep very much in mind what I suggested, my boy. And if it's too hard to decide, know that whichever you decide first, you can always try the other later." He smiled at the boy, rolled up the window and drove away.

Eduardo watched the car disappear. He wondered once again why his patrón was being so helpful. It seemed difficult for Eduardo to imagine himself deserving such generosity and patience from so important a man.

The small shop was close by. He approached the open door and looked in. There was a tiny workroom in the front, a separation extending out from one wall and then another small area behind that. He knocked on the door loudly and said, "Hello. Are you here?"

The old man emerged from behind the separation. Exterior windows along the wall let in plenty of outdoor light. He walked out smiling and wiping his hands on an ivory-colored apron. He had an odd-looking eyepiece attached to his head above one eye. "Good morning! I've been looking forward to having you here." As Don Alberto spoke, he removed the apron and draped it over his left arm. Rather than folding it to put it away, he simply laid it aside on the back of a chair as he walked by. Extending his right hand, he welcomed the boy, shaking his hand in greeting. While placing his left hand on the boy's shoulder, he patted it and then turned to escort the boy over to the two chairs that stood together in this small room.

"Let's sit and talk for a bit."

They sat facing each other, the old man smiling and at first saying nothing as if he knew not exactly how or where to begin. The boy, having absolutely no idea what to say, silently waited to be spoken to.

"My boy, does the idea of learning how to be an emerald cutter interest you at all?" Don Alberto asked intently. The boy said nothing, but the old man had spent many decades observing people and had learned how to gauge signs of interest. Based solely on the first meeting the day earlier outside of church, he had quickly decided that this was much more the mother's idea than the boy's.

The boy remained silent, but shifted in his seat and sat up straighter.

"I realize that you know nothing about what would be involved. So maybe it is unfair to ask such a thing until you have some idea what to expect. I'll tell you."

Eduardo felt relieved to have the older man setting the agenda. Listening well was something the boy could do. And the old man was correct. Eduardo had no idea at all what might be involved in this. He knew nothing but the classroom at school and the exciting vastness of the forest and mountains surrounding the village and the estate.

"I am growing old, as you can see. I will not be able to do this work much longer. I took an apprentice many years ago before you were born. But that boy married and moved away to work in Bogotá at something else. I never heard from him again. Meanwhile, I'd been teaching him for at least two years when he left. It was very frustrating for me and yet appeared not to bother him at all. I lost patience and refused to take on apprentices for many years. But the years passed quickly. And now I am old and have no son. I have no wife. And there is no other skilled gem cutter anywhere nearby. When I am gone, there will be no one who could teach. If I teach you and you learn well, you could carry on the work in this shop or could set up your own, here or in a city. You would have a solid way to earn a living anywhere and, if you are highly skilled, the products of your work would carry much value. I cannot imagine anyone wanting to live in Bogotá or even in a port city closer by."

Eduardo sat and listened, intrigued by the sound of the old man's voice and by the message he was conveying. The old man sat still for a brief moment, watching the boy's face. "You say little."

"I speak when I have something worth saying."

The old man chuckled and said partly to himself, "I wish everyone were that way." And the man breathed deeply seeming to try to remember where he was.

"There are four "C's" to consider when thinking about emeralds. Color, clarity, cut, and carat. When you get older, you'll find that people in the city and even farther away think mainly of the carat or the weight of the stone. They think that is what determines the value of the gem. It is not. The weight or size of the stone is the least important factor. At least as important is the natural character of the stone, which you can determine by its color and clarity. The color, which comes with the stone as one finds it, is very important. The darker the green, the better but only if there is great clarity within it. You can see the effects of clarity. But the clarity's cause has to do with the fact that all emeralds have particles included. A cutter has to chip away most of the rough stone to create a gem fit for jewelry. And that brings us to the value that we add as gem cutters: the quality of the cut. A perfect emerald will be symmetrical and will have completely uniform facets or flat faces. The cut must not be too shallow. It must not be too deep. All this together combines to create the most valuable, the most ideal gemstone. And I cannot overemphasize the fact that much depends on the quality work of the gem cutter. Of course, much depends on God himself, who creates the rough stone—and the cutter. But it is up to the cutter to work as the hands of God here on Earth making the most of what God has begun."

By this time, Eduardo was fascinated. What most interested him was the sparkle in the eye of the old man as he spoke about his craft. This old man clearly loved his work. That in itself was something to be admired. Eduardo would later come to appreciate how much this sort of passion was to be envied.

The old man stopped and caught his breath and thought. "Would you like some tea?"

"Yes, please."

He got up and walked back into the back room and lit the wick on a very small container of fluid and then placed the tea kettle on a rack over the flame. "The craft of gem cutting goes back for centuries and is usually taught by one master to one apprentice at a time. It is an art and craft that takes much time to learn. Are you patient enough to take the time?"

"How much?"

Gonzalez grinned, realizing he was beginning to tweak the interest of this youngster. "As long as it takes. Most men would normally take on an apprentice younger than you are now, because it can require years. But you seem bright. If you are interested and willing to work and to be patient, you could learn much in perhaps fewer years."

"Four or five?"

Don Alberto pulled the tea kettle off the flame, extinguished the fire and poured out the hot water first into one cup containing a metal tea ball with loose leaf tea inside and then moving the tea ball to the other cup and pouring water over it. He handed one cup to the boy and took the other for himself and began to sip, distracted and having already forgotten the boy's question, or having successfully managed to ignore him, possibly hoping the boy would shift to some other question.

"My boy, it's difficult to say. It depends on the natural talent involved in the student, the hours spent learning, how attentive he is, how focused, and so on...."

"Five or six years?"

"Why so specific? Do you have someplace where you need to be in five years?"

"It would take me four years to obtain a degree at the university."

"University?" asked the old man, at first puzzled by the suggestion of college study for a peasant boy like Eduardo. But then it occurred to him who the boy's patrón was. Anything might be possible. "Is that what you want to do?"

"I don't know. I'm not sure."

The old man sat back down and sipped more of his tea. "You have to decide. I'm not willing to invest my time and resources on another boy who is going to turn and leave all too soon."

"I want to study. But I know that I should not go and leave my mother to herself for the years that I would be away. She has been so wonderful to me. It would not be fair to her."

"That's very noble. You seem sincere. But I'm sure she would want you to do what is best for you. Would she not?"

The boy did not answer at first. He hesitated but then said, "Sometimes it is not clear what is best to do."

"Ahhhhh, wisdom far beyond years. The sad part is that in some people's lives, it is *never* clear what is best to do. At least in yours, I think you will know or will choose well even if you don't feel confident at first."

"Do you have questions for me?"

"How would I earn money while learning the craft?"

"I will feed you lunches here every day. You would eat at home before work and in the evening. And if you stay and work hard at learning and make progress, I will begin paying you a portion of my earnings each month. It could not be much. But then again you would spend less, living here so close. And, if you have patience, you'll become expert at cutting precious gemstones. And then someday, you can take over my business."

The old man had looked at the floor as he struggled to string together words to express what he wanted to convey. He began to speak about what most mattered. Alberto's eyes glistened as he looked up directly into the young man's eyes. He spoke of the boy's future as something he himself needed, as if this boy might, just *might,* be able to step into the role that the old man had hoped a son might someday play.

Eduardo, not knowing exactly how to interpret the look on the old man's face, did not understand at all why the old man's voice trembled slightly with emotion as he spoke. He was, after all, still only a boy, unable to appreciate the importance of leaving a legacy. Even so, Eduardo tried to imagine himself as the person that the old man was struggling to portray.

Don Alberto finished, but did not see the same glimmer of enthusiasm in the boy's eyes that he had hoped for. He lowered his gaze and asked with more detachment, "So, what do you think? Is that something that interests you?" He looked away briefly and then turned back, realizing how much he wanted the boy to be interested but hesitant to appear vulnerable to rejection. He tried to keep his face as expressionless as possible.

Eduardo surprised him with a simple answer, "Yes." And then the boy sat as if waiting for a more complicated question to be laid before him, since he had already dealt with the first one.

The old man, caught off-guard, asked further, "Are you certain? It requires hard work, patience, and staying in one place for what might seem like a long time to a young man."

"I love my mother dearly and owe her much. Trying to find a way to stay here and to be able to make a good living some day is a good investment."

Eduardo said this, feeling the words slip out coldly. In his eighteen-year-old heart, the idea of going away to a university, to be among interesting people and new studies and ideas, on the one hand frightened him and on the other drew him in with a force so overwhelming as to be difficult to comprehend. Yet, unlike most boys his age, he was able to appreciate the priorities that mattered most to him and was able to push down the compulsion to go away in order to find a more exciting life elsewhere. He was able to force himself to look for a way to make a rewarding life right where he was, or more to the point right where the person who had watched over him and cared for him was.

Without a husband, without parents to see about her, without family of any sort apart from him, his mother would need his presence and his attention and care in the years ahead. He was very much aware of the fact that he could not possibly have grown into the strong, healthy young man he had become without enormous love and attention from her. He must stay close enough to be able to return the favor through the years... and he planned to do just that.

Besides, there was something about this lonely old man that appealed to him. Alberto sat alone day after day, working on something requiring great skill and enormous concentration, and hidden away in this grimy, depressing old studio. Yet his eyes still shone when he spoke about his profession. There had to be great strength in this old man. At one moment, judging by the look on his face and the eagerness peeking out from behind those tired eyes, it seemed as if he were not so ancient after all. Yes, he could work with this man. He could learn from him, at least through the summer to see how it went. And, on top of all the rest, the old man looked as if he both needed and very much deserved help.

As exciting as going away to the university seemed, there was something terrifying about it. Eduardo had never been away from home. He had heard stories of bad things happening to very good people there, bad things caused not by accidents but by malicious intent. There was something more intimidating about that than anything he had ever encountered in the jungle. And so, "yes" was his answer to Don Alberto, and there was no need for more thought about it.

The old man's eyes shone even more brightly. He could not keep from clapping his hands together in happiness. "Good! You can start tomorrow if you want."

The boy hesitated a second and then asked what was on his mind. "Can I not begin now?"

"Ohhhhhh. I think we're going to get along very well, young man. Truly. Very well. Let's have some more tea and then I'll begin showing you the tools."

Don Alberto held out his large, rough right hand. It was rougher than one would expect for having performed such delicately challenging handwork for so many decades. "Welcome." And they shook hands, sat and finished another cup of tea and began the first day.

Don Alberto began by explaining the history of the emerald to Eduardo. He explained that emeralds had been in circulation as far back as 4000 years in Egypt and that this precious stone is found in various countries, but that some of the most beautiful and famous stones had been found right here in Colombia, in the province of Boyoaca.

"The emerald has always been seen as a symbol of eternal spring and even of immortality. It has always been thought to have special healing powers, especially among native peoples. Here in our country, stories about the powers of the emerald are legendary. It has always seemed a great irony to me that the emerald is viewed almost with awe by the people, even though the Indians—a very superstitious people—have believed that the mines, as part of the great underground, are influenced by the devil. Ha! I guess it makes sense that the devil himself would want to keep control of something known to be so beautiful and thought to possess tremendous power for good."

Eduardo sat and listened, mesmerized by the intensity with which the old man told his story. He tried not to bristle at the derogatory mention of "Indians." Don Alberto, although not wealthy, was of Spanish descent. Eduardo's mother was of the Motilone native people. She was only half Motilone. Her father was an Englishman. Eduardo was keenly aware of his mother and of her mixed heritage. He chose not to say anything about this. Not yet.

"In the 16ᵗʰ Century, a Spanish captain, Captain Juan de Penagos discovered the first emerald in our country, near Muzo, not far from here. One of his soldiers stopped when his horse was crippled by something he had stepped upon. The captain dismounted to see what was wrong and found the green "rock" the size of a boy's fist stuck in the horse's foot. And so it began. The rush to mine the precious stone." Don Alberto laughed out loud. "Ha! It may be that the real devil was Captain de Penagos himself!"

Don Alberto skimmed over the history of the precious gemstone and its importance and its legends and talked about the importance of the four "C"s: color, clarity, cut and carat. Hours flew by as if minutes. Eduardo heard why the stone was so fascinating, and why the cutter's craft mattered. The rough stone itself was amazing enough, but a properly cut emerald could be worth a great deal of money, more than Eduardo had ever imagined. That was why Don Alberto kept rough stones and stones in progress, as well as finished cut gems, safely hidden away in a huge safe far too large to be carried away. At the end of the day's lesson, Eduardo found himself engrossed in the story of the emerald and quietly thought to himself how the emerald amulet that had made its way to him fit into the legends he was hearing about. It was easier now to believe in enormous powers within the amulet, to believe in a value far greater than money, a power difficult to comprehend.

Later that evening, as Eduardo walked out of the patrón's home after supper in the kitchen, he ran across Don Edwin.

"Well, young man, and how do you like your apprenticeship as you begin?"

"A great deal. There is much to learn and the beginning is slow. That makes it harder than if I were working in the forest. But I like it. I like Don Alberto also."

"Good. It's hard for a young man to be patient in learning. Be as patient as you can be and learn well." Then O'Connor leaned down slightly and lowered his voice. "And know all the time that my offer always stands. Understand that there is only one time in each year when you can begin at the university. So if you don't begin this coming semester, you'll have to wait another full year. Keep that in mind."

Eduardo, genuinely trying to be positive about his apprenticeship and struggling to look at it as something for a lifetime, felt confused and a little disturbed by comments like this from his patrón. And so he said matter-of-factly, "I will keep it in mind. But I'm glad to be having the chance to learn a trade under so fine a workman as Don Alberto."

O'Connor patted him gently on the shoulder and smiled, saying, "Good boy. You do what you know is right, and make up your own mind as to what that is. Good night." And he walked on into his study, leaving Eduardo to walk out with his head down, wondering how it is that a person can know with certainty what to do or which road to take. Oh well, he did know for certain that he would not find the answer this evening.

Eduardo's mother could not possibly have been any happier. As he came home each evening, he looked content, always seeming to have enjoyed the time he spent with Don Alberto. After the first two weeks, they decided that it was not necessary for Eduardo to spend the entire day with the gem cutter. During the earliest part of his training, simply observing and listening carefully to instruction made up the biggest part of Eduardo's training. He also cleaned up the studio at the end of the day and helped with errands. The two-room space began to look cleaner than it had in years. Eduardo even came in early to clean the inside and outside of the windows. Don Alberto had not realized how dirty they had become. And he appreciated the extra light in his work area. He realized, as each day went by, that he was feeling years younger and was looking forward to beginning work each day.

There had been a time years before when Don Alberto would have been impatient himself with the learning process, with the fact that a young person requires so much time to absorb what has to be learned, and that the young learner requires patience and understanding from his teacher. Fortunately, Alberto was sensitive to this now, in his later years, and appreciated having a young person around each day. He could not picture himself being anything but pleased by having the opportunity to teach a youngster an honorable way to make a living, preparing a young man to have a way to take care of himself and any family that might come along some day. He found himself taking pride in this young man, in his attitude and his work ethic, more quickly than he had imagined that he might.

At the end of the second week, Don Alberto asked Eduardo if he would rather work only in the mornings, leaving him free to work elsewhere in the afternoons, since at this stage of the learning process that might be sufficient commitment each day. Eduardo thanked him for this offer, understanding that it would make no difference in what he might earn from Don Alberto and also that it would leave him free to vary each day. He liked that idea. He enjoyed his time with the old man and enjoyed watching him work and learning from what Don Alberto told him. He also enjoyed being allowed to work with a rough stone occasionally, trying his hand with stones selected by Gonzalez that were likely to be suitable for an apprentice to use for practice.

But it was tedious work for a young man scarcely beyond boyhood. Eduardo liked the idea of looking for some way to work outdoors in the afternoons. The opportunity presented itself when he visited with his mother that evening about what Don Alberto had said. She suggested he speak with O'Connor to see if he could help.

Eduardo had become more accustomed to visiting with the patrón. He no longer trembled inside when he spoke with the gentleman. This time he felt comfortable approaching O'Connor directly and so, after supper, knocked on the door of the man's office. He was, though, still timid enough to hang back almost out of sight until invited in.

"Yes?"

Eduardo stepped forward into the light, standing in clear view. "May I come in?"

O'Connor answered warmly, "Of course, Eduardo. What do you need?"

With this, he rose and moved over to a chair by a round table and invited the young man to sit in the other chair. "How can I help you?"

Eduardo knew it was only a saying. But he wondered whether the patrón had actually known in advance that the boy needed his help. "I need advice."

"Certainly. About what?" O'Connor realized the boy was having trouble spitting out what was on his mind and tried to reassure him by his tone and manner that it was all right to speak up.

"Don Alberto seems pleased to have me as his apprentice. And I am happy to learn with him. But there is not yet a great deal I can do to produce for him. He said it would be acceptable for me to look for other work for half of each day and that I could still accomplish everything needed in terms of learning his trade just with a half-day spent in his studio."

"Sounds reasonable. And you seem to agree."

"Yes. The study is slow and is always indoors. It would be good to have work in the afternoon letting me be outdoors. Is there any way you could help me to have some job like that?"

"Of course there is. There is always a need for workers down in the mines. But there is much work to be done above the mines. Would you be interested in that?"

"Yes. Anything that would give me physical work to do and fresh air and sun."

"That's not a problem at all, my boy. It will be difficult, though. You can expect to be exhausted each evening. You'd certainly not be bored. It would give you a taste of what it is like to work with both your hands and your back."

"Whom would I have to speak to?"

O'Connor could not help laughing. But as he saw Eduardo perplexed by the laughter, he stopped abruptly and tried to put on a more serious face. "You've spoken to the right person. When do you want to begin? The mine is no great distance from here."

"Monday?"

Not mentioning that each of the mines worked seven days a week and seeing no need to suggest to young Eduardo that he could work through the weekend since this was Friday evening, he simply answered,

"Done. The foreman will be looking for you early Monday afternoon. Here's where it is." And he pulled out a map which showed clearly where the small mine was, within walking distance from the village. Eduardo studied it quickly, realizing exactly how to get there and back. He then looked up, smiled, said "Thanks", and left the office. As he neared the door, O'Connor called to him.

"Eduardo, just a second." The boy stopped in the doorway and turned to listen.

"I'm very proud of you. Very proud indeed. I should say that out loud instead of merely thinking it to myself. I want you to know that each job you do will prepare you for life in some way. You may someday become a gem cutter. But the work outside will be good for you physically. And it will give you an idea of the business I'm involved in. Please understand that if you do someday decide to pursue an education, I would eventually make a place for you in my business. Everything you will have learned by then, including this work will have prepared you. Keep all of this in mind."

"Thank you, sir. I will," Eduardo said, not just being polite. This was something he had never expected, and left doors open no matter what he might choose. He felt relieved as he went to sleep that night. Knowing that any decision he might make now wouldn't close every other opportunity somehow made the world around him seem more secure. Being honest with himself, he had felt more than a little confined, even though he had freely chosen and understood why he was choosing to do it. For now, he could enjoy what there was to enjoy each day. And there was much to enjoy. Life looked freshly promising as he slipped off to sleep.

The following Monday morning, Don Alberto allowed Eduardo to begin the day by examining a rough stone, encouraging him to note everything he had been taught. Then he invited him to begin the work of cutting the stone, of taking the tool and making the first cut. Eduardo, wanting very much not to ruin a perfectly good rough stone, hesitated before making his first strike.

"Go on. I've selected a stone that is acceptable for learning. Don't be afraid of it."

Eduardo, with the stone carefully secured in the brace, and with his magnifying eyepiece placed too firmly in his tightly squinted eye, made the first strike. He looked up at Don Alberto and grinned a triumphant grin. Nothing bad had happened.

"Continue. You know what to do."

More confident now, Eduardo steadied his hand, hit the stone and broke it in two. A disaster. This was precisely what a cutter was not supposed to do. He felt his heart sink and at the same time felt so angry that he wanted to hit the table as hard as possible with his fist but controlled his anger.

"That's all right. Don't worry. We all learn by our mistakes. It takes extreme attention to detail Eduardo. It takes a calm head and heart, a steady hand, and a clear, discerning eye, and much practice. Meanwhile, you have begun. It is always difficult to cut any precious stone. But the emerald is especially delicate. Look. There are inclusions within this polished stone. They help give it its fire. But they also make the gemstone more delicate than many stones. So we have "the emerald cut," a softer, more delicate cut that keeps the cutter from ruining the stone. Now here, let me show you. Watch carefully."

Waiting for the boy to get up and to stand aside, the old man sat down and quietly took a similarly rough stone, secured it in place and made his first cut and then his second and then his third, deftly chipping away only the slightest pieces of roughness, coaxing a thing of beauty ever so delicately, slowly, meticulously out of the rough-edged, hard and unforgiving rock.

"Think of the rough stone as a canvas, son, if that helps. A canvas has to have that first brush stroke before anything can begin to appear on its surface. Eventually, a specific place or person, completely recognizable, emerges out of nowhere, but only after a thousand subtle strokes by the painter. It takes time and patience. It requires love. Love for the very special uniqueness of each particular stone. Love for what it can become with a little coaxing. Love for the work itself and for the sense of satisfaction after having completed an exquisite work of art. Think of it as a miracle, my boy. And you are the miracle worker making it happen."

Recovered from his frustration now, Eduardo, standing just over Don Alberto's shoulder and watching his every move, corrected the old man. "It's a miracle. But you're the miracle worker, not me."

"For now, for now. Stay with it and pay attention."

The morning flew by. It was as if everything in the world disappeared except for that old man's expert hands and the stone—the object of his attention and talent. A beautiful precious gem began to emerge from a rough stone after each cut by the gifted old craftsman.

Finally, it was time to eat. The stone had been worked as much as was necessary for one morning. The old man knew that even the most skilled expert must not rush his work and that the key to great results was a steady, step-by-step approach. "Let's eat. I'm hungry."

He prepared leftover soup from his dinner the night before and pulled out a loaf of day-old bread and some cheese. They sat at the work counter and ate together. The old man began telling the boy about his youth, about his own apprenticeship and how frustrated he had become so long before. He remembered as if it were yesterday the pain of failing to get the results he wanted to achieve. He had listened carefully to the master and had watched with enormous concentration. Don Alberto's master had been a gifted gem cutter but a terrible teacher, unable to offer advice that was meaningful; unable to present comparisons to other efforts that might help the student better grasp the correct attitude and frame of mind to adopt before striking a stone. And yet young apprentice Alberto Gonzalez persisted. He mentioned to young Eduardo that being persistent in pursuit of excellence was more important, in his experience, than anything else—more important than effort, more important even than talent.

Eduardo sat eating and listening intently. This old man was more fun to listen to—and to be around—than the boy had thought any adult could be. Lunchtime passed quickly. It was time to make the walk to the small mine outside the village. "Good day, Don Alberto. Until tomorrow."

"Good day, my boy. Be careful. Work hard, but take care of your hands. Wear gloves. Here, take these," he said as he stepped over and pulled some out from a drawer.

Eduardo took them, stuffed them into his pocket, and left.

The days passed smoothly for Eduardo, working and learning with Don Alberto in the mornings and then doing hard physical labor near the entrance to the mine in the afternoons. O'Connor had not wanted the boy descending into the dark, dangerous mine because he feared for his safety. He had come to care a great deal for the boy's well-being through the years and held the boy's mother in high regard as a loyal servant. He just wanted to give the boy a chance to see what hard labor involved and also, in the back of his mind, wanted the boy to be as exposed as possible to mining.

He very much hoped that someday Eduardo would go on to the university and return home to help run the business. There was no reason to assume that the son of an Indian woman would be capable of accomplishment such as that—not in most people's minds. But this was clearly no ordinary boy. O'Connor had watched him grow and knew him to be unusually bright, quick to learn, and strong of character. This boy had the potential of becoming an exceptionally fine man someday, possibly even a better man than Sean could have become. Even if only thinking that to himself, it hurt O'Connor to consider the truth about his dead son. The very memory of the loss of Sean was more than he could bear, and so he struggled not to think about him at all. He found himself focusing more and more on how to develop young Eduardo into a surrogate son and into an educated gentleman capable of becoming a great leader.

Hard work strengthens character, or so O'Connor firmly believed. As far as Eduardo was concerned, he didn't particularly enjoy the hard labor. He did enjoy the sunshine and fresh air and the penetrating ache in his muscles at the end of the day. Sitting and listening carefully to the master gem cutter during the mornings and struggling to learn the intricacies of cutting fine emeralds were more draining than the strenuous work in the latter half of the workday. Days and weeks flowed one into another.

One afternoon Eduardo, chopping wood with a large axe, grew tired late in the day and let the axe slip. Without great force, it nonetheless hit his left leg hard enough to make a cut. Screaming and falling to the ground, he dropped the axe and tried to reach down toward the damaged, bleeding leg. Another man working next to him ripped the lower part of his shirt and tied it around the wound as quickly as possible.

Eduardo writhed on the ground. His leg bled profusely. Although there was normally a truck at the site, a worker had driven it to the nearby village to pick up supplies. There was a cart and a horse for moving material near the mine area. The man picked up Eduardo and placed him in the back of the cart, jerked the reins to startle the lethargic horse, and hurried with Eduardo along the dirt road toward the village.

There was only one doctor in the village, and the worker drove the cart directly to the physician's office. He carried Eduardo in and lifted him onto a table, going past patients sitting quietly and undisturbed, accustomed to serious accidents involving persons around the mine. The doctor, who had been seeing a patient with a bad cough, hearing what had happened, rushed in to see about the seriousness of the boy's wound. He tore the pant leg and cut off the tourniquet that had been hastily applied by Eduardo's fellow worker. The wound required stitches.

"Angélica!" the doctor shouted to his one nurse. "Come quickly!" She rushed into the room and immediately began to help clean the wound, applying antibacterial liquid to the wound itself and to the surrounding area. She washed the leg well and poured more disinfectant on the wound. The red tint of the bacteriacide painted the boy's leg a slightly different shade of red from the color of fresh blood. The blood coming out was not bright red. That meant that an important artery had not been hit. But the wound, although relatively superficial, could become serious if ignored and if not cleaned, disinfected, and closed quickly.

A new tourniquet was hastily applied slightly above the wound. The doctor began stitching together the raw, rough-edged pieces of crudely insulted flesh as if sewing together a piece of poultry for roasting.

Meanwhile, a mild sedative had been given to Eduardo and then a local anesthetic prior to the stitching. He was calmer and was resting quietly on the table now as if the entire event had never occurred. The doctor completed his work calmly, focusing on each stitch, on each tug of the thread until the wound was closed completely. More disinfectant was applied liberally to the area by the nurse, and then the doctor stood up straight and said, "Young man, you are very fortunate. You could have bled to death. You absolutely must take greater care when using an axe. Big, mature men have great respect for an axe and for its power to injure. You must learn to respect it too."

Eduardo, still groggy from the sedative, listened and answered mechanically "Yes, sir." But it was as if the physician's words were coming from someone and somewhere else entirely and from a great distance. Or perhaps it was that Eduardo himself had slipped far, far away. Nothing seemed connected. Nothing seemed real. There was still a dull pain from his leg. But the aggressive pain had subsided. He grew sleepy and began to lose consciousness.

The doctor, cleaning his hands and arms to remove the rapidly drying blood stains and to disinfect himself, stood over the boy and felt his forehead, took his pulse, determining that the boy was stable and was simply resting calmly now in a deep drug-induced sleep. His breathing was normal. His pulse and blood pressure were fine. The wound looked acceptably repaired. The physician turned to the nurse. "This is a boy from O'Connor's estate, isn't it?"

"That's what the man said who carried him here."

"Let the boy rest and check him once in a while for the remainder of the afternoon. Have someone advise O'Connor."

With that, the doctor turned and left the room to get back to his other patients.

Eduardo awoke in his own bed, turned his head, and saw his mother reading quietly in a hard-backed chair at his side. "Hello!" she said as if surprised that he was awake. "How do you feel?"

Still groggy from the sedative, although now awake enough to hear and to speak, he answered, "My leg hurts. My head hurts." He struggled to sit up to look at his leg and began to throw back the covers. "Whoa! Wait a minute. You rest this evening and tonight. You're doing well. The doctor cleaned the wound today. I've cleaned it again. Here, drink this." She bent over to give him a warm cup of weak tea with sugar, and he took a long, deep swallow. He then sat back, leaning against the double pillows she had placed beneath his head and shoulders when he was first brought home in late afternoon. He blinked hard, trying to wake up. The hot liquid revived him and the sedative now was wearing off. "Did I pass out?"

"No. You just took a long nap after the doctor gave you something to relax you."

He tried to think of what to say but had difficulty thinking clearly, unable to see past the throbbing pain in his leg. "Will I be able to go to work with Don Alberto tomorrow?"

"No, son. The doctor said you should stay off the leg for a few days, walking a little each day here in the house and no more than that. I'm to feed you well, give you liquids, and let you rest and heal. I have to do my work. But I can see about you from time to time tomorrow. You'll have to behave well while I do my chores."

"I will. I wish this had not happened. I feel weak."

"That has more to do with the medicine than with your leg. Besides, I have also given you something in your tea that will help you relax and sleep through the night."

"Mamá! You shouldn't."

"It's very gentle. It will do nothing but to help you go back to sleep soon."

She had not finished her sentence before she noticed his eyes becoming heavy again. His breathing deepened and slowed slightly. He shook his head slightly trying to revive himself. But there was no point. "Here, have another sip."

Too weak to argue with her, he sat up a little and drank the tea. He drew enough of it down to quench some of the thirst that had accumulated during the afternoon. He lay back again and took a deep breath as if preparing to relax and to slip away again. Eyes heavy, speech ever so slightly slurred, he said softly, "I love you, Mother. Thank you."

She said nothing but only smiled, carefully pushing his hair back away from his forehead. "Rest now."

The days were quiet for Eduardo over the coming week. He read. Don Alberto came to visit him the following afternoon and sat for an hour talking to him about a time when he had had an accident as a boy and had almost died. Eduardo listened to the old man's stories with as much attention as if he were learning the craft of storytelling in addition to learning the craft of gem cutting.

After that first night, he was allowed to be perfectly alert during the day. He ate well. He drank all the water and tea he was given. By the end of the third day, he mentioned to his mother that his leg had been hurting more rather than less, and he asked her to look at it.

She pulled back the covers, pulled up her son's baggy pajama leg and pulled away the bandage. She tried to conceal her reaction, knowing that Eduardo was watching her face closely. Nevertheless, she flinched. The skin around the wound looked pink and swollen. As she removed the bandage, she saw small white spider-like streaks beginning to extend outward from the wound in at least two or three different places. She was not a physician but knew that the doctor must be called immediately. She had one of the other servants at the house sent to fetch the doctor.

The doctor hurried to the O'Connor estate as quickly as he could when he heard what was happening. By the time he rushed into the cabin and found the boy lying there red-faced, he felt his forehead and realized that the boy had a high fever. He looked at the leg and saw the spidery streaks extending outward from the wound, where infection had set in despite his best efforts to avoid it. Eduardo's mother watched intently alongside the physician and said quietly, "The streaks are longer now than they were when I first saw them." The doctor, seeming to ignore her, pulled out his bag and searched for the materials he needed. "Get a towel or thick cloth and place it here under his leg." By this time, he had out a scalpel which he quickly disinfected by pouring alcohol over it on both sides. He rubbed alcohol on both his hands and over the wounded area and leaned over saying to Eduardo as calmly as he could, "Now, son, this will hurt. Be brave." He placed more alcohol over the area and then meticulously cut a barely visible incision, allowing the area to bleed and to drain away the pus and the poison that was rapidly forming. The boy's infected leg was developing blood poisoning that could not be allowed to progress. He poured a substance in powder form over the wounded area and opened up one of the few sterile gauze pouches he had and placed the gauze over the old wound alongside the new tiny incision. He then wrapped cloth around it and taped it loosely, and gestured to the mother to follow him outside the cabin.

"We have to get him to a hospital. Is O'Connor home or away on business?"

"Away. He's in Puerto Lindo. Why?"

"Because he has a good car. That's why. We'll have to use my truck. And I can't be gone for as long as it would take to get the boy there and then to return. Can someone drive my truck with you and with the boy in it?"

"Yes. There is one man here who can help. But how will we get there? I don't know the way."

"I'm going back to the village and to my office. Have the man there as soon as possible today. I almost never use the truck. It's old. But I think it can make it." He turned to leave her, but hesitated long enough to add, "And hurry. I'll get word ahead to the hospital and will prepare directions for the driver."

She got in touch with her fellow servant and explained the situation. He ran the entire distance into the village and arrived panting and exhausted at the doctor's office only to find the doctor looking both disappointed and angry. As he'd gotten back to the office, he tried to start the truck himself. He tried once and then again. It would not crank. He explained to the man that he could return to the estate and that the doctor would see if he could find another vehicle.

As he watched the man walking back, he wondered what to do. The one doctor in another village who had a car was twenty kilometers away.

Eduardo's mother felt her heart sink as she heard the man telling her that they would have to wait. She checked Eduardo again and found him burning up with fever. As she looked at the swelling leg, she realized there would probably not be time to get the boy to the city. Bogotá was entirely too far away as well. Panicked, she felt desperate and sat down to collect her thoughts.

Then, suddenly wondering why it had not occurred to her before, she remembered the amulet she had carefully locked away in her one small safe. She was not an educated woman, but she could read and write. And her mind was sharp enough that she doubted seriously the ancient superstitions of her mother's people, of the Motilone tribe. They believed in amulets. Yes, they also still believed that the devil controlled all that was underground, including the mines. Whenever catastrophe struck around a mine, they sincerely believed that the devil had risen up in indignation against the impertinence of mere mortals invading his territory, his underground. She also accepted the Church and the teachings of the priests and nuns. She knew that she should simply pray for help from God above. And yet terrified at the thought of losing her one and only child, her precious son, she decided to try the emerald amulet. She took it out of the safe where she had kept it for Eduardo for the future.

The future had arrived. She gingerly took the amulet in both hands and draped it around Eduardo's neck, pulling up his head slightly to get the chain into place. He winced slightly. Although his neck was not injured, with his fever raging, she knew that every muscle and bone must ache. She took his hands and placed them over the amulet.

"Take this into your hands, Eduardo, and concentrate on the amulet." Conscious, although with both his eyes closed, he did as she asked. She thought to herself about the saying he had repeated to her. She had never known anyone with less malice in his heart than her own son. She was not aware of any vice that her boy had had time to develop.

Unwilling to rely solely on the amulet, she found herself also praying to God to save her boy and then—not knowing exactly how to express it—prayed that God would not hinder the amulet's gifts.

She sat beside her son for hours, watching and listening to the sound of his breathing, occasionally touching his face, frequently placing cool wet cloths on his hot forehead and repeating to herself or to God or to the amulet, how important it was to save her only boy.

Unable to restrain herself, she at one point reached over to touch the amulet and realized that it felt warm. As daylight slipped away and darkness fell, and before she lit a candle, she realized that there was a soft, almost imperceptible glow emanating from the emerald.

The evening passed. Another woman servant came with a plate of warm food for her. Not at ease enough to eat, Eduardo's mother had to be coaxed into trying it. As she ate, she realized she had needed to eat. She finished the small meal and drank the milk the woman had also carried to her. Absentmindedly, she thanked the other woman and continued watching Eduardo sleep. The other woman stood there for a minute or two also watching and praying quietly before leaving.

Hours passed. Eduardo's mother awakened herself, realizing that she had nodded off to sleep. She stepped over to see how he was doing and touched his forehead and the side of his face. He was sleeping more peacefully now and his forehead no longer felt hot.

Beads of sweat rolled off his head one by one. His fever had broken, and he was resting well. Sensing that the crisis might have passed, she sat back down and ended up dozing for long periods of time through the night until fully awakened by the sound of a rooster crowing. The predawn light pushed away some of the lingering darkness. The longest night she could remember had finally come to an end, and Eduardo seemed well—without fever, sleeping peacefully and breathing normally. She gently lifted the covers from the side to see how her son's leg looked. The swelling had subsided. There was no extension outward of the tiny streaks around the wound. And the streaks that remained looked paler and less obvious.

Trying not to awaken him, she carefully reached over and slipped the necklace from under his head and pulled it off. Holding it in her hands, it felt cool to the touch. She smiled. It seemed to have done its work. Not knowing what to think, she felt enormous relief at having stowed it away safely, on the off chance that there might be some sort of truth to the tale... truth to this amulet's ability to heal, to protect.

If whatever magic this emerald possessed were real, then the saying that had been given to Eduardo that day when he was small must be true as well. If so, then one of the three times the amulet would offer protection had now been used. Throughout his life—what she hoped would be a long life—there would only be two more crises that could be addressed with the help of this strange object.

The sun was up. Light was beginning to stream in through the window on the eastern side of the cabin. As she rose to leave the cabin to find something for breakfast and to bring hot tea for Eduardo, she heard the sound of a truck approaching rapidly. Standing in the doorway to the cabin, she watched it pull up and saw the doctor climb out of the driver's seat quickly. "He made it through the night?"

"Yes."

"Thank God, but no thanks to me."

She smiled and thought to herself, "I hope it was God."

The doctor walked in brusquely and awakened the boy so that he could examine him. Eduardo, dreadfully sleepy, still exhausted even after a long night's deep sleep, had difficulty waking up. "Here, put this under your tongue," he told the boy as he picked up the boy's wrist and checked the pulse. He took the boy's blood pressure, and, seeing all things normal now, began to peel away the bandage to examine the condition of the wound and surrounding area.

He looked over the area and then stood up straight and turned to the mother. "I can't believe it. Look." The wound still looked angrier than it should. But the streaks that had extended outwardly as if reaching up to take the boy's life had completely vanished. The swelling was almost gone. "My God. I've never seen anything like this."

Nevertheless, he sent her to get boiling water. She returned with it within minutes. He carefully cleaned the wound and added alcohol, then placing a large sterile bandage over the wound, loosely strapping it onto the leg with surgical tape. "Never in my career have I seen something like this reverse itself so quickly. It's truly a miracle. Anyhow, I don't think we should take the long dirty ride to the city now. If we let him rest, get him fluids and keep him and this leg perfectly clean, that may be the best approach for him now."

"Good. I'd rather have him home where I can see about him," she added.

The doctor put his things into the black bag and pulled down and buttoned his shirtsleeves. "You must be one fine nurse. Or this must be one truly exceptional young man. We do need to keep a close eye on the leg, though. I'll check in on him again tomorrow morning unless you need me sooner." And he reached over and squeezed her shoulder and said warmly, "Congratulations. You're a lucky woman and an excellent nurse." He looked at the boy's face, now with normal color again and said, "And you are most definitely one fortunate young man."

As she accompanied the doctor to his borrowed truck, she thanked him and watched him pull away, more carefully than he had raced into the estate less than a half-hour earlier. She wondered to herself which had worked the miracle—the God she could not help praying to and believing in or the amulet; the amulet that had come from God knows where. Not able to determine which it was, she decided it was best only to be thankful that she still had her "boy," her only son. She wondered if there were in fact a deeper purpose as to why her son had been blessed by whatever had been the source of his protection. Too much to worry about. For now, she needed to get Eduardo bathed and fed. There was work to be done.

III.

As the next three and a half years progressed, Eduardo was no longer surprised by the intense heat and humidity in Puerto Lindo. On the other hand, he had not yet acclimated himself to the tropical environment, to the humidity that could rot socks, to the heat that oppressed even those who had lived there for decades, knowing nothing else. With the windows open, the classroom in the university was still almost unbearable. He sat as closely as possible to the window while struggling to complete his final exam for his next-to-last semester. He had already done well as a college student, although not quite well enough to be near the top of his class. The idea of competing with someone else was foreign to his nature. And yet he had fought against the many distractions of the city and of campus life.

In the city, his fellow students managed to discover the charms of excessive drinking, and not just on the weekends. They had learned to settle for women not only of dubious honor but of unquestionably bad looks and odor rather than to do without that type of diversion altogether. There were no women students in the university. His fellow students made fun of Eduardo and his monkish dedication to relentless study and honorable conduct. He wondered what attraction these young men found in such frivolous and...to his way of thinking... unsatisfying pursuits.

He loved passionately his opportunity to learn. He had managed to avoid debt only because of the patronage of Edwin O'Connor. No student failed to find moments to remind him of his status as a "scholarship student". And yet his scholarship had been offered as personal patronage of a wealthy landowner. Eduardo's handsome face—in spite of his green eyes—betrayed his mestizo background. One of his parents had obviously been white, the other native. He could not conceal this fact and did not care to.

He arrived unprepared for the challenge of coping with the attitudes of wealthy sons of prominent families... attitudes involving presumption of superiority both in terms of race and wealth. Several of them had in their backgrounds similarly diluted whiteness, while managing to ignore that trait in themselves. In overall looks and manner, certainly in the way he carried himself and especially in the way he would express himself, Eduardo might conceivably have passed as one of them in another setting. But he clearly was not one of them. He knew it, and they knew it. And they seemed to take particular delight in finding ways to remind him about it.

Given the situation, he made no attempt to persuade himself that he was one of the elite or even that he might want someday to be a member of that social class. The idea of preparing himself for a career and for obtaining great wealth and position strongly motivated him throughout the first three years of college. But, having had to put up with what he had seen as disgusting behavior on the part of most of the wealthy students, he concluded that doing whatever had to be done in order to obtain great wealth would make him similar to them only in the worse sense: turning him into a money-grubbing, shallow, self-centered snob... in other words, a thoroughly repulsive person.

As he sat near a window, with a slight breeze no more than hinting at its presence, he stared at the green lawn outside and the trees beyond, missing home for the first time in a while. He caught himself daydreaming about what it would be like to return home and to be happy making a living there as an adult.

He shook his head as unobtrusively as possible and tried to concentrate on completing his essay for the exam. He had almost finished but felt tired and distracted. Finally able to focus, he read the same words and then wrote the resolution of the essay.

These years had been wonderful for Eduardo. He learned not only facts but how to reason. He had, beyond everything else, learned how to doubt. Unfortunately, the newly developed capacity to doubt in turn created great confusion. He reached a point where the world no longer appeared as simple and straightforward as it once had seemed. He learned to question people and ideas he had never thought of questioning before.

He learned that the conquistadores who invaded his homeland so many centuries earlier had exploited resources, including the many people already established. He learned that foreigners in general did not immigrate in order to acquire property, factories, or mines for the benefit of the nation but instead for their own personal benefit. This had not been taught to him as simply one viewpoint to be considered among many others but as objectively undeniable truth.

And, without his courses of instruction or any particular professor drawing special attention in this direction, his own thinking carried him toward questioning whether any foreigner, including his own patrón, Edwin O'Connor, had ever had any interest at all other than his own wealth and how to increase it. This realization disturbed the young scholar. His instincts told him that home was a comfortable, safe place, a pleasant sanctuary and soothing memory. And that this was all made possible as a result of O'Connor's wealth and protection. On the other hand, Eduardo's mother—the one person whose motives Eduardo never doubted—had in a real sense been exploited throughout her life by this same man, as had all the servants working hard every day in return for nothing more than basic housing and food.

Eduardo learned to try to separate his thoughts from his emotions and achieved a certain amount of success in this. His emotion told him to appreciate O'Connor and all that Don Edwin had made possible. His sense of reason told him to be suspicious of the man and not only to question his motives but also to feel certain that the gentleman was not interested in anything other than his own economic interests.

Although Eduardo now considered himself a thinking person, he found himself from time to time wondering whether this had been such a positive development. It introduced uncertainty into his life: a degree of uncertainty that had never existed in his thoughts before. Yet he could not seem to reason away that uncertainty. With new knowledge and his expanded mind (and world), life not only seemed but was infinitely more complex than it had once been. There were days when he was so confused by the war being waged within himself—a war between emotion and old beliefs on the one hand and reason and new doubts on the other—that he almost wished he had remained in the small village close to home studying each and every day, doing nothing other than learning the art and craft of cutting precious gemstones. He had moments when the idea of sitting beside the old emerald cutter, observing him and then miraculously realizing exactly how the difficult "emerald cut" had to be executed and then executing it perfectly seemed more than satisfying. But then again at other moments even this assumption he began to doubt.

This was not a good afternoon. The day had been cloudy and damp. Humidity hovered heavily in the air in spite of the sun's efforts to burn it away. Then a storm out at sea gently edged toward shore and the clouds made the day look even darker and more problematic.

He completed his exam, folded it neatly and rose to take it to the professor, who sat behind the desk in the front of the room, reading, completely engrossed by the subject matter of whatever lay inside the book in hand. The professor offhandedly acknowledged receipt of the exam paper, grinned, and promptly returned to the world inside his book, managing to say to the student "Good afternoon" along the way.

Eduardo exited the building, heading back to the small dormitory. Hands in pockets, lost in thought, eyes focused on the ground immediately in front of him as he walked, Eduardo heard a familiar voice behind him.

"Eduardo! "¿Cómo le va?" the man asked in Spanish. The student turned to look and saw a smiling Edwin O'Connor.

"Sir! What a surprise to see you here," replied Eduardo in English, surprised that O'Connor had greeted him in Spanish. The patrón always had addressed the boy in English, although with a notably Irish brogue, something Eduardo had always presumed to be the normal manner in which to speak English until he had taken formal classes in English conversation under a professor originally from London. Eduardo knew that a key part of Don Edwin's business involved dealing with export brokers and financiers located in Puerto Lindo. He remembered Don Edwin's having to be away from the estate at least once a month on business in the port city, sometimes more often than that. It had occurred to Eduardo, since arriving at the university, that Edwin's relatively frequent trips to the port city might involve some significant degree of pleasure mixed with business, although that thought would never have crossed his mind before, prior to his realizing how easily distracted his fellow male students could be by the various "extracurricular" activities available off-campus.

"What a surprise to see you here. Is there something I can do for you?"

"What a boy! What could you possibly do for me, except for making me proud, as you always have? On the contrary, I just had a moment and wanted to see how you were doing."

Surprised by the spontaneity of this statement, Eduardo immediately suspected that there must be some motive behind the surprise visit and wondered what that might be.

"I'm doing very well, thank you. Much thanks to you."

"Rubbish, son. Any success at all that you have here is entirely your own doing. All I did was to buy the ticket. It's up to you to take the trip and to make of it what you will." Edwin hesitated, considering the wisdom and magnanimous nature of what he had just said. "Would you like to join me for a coffee at the café I noticed on the edge of the campus?"

"Of course, sir. That would be an honor."

"Young man, you don't have to be quite so formal with me. A certain amount of respect is appropriate for someone your age relative to someone my age. But, beyond that…"

"I'm sorry, sir." Eduardo replied, not at all sure what it was that he had said that had prompted that comment.

"Never mind. Let's go," O'Connor said as he stepped briskly away softly tugging at Eduardo's right arm with his left hand and then letting go.

"And how have things been with you, sir?"

"Very well. Thank you for asking."

"And with my mother, if I might ask?"

"She's well, boy, very well. I'm afraid I may work her too hard. But that can't be helped." And then he looked over toward Eduardo without slowing his pace. "I have encouraged her to slow down. I don't want to require her to do so much now… keeping the same pace you know. I realize that she needs to slow down. But apparently she does not realize it. She continues working as if she were still twenty. To be quite honest, I worry about her from time to time." He had turned away while saying this, almost as if trying to distance himself.

Eduardo glanced aside at the man's face to see if he could read what lay behind it, but could not see any sign. Don Edwin continued speaking and looking straight ahead. Eduardo thought little of it. He had become accustomed to feeling puzzled by this man, by everything about him, but especially about the man's attitude toward him and his mother.

"Well, sir, that's a coincidence. I worry about her a great deal too. Especially since I'm so far away all the time and I'm not able to see about her."

They were approaching the café now and Don Edwin reached forward to grab the door knob to pull it forward. Then he held the door, waiting for Eduardo to enter. "Go ahead, please."

This gesture completely befuddled Eduardo. This man who was the fountain of every good thing that the boy or his mother had ever enjoyed, was the same man who—according to everything Eduardo had absorbed from his studies—represented all the worst of human tendencies, everything that was purely material, exploitative... everything foreign. "Thank you, sir." As he entered the same café he had entered often before, either alone or with friends, Eduardo felt as if he were somehow changed into someone important, someone who actually mattered. To have the door held by such a caballero, by such a gentleman, and to be invited in as his guest was more than Eduardo had been prepared to absorb today.

"You are a young man now, Eduardo. You've almost completed your schooling. What do you have in mind next?"

Eduardo looked down at his hands. "To be honest, I don't know. I have thought seriously about returning to the village to teach."

"Well, that is certainly a noble profession. You realize that you're prepared for much more than teaching in a one-room school, though. Don't you?"

"No, sir. I'm not quite sure what you mean."

"Well, you've studied a bit of everything here, as I understand, including economics and business."

"Yes, although those were definitely not my favorite subjects."

"Well, no matter. At any rate, you've been exposed to them and to languages. You could be quite an asset to my business if you wanted to be."

"How so?"

"I run my mines largely by myself, Eduardo. Of course, I have foremen at each mine. But much more is involved than merely managing the workmen at each site. That's why I have to be here in this port city so often. I export my emeralds all over the world. You could help me a great deal either by living in Puerto Lindo if you like or even by living back near the village. I'm not getting any younger. As I've mentioned before, I'd like some day to be able to turn over my business to someone I know and trust. I'd like to know that what I've built will continue after I'm gone. I might even want to retire at some point, rather than working up until the day that I die."

Eduardo hardly believed what he was hearing. "I don't know what to say. I don't know what to think. I have not prepared myself for a career in business."

"You're already better prepared than many. You are well educated and present yourself well. You've mastered more than one language. I could teach you the rest. A sort of on-the-job graduate program. What do you say?"

"Sir, I need to have some time to think it over. On the one hand, I'm flattered to have such an opportunity offered to me. On the other, this is not something I had ever considered."

Not surprised to see the boy at a loss for words, O'Connor leaned back in his chair and crossed his legs. "Don't worry. You haven't yet graduated. And I don't require an answer right away. As a matter of fact, there is no rush. Do keep it in mind. I'd love to have you with me. I have to admit that I am very proud of you. I always have been. And now you've grown up into a fine young man, well-prepared for life. I'd like to see my business prospering through another generation. But at the same time I'd like to know that you're doing as well as you can for yourself and your mother."

Eduardo, his mind racing, struggled not to say it out loud but could not help thinking to himself, *"This is an offer that would be made to a gentleman's son, not to a son of a servant."*

"Sir, I do need to consider the offer. And thank you very much for mentioning it. You overwhelm me at times with your generosity."

"Oh, rubbish! You're a good person and a deserving one. I would have done this and more for my own son, but I no longer have him around to help."

"I also miss Sean very much."

O'Connor said quietly as he smiled, "But it has been a pleasure having you nearby ." And with this, O'Connor's face suddenly showed a look of surprise, as he realized he had forgotten something important. "My God, I almost forgot!" he exclaimed, reaching into his inside coat pocket to pull out an envelope. "Here is a letter from your mother. She insisted that I not forget to give it to you and I almost did."

Eduardo accepted the envelope, thanked O'Connor, and placed it into his small book bag without opening it. "I really must go now. Please forgive me. I have an appointment with a professor who offered to help me with a paper I'm writing. It's the final assignment that I have to address."

O'Connor rose from his chair, straightened his back and said, "Of course, I understand. Run along. I'm sorry to have kept you for so long."

"I owe you so very much. It's always a pleasure to be able to visit with you."

O'Connor said, "Run along now. Take care. And do give some thought to what I said."

✻ ✻ ✻

Eduardo sat that evening in the library finishing up his paper. He had not opened the letter from his mother, knowing that he had to complete this assignment first. A teacher from an earlier literature class had offered to help him proofread his history paper. With that accomplished, he went to work completing his own proofreading and final editing. As he wrapped up the last page, he realized he was hungry, and then remembered that he had not eaten supper.

Packing up the materials, he then pulled out the letter, unsealing the envelope and unfolding the paper, preparing to read the note. Before reading the actual words, he could not help smiling about how neatly his mother's script appeared on the page. Although she had not had the opportunity to pursue an education, she was literate and would have done well in school if afforded the chance.

"My Dearest Son,

I miss you so much during the weeks when you are away from home. As Christmas approaches, I can barely stand the wait until you'll be home even though it's only for a few days. Don Alberto is ill. He has aged much in recent months and is failing quickly. I hope that he makes it to the first of the year. He cannot eat most of the time and has lost much weight.

Whenever I have a chance to see about him, his eyes light up as he asks about you. He has tremendous hopes for you, my Son. He had hoped to teach you his trade. But he does not seem to resent at all the fact that you wanted to go in a different direction.

I can see the pain and discomfort in his eyes. Yet it is wonderful to see him as he thinks about you. Please come home as quickly as possible for the holidays. I miss you desperately and look forward to seeing you. I want you to be able to visit with Don Alberto so that you can give him all your love and can wish him well in person.

I love you more than words can express. Come home safely. But come home soon.

Lovingly,
Mamá

Eduardo was planning to leave in two more days for home on a bus that would stop near his village. He wondered why his mother had felt the need to write this letter so close to the time that he would be coming home anyway. The thought crossed his mind that old Don Alberto might be gone before Eduardo could arrive home. Eduardo thought how wonderfully patient the old man had been while beginning to teach his craft. Good-humored and as affectionate as if he were a grandfather. Eduardo also wondered if his mother was in good health herself. There was in her letter a tone of desperation, a sense not only of missing her son but of needing to see him right away. The letter had an unsettling effect on Eduardo.

Picking up the remainder of his pencils and papers and leaving the library, he went back to his small dormitory room. A note remained on the bed of his roommate. "Gone home for the holidays. Merry Christmas." He had not become close to this fellow student from Bogotá. The differences between the roommate's life in the city and Eduardo's life in the mountains and rural area of his childhood were far too great. It was not only a difference of environment. The city boy was uninterested in learning and was profoundly uninteresting to Eduardo.

Eduardo simply could not comprehend anyone taking for granted the open-ended opportunity for self-education here in this community of "scholars." In fact, the only scholars on the campus were the professors and a very small handful of students. The remainder of the students seemed to Eduardo to be there simply to take up space and to entertain themselves—to spend someone else's money. And a very great deal of money it was at that, or at least so it seemed to Eduardo based on what he had heard.

He dearly loved his time in the university, not for its social life but for the chance to learn so much, delving as deeply into the subjects as time and energy would allow. He had won recognition each year for superior academic performance. But that meant little to him. What was rewarding was the acquisition of knowledge itself and the opportunity to use his mind.

If there were anything missing in all this, it was only that he had not been able to see clearly where it was leading him. What was he meant to do after his time in the university? He had no interest in becoming a lawyer or a doctor. He loved the Church but had no interest in training for the priesthood. He had often wondered what it might be like to be a teacher and had thought that this might be the only profession that would allow him to continue throughout his life studying and learning everything of interest to him and then being able not only to share acquired knowledge with others but also possibly to spark the same love of learning in the one or two outstanding students who might come under his influence. If he could spark that interest in even one student every year or two, that might be more of an accomplishment than many people achieve in a lifetime.

It would be difficult, though, to teach not only the brightest and best students but all the students in a small rural area. And Eduardo had been very much aware of how starkly he stood apart as a boy growing up and learning well, interested in his studies, unlike other students around him. He understood that he would be lucky to have even one student interested in learning each year and that the vast majority of students would be incomprehensively dull and uninteresting not only as students but also throughout their lives.

On the other hand, if he left teaching aside and instead took up Sr. O'Connor's offer, he could not even picture what it might be like to be involved in the business. One thing he felt certain about was that there would probably not be any more interesting people involved in that line of work than there would be interesting students in a rural classroom.

No matter how he considered it all, there did not seem to be a clear path for him to follow. It was bothersome, tedious; making a decision about what to do with his life.

Meanwhile, he needed to finish this semester in order to get home one day earlier than he had originally planned. He ate a simple supper that evening in a café beside the university, using cash that O'Connor had handed him that afternoon. The patrón always paid the university all the boy's bills on time and directly to the business office. And yet he frequently delivered spending money to Eduardo, either in person or through the mail.

Eduardo could not, to save his life, understand what it had been that he had done to deserve such generosity. He was quite sure that he did not deserve it. But he was certainly not going to waste it. He normally held on to any cash he was given for as long as possible, saving at least part of it for a stash to give his mother at Christmas time.

But this particular evening, he felt famished and indulged himself by dining on a hot dinner of fish, rice, vegetables and tea. He went to bed that night, exhausted but well-fed, and content, knowing that he had done well in all his classes and did not need to wait around for his grades. He would leave on the bus in the morning and would head home to surprise his mother, hopefully arriving in time to be able to visit with the old man, with Don Alberto.

The bus pulled up to stop at a crossroad. The smaller dirt road would lead to Eduardo's village. He got off the bus, carrying his only suitcase in one hand and his book bag slung over his shoulder. The small road , gently inclining toward the village, was about four kilometers long. The weather was mild, and Eduardo did not mind the walk at all. He was young and strong, and he was arriving home for the holidays. It would be good to be home, and he would gladly have walked much farther had it been necessary.

The village was on his way to the O'Connor estate. So he decided to go first by the studio, by the apartment where Don Alberto had always worked in the front and lived in the back. He arrived at the door. It was closed. He knocked but no one answered.

He tried the knob and saw that the door was not locked. He opened the door softly and spoke quietly, "Don Alberto, are you at home?" No answer. Again he asked, this time a little louder and stronger, "Don Alberto, hello?"

This time he heard someone stir in the back. "Who is there?" came an old man's voice weakly from the area where his bed had always been.

"It is Eduardo. I'm home from school and wanted to see you."

The voice called out with a joyful lilt to it, "My boy! How marvelous! Please, come in. Come back to me. I cannot come to you."

Eduardo stepped inside, placed his one piece of luggage just beside the door. He walked back to the area where he knew Don Alberto had kept his bed in the farthest corner back of his small apartment/studio. He stepped into view of the old man and Don Alberto smiled, raising his hand beckoning the boy to come closer. "Here, come closer where I can see you."

Eduardo stepped up to the side of the bed, grinning from ear to ear.

"My God. You are a fully grown man now. How you've matured. And looking very much the scholar. How wonderful that you have pursued your education. It's so good to see you." Alberto's voice weakened toward the end. Eduardo realized that the old man was extremely ill. He was pale, thin, and too weak to raise himself up in bed, much less to get out of bed. But his eyes showed excitement as young Eduardo stood there to visit him.

Eduardo realized that there was much love within this man, love that had found little outlet in recent decades. There must have been much love within him in order for so much to rise to the surface so easily over someone so insignificant. And it wasn't too difficult to understand why. He had lived alone for so many years, his wife having died long before. He had no children. And although he was married to his craft, to his trade; his work was not enough. Clearly it had never been enough for a person who could feel so warmly toward someone else's child and one at that whom he had known for only a short time.

Eduardo pulled up the one chair by the bed and sat down. "Tell me about your studies," the old man said to him.

"Well, I'm enjoying all of them, especially history, but all of the subjects."

"Why history?"

"I'm not sure. Most of the students seem bored by it. But for me it opens not only the world outside this place but also all the worlds that have come before."

"Oh, my God, a philosopher too."

Eduardo laughed softly. "Yes. I like philosophy as well. It's as if the great philosophers, even from the most ancient times are there with you helping you to think through important questions."

"I envy you, boy. When I was your age, I wanted so much to be able to go away to any university, but especially one in particular in Bogotá."

"And why didn't you?"

"Why do you think?" asked the old man , almost scolding with his glance. "Money...and also..."

"What else?"

"We did not have enough money even to consider it as a possibility. But if there had been a scholarship available—perhaps from a patrón such as yours—even then my father would not hear of it. He distrusted educated people. He had always worked with his hands. He did not trust anyone who did not work with their hands. I never understood that. He resented success in others. And he saw education as something placing others above him, as if better than him. The priests were educated. And the foreigners, especially the British, were educated and ran everything and everybody. No, I don't think it was distrust. It was resentment. He deeply resented anyone who was more successful than he could ever hope to be. And I guess, now as I look back, I guess he could not stand the possibility of my obtaining education and thinking myself better than he was. It was a strange sentiment. I never understood that about my father. I would have loved to be able to study, not to become wealthy or to control others but only in order to learn."

Eduardo was amazed at how much more alert Don Alberto seemed when talking about his own youth and about what had sparked enthusiasm in him as a boy, and what obviously still held the same fascination for him as an old man in decline. "How did you become a gem cutter?"

Alberto shifted in bed slightly and tried to raise himself somewhat but could not. Eduardo got up and lifted him, reaching underneath the man's arms and pulling him up, then fluffing the pillows underneath his head. Seeming more comfortable, Alberto focused and answered, "Again, my father made that decision for me. He did not consult me about it. One day I was taken out of school without explanation and then was taken directly to an older gem cutter. The gem cutter explained to me that I would become his apprentice and would learn an important craft that could someday allow me to feed myself and any family that I might have. There was nothing for me to say about it. I accepted that as my destiny and tried to make the most of it."

Don Alberto stopped and shuffled the covers. "I learned well and became a very good gem cutter. I married. We had a child, a boy, who died in infancy. Then my wife the following year became sick with typhoid and died quickly. I considered moving away either to the coast or to the capital city. I was still a young man , but I already felt too set in my ways to consider moving, re-establishing myself somewhere different. And so I decided to remain here alone and then concentrated all my talents, all my time, toward becoming the best gem cutter anyone could be."

"I don't doubt that at all."

Don Alberto grinned. "I understand the products of my work are much desired elsewhere. Edwin O'Connor has told me that he has had great success with some of my best gemstones. I suppose I should be proud of that."

"Of course you should. I'm sure there's no finer gem cutter in the world."

"Well, I don't know about that. But it should be enough to be considered truly competent. At any rate, that's all I have," he said smiling as he turned his face toward Eduardo's. Eduardo could see his eyes glistening with the hint of a tear in each.

Eduardo took his hand. "Are you hungry?"

"Not really. No."

"When did you eat last?"

"Oh, earlier today. The priest brought me breakfast this morning and said he would come see me this evening."

"Good God. You must be starving. Let me get you something quickly."

"Really, Eduardo, I don't feel well at all and have no hunger."

"Nevertheless, you have to eat something. I'm home for several days. I will come each day to see you and to bring you something. But now, I'm going to run to the bakery shop to get you at least some bread." With that, Eduardo did not wait to discuss it further. He simply squeezed the old man's hand, which he had been holding loosely, and left briskly, saying as he went out, "I'll be right back. I have to get home to surprise my mother. I'm home a day early."

"Eduardo! And you came here first? You should be whipped."

"I'll be back."

Doing as he had said, he hurried to the shop and bought a small baguette and a chunk of cheese and some cider at another shop, and awkwardly carried it all back to the old man's studio. "Here," he said putting the bread and cheese and drink down on the small table by the bed. "I'll cut some slices for you, but you have to be the one to do the eating. You promise?"

"I will, if you insist," the old man said accepting a small piece of bread with a tiny chunk of cheese on top. Eduardo helped him with the warm cider, letting him have a couple of sips and then said, "I must go. Now you eat as much of this as you can and drink all of this."

"You're a good boy, my son. You don't mind if I call you my son, do you?"

"Of course not. Now you behave and rest. I'll be back tomorrow."

As Eduardo left, he turned back quickly at the door and said once again, "I'll be back. You must get stronger now."

"Good night. Say hello to your mother for me."

And Eduardo picked up his suitcase and book bag and left for the estate. It was beginning to get dark by now and he needed to hurry, hoping to arrive at his mother's cabin before the day's light had completely vanished.

Eduardo stopped by the cabin to leave his bags before heading to the O'Connor house. He knew his mother would be working in early evening assisting with dinner and knew he would not startle her by finding her alone in her own cabin at this hour. As he entered the house, he glanced in at the door to Don Edwin's office, knowing that O'Connor was supposed to be in Puerto Lindo, but compulsively he checked to see anyway.

He breezed down the hallway and into the doorway to the kitchen, holding it open. Grinning, he said, "Mamá!"

Looking up from the chicken she was preparing, she tried not to scream as she exclaimed, "Eduardo! My boy." She hurried over and hugged him tightly, planting a big kiss on his cheek, but only after he had done the same to her. She let go and held him back a foot or so to gain perspective. "You look thin. You haven't been eating. Come sit down and eat something."

"I'm fine." Fortunately, he had the presence of mind to hold back from saying spontaneously, *"But you look more tired than ever."* "I'm fine. I eat enough. But I work. Just as you do, although mine is easier work, I have to admit."

She straightened her back and tilted her head slightly and said with authority, "It is important work that you are doing. For a young man, there's nothing more important than studying. You'll have a chance to be a fine gentleman someday."

"I'm not sure what that means. But I agree with you that I'm doing important work." Then smiling, he added, " Or, even if it is not so very important, I do love it anyway. I love school. I'm sorry it'll be over for me so soon."

"Here, first of all, you must eat. Sit." And she quickly put together a plate of vegetables, bread, and milk. "The chicken and the plantain are not prepared yet. But you can eat this now."

"All right," he said almost reluctantly, sitting down and beginning to eat. He was hungrier than he had realized. He did not tell her that he had eaten nothing during the day other than the hot chocolate and small hard roll that he ate for breakfast right before leaving Puerto Lindo very early in the morning.

"I received your letter. And I was worried about you. Are you all right?"

She busied herself with the cutting of the chicken again and said to him as she concentrated now on the work in front of her, "I'm fine. I'm worried about Don Alberto. I've gotten to know the old man since he took you in. He's a very sweet old man who has come to Mass every Sunday in recent months, until this past month. He is very, very ill."

Eduardo considered whether to tell her that he had stopped by to see the old man first and then decided to say it. "I was passing through the village on the way here and stopped to see if I could say hello to him briefly."

"Wonderful! And how did he look today?"

"Terrible. He's exhausted. He seems to be unable to get out of bed. But we had a good visit. I must go each day while I'm home. I promised I would take him food when I go."

"He's in bed all day now. He's still able to get up to relieve himself when he needs to. But the church is supposed to provide him with at least one meal a day. Are they not?"

"He said the priest had come to see him and brought food in the morning. But I want to visit him. Don Alberto is a good man. I cannot believe he had lived in the village for so many years without our knowing him."

"He was a very reclusive man, staying in his studio, working, not attending Mass until I suppose he realized that his years were numbered."

"We didn't visit long. But he mentioned that he had wanted to go to a university when he was young and could not afford it. He seems to feel very proud of me and my studies."

She reached over and touched his hand lightly. "Oh, my son. I am so very proud of you and your work at school."

"But I thought you wanted me to apprentice under Don Alberto."

"That was the only opportunity I could imagine for you that would give you a way to make a good living and that would provide you with a way to live here nearby."

Before taking the time to think it through, Eduardo connected this with his visit with O'Connor.

"Don Edwin, when he handed me your letter, told me something that surprised me."

She stiffened slightly and looked straight at him. "What?"

Puzzled by her reaction, he chose to ignore it and went ahead with what he had begun. "He told me he would like me to apprentice under him for his business. He offered me the chance to work for him and to learn how to run his company."

She stood, dumbfounded, her hands still greasy with the fat of the chicken she was working. Obviously not knowing what to say, she said almost absentmindedly, "Are you sure?"

Eduardo chuckled. "Yes, mother. I'm certain. I would be working for him as an employee in training. But he jumped ahead several years and said that he would like to be able to retire someday and that he would like to see me prepared to take over the management of his company if I were able."

Clearly uncomfortable with that proposition, she asked, "And what did you say?"

"I said nothing really other than to thank him and to remind him that I've not yet finished my studies. I also reminded him that I had not considered a career in business and had not made any effort to prepare for it. He didn't seem to mind that at all and said he could teach me what truly matters."

"I see. You sound as if his offer interests you."

"Well, it was an honor to have it suggested at all. I haven't had time to consider it properly. I'm not sure that I could be a businessman."

"Did he suggest at all why he would offer something like this?"

"Not really. He did, though, say that he has been impressed with me through the years and that he takes pride in who I am and in what I've accomplished."

"Well, that comes as quite a surprise. And it makes it difficult for me to say what I had been thinking."

Eduardo stopped eating and sat, turned in full face toward his mother, giving her his undivided attention and asked, "What, Mother? What have you been thinking?"

"You have always loved learning, Eduardo. You were such a bright, questioning child. And you were always such a wonderful student in the grammar school here. Your teacher always told me that. And now, partly by the grace of God and also with the help of Don Edwin, you're obtaining a university degree. I have thought that you might make a fine teacher somewhere near here."

He stopped and considered for a moment, realizing that she had put a great deal of thought into this. "Well, I would not be able to make such a good living, would I?"

"No. But you love learning, son. And it would be wonderful to have you nearby giving other children the chance to open doors for themselves. Don't you think it would be?"

"You want this, don't you?" he asked, realizing as he said it out loud that it would have better been a question kept to himself.

She looked at him, saying more than she had meant to say so soon after his arrival home. "Son, I'm not getting younger. I have no husband. If you work for Don Edwin, in the early years at least he would have you gone all the time. You would fall in love either with someone or someplace far away. It may be selfish of me. But I need you somewhere close by. Whether a gem cutter or a teacher, you'd be here at home." She immediately regretted sharing this sentiment as she glanced and saw the uncomfortable look on his face.

"I'm not trying to get away from you. Not at all."

"I know you could be a good teacher. I know you, I think, maybe better than you know yourself. Whether it would be here or somewhere else, I think you'd be happy as a teacher."

Finishing his plate and leaning back, he suddenly felt not only full but extremely tired. "Well, to be honest, I have no idea what to do next." And he got up to leave. He gave her another hug and said "No matter what I do, I'm not going to abandon you. Don't worry. I'm going to bed for now. Good night."

"Good night, son. Sleep well." She knew in her heart that her son would do whatever was best. She also knew that, as young and strong and handsome as he had become, a girl would grab his attention at some point. She only hoped that this would not happen too far away from home. And, as much as she wanted to continue having him close by, she believed deeply that her son was meant for something more significant than selling gemstones, even if skipping that career meant never possessing wealth.

Eduardo went each day to visit Don Alberto, bringing him something to eat. He spoke with the priest and they agreed to split their visits, with the priest going by each morning with breakfast and then with Eduardo going by late afternoon with something more substantial. After two or three days, Don Alberto seemed a bit stronger and was sitting up in bed to greet Eduardo each time he arrived. He had slightly better color, and Eduardo one afternoon tried to get him up to walk around the room. This challenge exhausted the old man the first time. But he asked for it the second day and was able to take a few steps around the studio during each of Eduardo's visits.

Finally, Christmas Eve arrived. Eduardo went by and found the old man lying in bed looking pale and tired. "Why are you not sitting up for me, my old friend?" he asked.

Don Alberto smiled and said, "If you want to help me raise myself up, that would be all right. I have not felt well at all today."

Eduardo lifted him under the arms and pulled him up and arranged the covers, trying to see if that helped. They visited about small things for several minutes. Then Don Alberto sat still, looking for how to say what he wanted to say, seeming to study his hands, as if somehow the words he needed might be found there.

"Eduardo."

"You look so serious."

"Not so serious. I don't believe I have much longer. And I want to tell you while I am able. Your attention has meant so much to me. I had spent years alone, with only my work and myself. At first, after my wife and child had died, I was lost and felt horribly alone, abandoned. With time, that feeling died too. I was left merely surviving, day after day—in good health and enjoying being alive, but only getting through each day. I no longer felt anything. I stopped going to Mass and left behind my faith. The God I loved abandoned me by taking the ones here on Earth who I loved so much and by leaving me all alone. I resented him, until after so many years I could not even feel that resentment anymore. One Saturday evening I wandered back into the church for the evening Mass and it felt like going home again. I felt warm and safe and not so alone. And then he brought me you, first your mother seeking me out and then you. I don't want to die without letting you know how important it has been to care about a person again. You are not my son. But you have seemed to care about me almost as if you were. And I want you to know how much I appreciate it. I've spent much time by myself in the past four or five years. But I haven't felt so alone as before. I do not feel abandoned anymore. I feel very lucky."

Eduardo, uncomfortable with the whole tenor of this conversation, interrupted, "Don Alberto, it has been a pleasure to know you, but I'm going to know you for many more years. Why are you saying all this now?"

"Don't interrupt. I'm very serious about wanting to get this said. Don't ask me how I know. But an old man can know things no one else does. And I know that I don't have a great deal of time left." He caught his breath and Eduardo relaxed and smiled and sat back in his chair to let the old man continue. "I've been a very lucky man. But I have come to care enough about you, my boy, to want so much more for you."

At this point, he sat up as if there were no problem at all with his health. His eyes brightened. "I want you to understand that the greatest wealth any man can have is to be connected with someone he loves, to have a family and to have a way to feed that family. And to be a part of a home, a place where he and then his family after him can be connected not only to each other but to life. Not running away from life, not hiding. Not distracted by money or the hunger for it that can devour everything that matters most. As you finish your degree, you're going to have the world opening up for you. You may feel confused at times and not know what to do. Just remember what matters most and only look for that—someone to love who loves you in return and then possibly children, God willing, who will give you even more to work for and love. Your work, whatever that is, should focus on helping others. I don't want to waste breath trying to tell a young man what to do with his life. But I think you would be a wonderful teacher. You should share your love of learning with others. See if you can make it like a great infection, infecting children with a hunger for learning." Already tired from the emotional exertion, the old man looked spent and began to relax and to slump slightly to one side.

Eduardo got up and helped Don Alberto sit up straighter and tried to offer him the meal he had brought. But this time Don Alberto had so little interest in food that he only nibbled slightly at the roasted chicken leg and at the cornbread. Taking a few bites and then a few sips of the water that Eduardo had given him, he sat back and breathed as deeply as he could manage and said, "Thank you. That's all I can have now. I'm very tired. I should sleep."

Eduardo felt the need to reach over and to kiss the old man on the forehead. He did this and straightened the covers for Don Alberto and said, "I want you to rest well and to feel much better for tomorrow, Christmas Day."

The old man nodded, made another slow attempt to take a deep breath, and said "Merry Christmas, my good friend. Come back to see me. Good night."

Eduardo bade him farewell and walked back to the estate. It was too early for the Christmas Eve Mass, and he wanted to walk with his mother to the small church that evening. He arrived back at the large house and saw Don Edwin in his study as he walked by. Realizing that O'Connor had noticed him, he said respectfully, "Good evening, sir."

"Good evening, young man! And how are you this fine Christmas Eve?
"Very well, thank you and you?"

"I arrived this afternoon. I'm sure you did well on your examinations?" he asked, having gotten up and approached Eduardo, standing just inside the doorway. He did not invite the boy in but was greeting him warmly and seemed genuinely glad to see him.

"Thanks to God, I believe I did very well."

"I'm sure you did. You always do. I think you might do well with or without God's intervention, to tell you the truth. But then maybe I shouldn't say that." The don began to return to his desk. "Attending Mass with your mother this evening or tomorrow morning?"

"This evening, sir, after supper. It is a very late service."

"Yes, I know. I used to go every Christmas Eve. Well, enjoy it. Good evening." And he sat down behind his desk and turned his attention as completely to the paperwork as his attention had ever so briefly been turned toward young Eduardo.

"Thank you, sir. Merry Christmas Eve to you."

"Same to you, my boy. Same to you," he answered absentmindedly without looking up from his papers.

Hot soup served as supper early that evening. This was prepared, served, and the kitchen was cleaned by mid-evening. Eduardo and his mother walked to the church and found it full of people as they arrived. They were handed candles as they entered and were expected to hold them in their hands until the service had begun.

Eduardo enjoyed the warm, comforting environment of the small chapel and the very special service. He did not share, though, with his mother the fact that he had begun to wonder about a great many things during his three and a half years in the university, including the beginnings of doubt about his faith. His mother, raised within the Church and within the faith, had no doubts. Her mother and her grandmother before her had all acquired the foreign faith brought over centuries earlier by the Spanish conquistadores—an imported faith, a foreign idea like so many other foreign ideas.

And yet he had not entirely let go. The security and protection of his mother's faith had enveloped him for as long as he could remember. It was something deeply ingrained inside him, and it was difficult to let go. He did not want to lose it. Even so, as he stood in the midst of one of the most important Christian services, he thought back to that bizarre situation in the cave so long ago—that dark, lonely cave, with the mysterious old woman and most importantly the almost devilish power of the amulet. How could God be so real and ever-present when something like this could happen? Did he send it as a sign of his protection? That made no sense at all.

Eduardo knew that the ancient beliefs of his ancestors were that the devil not only dwelled underground but also lorded over the underworld, including the mines. Was the old woman Satan in woman's clothing? Or was there a separate power that had nothing to do with God or with the devil, with potential for good works?

He had grown accustomed to considering complex questions during his time at school. But speculation about this particular subject seemed to lead nowhere. He only became more confused as he let his mind wander into unfamiliar territory. And, at any rate, why would it matter? What mattered more now was to be here this evening with his mother, who he still cared very much about, and to be in this safe, loving place He knew it felt good to be at home, to be alive and relaxed, safe and well.

He thought about Don Alberto during the Mass and wished the old man could be with them, and found himself mentioning Don Alberto's name out loud when the priest came to the part of the Mass where prayers were offered up for specific persons.

He wished that the old man could be sitting there with them—healthy, well-fed, and happy to be with someone, if not with his own family then among people who loved him. He wished he could have the old man for many more years. But he knew this was not going to happen.

Eduardo listened carefully to the words of the Mass. He participated in the ritual, in the liturgy. But even as he listened, he still had room for other thoughts. He considered what it would have been like to have completed his apprenticeship with Don Alberto. He wondered whether that might somehow have lengthened the old man's life. He thought about what it might be like to master the craft of gem cutting and to be able to develop the reputation that he now knew Don Alberto had in Puerto Lindo and beyond as a gifted master cutter. He wondered if Don Alberto, as a young man himself, had been as good at his work as he later became after years of practice. He realized that only four years would not have been enough time to develop the enormous skill that Don Alberto had mastered. It had taken much more than time and hard work to produce the level of expertise that Don Alberto had produced through his years of labor. It required more than training. It required tremendous talent, a gift. He wondered if he would have been able through years of hard work and concentration to develop the same level of expertise and then beyond that the widespread reputation that the old man had achieved, whether he had the old man's gift or not. He doubted it very much.

No, he had done the right thing in choosing instead to take advantage of Don Edwin's generous offer for assistance in attending the university. He loved the three and a half years of study. He loved learning. He loved using his mind. There were so many questions to ask, to pursue and so little time. Or so it had always seemed. In fact, here was Don Alberto this afternoon having said much the same thing: that Don Alberto's life had been too short; that there had not been enough time. Or was that really what he'd said? No, what he had said had more to do with how to use that time than about how much there was of it, more to do with quality than with quantity.

To love. To be loved. To have a family. Eduardo had not given this much thought. He had been so completely preoccupied with his studies that he had ignored meeting girls. But Eduardo's studies consumed him, and he remained completely satisfied with that.

Perhaps Don Alberto was trying to share something important with him today, something directly related to all this. Oh well, the Mass was ending. Eduardo managed to walk up to receive communion without losing his train of thought. He had been through the liturgy so many times with his mother that it did not require active thought. They returned to their pew.

He wondered what it might be like to do what Don Edwin had offered, to apprentice under him in the business. He wondered what it might be like to follow that route and to learn and to do well and maybe someday to become a partner in the business, maybe someday to become heir to the business and the fortune that would go with it. How ridiculous! Why even bother thinking about something like that? He could not imagine what had prompted Edwin O'Connor to suggest such a thing. Don Edwin must have some motive of self-interest, some understandable reason for offering something so outrageous. But what could that reason be? Just that he was impressed by what he saw in Eduardo? That could not be right.

Mass ended. The congregation dispersed. Eduardo's mother hugged the priest. Eduardo left the small church aglow with the warm secure feeling he had after each Christmas Eve service. Had his mind wandered too much? What did it matter? He couldn't control it. There was so much to think about now, so much to consider. And yet, now, walking alongside his mother toward home, he thought about the small present he had bought for her. He had bought it with money saved from the allowance that Don Edwin provided for him each month. As they arrived at the cabin, it was clear to him that his mother was exhausted after a long day's work and a long evening's praying and listening. But he could not hold back til morning.

"I have something for you!" He reached under his bed and pulled it out. It was wrapped very simply in brown paper to protect it. No bow. No adornment. She opened it hurriedly and held it up. It was a white blouse with hand-embroidered threads in various colors and was gathered at the neck.

"It's beautiful! Oh, you did not have to do this. But look," she said as she held it up in front of her.

"Try it on." She did and it fit her well.

She looked at him, tears in her eyes, and embraced him warmly, rocking him gently from side to side, saying regretfully, "But I have nothing for you."

"My God, Mother. You've given me so much. It's wonderful just to be able to be here and to have you in good health." And he sat admiring the blouse he had brought her. She proudly held it up against her front. It made her look younger, even though years of hard work had begun to show in her face, or even more in her spirit. She looked at him and began to leave the room. "Just a moment."

She came back with something small in her hand. "Here, I want you to have this." She handed him a small silver money clip. It had a very small but lovely emerald set within it. "This was your father's. It's time for you to have it."

Eduardo, completely at a loss for words, sat holding the small object. He looked up at her. "My father's? Why would you have not shown it to me before this?"

"It is very special to me. But I want you to have it. You are old enough to have it as your own now. It is intended to be used by a man. And it should become yours now."

Now it was Eduardo's turn to have moist eyes. "I don't know what to say."

He held it and asked, "What was he like, Mother? You never told me about him."

"I'm sorry, son. I cannot even now. It hurts to think of him. But I am so proud of you and of the man that you are becoming, a better man than your father ever was."

Seeing the look in her eye that told him that there was no point in pursuing the subject further, he left it alone and instead turned his attention to the small object, studying it as if he might learn something about his father from it.

"Good night, son. Sleep well." And she went into her bedroom and shut the door. Eduardo turned the money clip in his hand. It spoke of success. It was in fact the type of item a gentleman would carry. A working man would never put together enough spare cash to own something seemingly so frivolous. No. This told Eduardo that his father, no matter what he had done to hurt his mother, had been a "gentleman" if not by birth then by having succeeded in business or some profession.

But this was all pure speculation. Eduardo had always hoped that his mother would tell him more about his father. This was the closest she had ever come toward sharing anything at all with her son regarding the forgotten man. Clearly she had never forgotten him. Or it would not still hurt to think about him. And Eduardo knew that his father had left his stamp on the son, if only in the green eyes that had always set Eduardo apart, at least in Eduardo's own mind.

☆ ☆ ☆

The following morning, Eduardo had breakfast with his mother and then greeted Don Edwin, wishing him a Merry Christmas. He left to walk the trail toward the village. He knew the priest would be busy this morning and would not be able to visit Don Alberto. Eduardo had spent Christmas Eve with his mother and wanted to wish Don Alberto Merry Christmas this morning.

Arriving at the door of the studio, he knocked, not expecting an answer but hoping to avoid frightening the old man as he entered. The door was locked, but Eduardo still had the key. Entering the front of the place, he shouted "Merry Christmas" as he walked through the studio toward the bedroom in the back. There was no reply. He assumed the old man must be sleeping soundly. He walked more quietly the remainder of the way and then entered the area where Don Alberto kept his bed.

As he approached the bed, he stopped a few meters away. The old man's eyes were opened in a blind stare. All color had drained from his face. His mouth lay open. The overall effect was as if the old man were astonished at how pathetically his long life had ended. Eduardo knew even from that distance what he did not want to know, what he had dreaded but had not allowed himself to contemplate. The old man had died during the night, sick and alone. It was difficult to imagine such stark isolation. It would have been, for most people, as Eduardo knew, the most horribly sad way to die. Had he fallen asleep the night before as with every other night of his life? Why on this particular night would Alberto suspect that this would be the night when it would end?

Eduardo gathered up his strength and put the small bag of food down on the floor. He stepped up to the bed, reached over and gently lowered the old man's eyelids. He took a small towel from nearby, tied it loosely under Alberto's lower jaw and around the top of his head, trying to close the mouth, trying to reconstruct some semblance of dignity in death. Mouth and eyes discreetly closed, Don Alberto lay with a peaceful expression on his face, as if finally resigned to his fate, accepting, no longer able to resist...as if away from here and yet still here.

Eduardo pulled up a chair and sat at the old man's bedside and wept for the old man but also for himself. If the teaching of the Church were correct, then Don Alberto was surely on his way to a far better place. Eduardo, as he cried softly to himself, desperately hoped that this was true. The alternative was unthinkable: to consider the possibility that this person, this very special man could have lived entirely alone for so many decades, always remaining the same sweet person he had been all his life and then that this life could end in silence, unnoticed, simply vanishing into nothingness. This would be too much to bear. And so at this moment Eduardo chose to hold onto his faith.

Eduardo had heard in classes at the university that the teachings of the Church were elaborate fairy tales manufactured to comfort people about the severity and finality of death, and to help ease the pain of losing loved ones. He had also heard that this fantasy had been invented to help each person feel less anxiety about the inevitability of his own demise, to help ease the pain of the realization of one's own mortality.

He had heard and considered all this carefully. But, especially at this moment, it mattered little whether the Church's teachings were fairy tales or not. The loss of someone so dear, so caring, so capable of offering love to others, was more than Eduardo could endure. It was impossible at this moment to consider anything other than the inevitability of the grace of a loving God embracing this sweet soul. Fantasy? No, it had to be true.

Yes, Eduardo had learned how to doubt, how to question, while learning how to reason. He had to admit to himself, however, within the horrific silence and solitude of this deathbed scene; that it did matter whether the Church's specific teaching about heaven was objectively true or not. There had to be more than the ugliness of death for Don Alberto. And so heaven must be real.

Eduardo realized how ridiculous it seemed to believe this and at the same time to be willing to accept belief in any real power that might reside within the emerald amulet. The priest would be enraged to know that Eduardo possessed such a blasphemous idol, and that he, in a sense, worshipped it by believing in its power to protect, defend, and save.

The question occurred to him as to whether the amulet could have saved Don Alberto, as to whether it could have added health and years to his already long life. Eduardo began to feel guilt for not having thought of this earlier. He felt even more guilt as he considered further the realization that he would have hesitated to turn over to someone else any protection the amulet might offer. Lending it to someone else could mean using up one of his own opportunities for any protection it could provide. Or would it? It might. And so he admitted to himself that he would not have made it available. The realization of this selfishness made him feel much worse.

At any rate, it was a waste of time to consider all this. The old man died and was gone. There were other, more urgent, things to consider. Where his soul would go was not something Eduardo could change or fully comprehend with certainty. What needed to be done in terms of real-world responsibilities was very clear, though. Eduardo must go to the priest to see about arrangements for the body, and he must do this right away.

He picked up his sack and left the studio, locking it behind him to go straight to the chapel, where he sat patiently outside waiting for the priest to complete Mass. With the priest having greeted his parishoners outside the church, Eduardo approached him and told him the news. The priest, with more experience in this sort of situation than he cared to have, told Eduardo to go home and that he the priest would see about the necessary arrangements himself.

Eduardo instead offered to go with the priest to help him in any way that he could. There were details to be seen about, everyday details that require attention, consideration and concern. A celebration of birth of a savior was now defiled by a death of a friend, a mentor. For this one old man, his life on Earth now was over. It was done.

✷ ✷ ✷

The next morning, in front of Don Edwin's imposing desk, Eduardo sat erect in the high-backed chair, fully distracted by the prospect of the burial of a friend. He tried to show respect toward Don Edwin. He tried only to listen and not to speak. He heard the patrón's words of comfort and softly offered advice. Doing his best to pretend to hear each and every word, he found himself thinking about that lonely old man who had somehow managed to lose himself completely in his work, in his craft, until the end when regrets began to creep into his thoughts, regrets about the loss of life with a family, about the loss of tenderness from a loving spouse and a loving son, about the waste of a long life virtually devoid of interaction with others. You would think that a man living in this way, living the life of a hermit focused entirely on the details of his work, would become through the decades a cynical man. That had not happened. He had simply made it through the years without all the love that he naturally wanted, without all the careful attention of family members to each other. And yet his capacity for concern about one young boy and for that boy's future still survived despite all the misplaced opportunities to show love and concern. He had wanted to teach Eduardo how to excel at something, how to carry on the artful skill that could be transferred from one old artisan to a younger student. He wanted to see the young man able to make a good living. But, at the end, his most important desire had been to encourage Eduardo to value human contact above all else, and to hold onto and to embrace faith in God. To be prepared to work endlessly with enormous effort and attention to the quality of work produced. But to keep in perspective the reason for doing the work in the first place—to be able to care for a family—first to have a family and then to provide for it.

Don Alberto had taught Eduardo to love craftsmanship and hard work more than money. Not such a bad lesson to teach. Eduardo could not know at this age, but he suspected that the old man had tried very hard to share at last with his young student the most important lessons he had learned himself only after so many years of experience—lessons of time lost but not wasted entirely, of a good life lived by a fine man, but of one who died more full of regret than pride. This example was foremost. It was one about a man who had wanted desperately to prevent this young person from similarly wasting a life.

Don Edwin was speaking at length about something. Eduardo almost startled himself as he realized his mind had wandered so far from the subject at hand that it might have been obvious that he was disoriented and inattentive.

In fact, O'Connor stopped speaking for a moment, smiled and then said, "Your mind is elsewhere. That's all right. It's understandable. You've lost a dear friend. Your mother has told me how much the old man had come to mean to you. Based on what she's told me, I almost wish I had gotten to know Don Alberto better myself. You're distracted. You should go, and I'll leave you to your thoughts. You and I will speak later, perhaps tomorrow."

"The funeral is tomorrow."

"Ah yes. I'd forgotten. That won't take the entire day. But you're probably right. Let's plan to talk when I get back home at the end of this week. I must go briefly away but will be back Thursday evening. Take care, my boy. I feel for you. I know how painful it can be to lose someone you care about."

"Thank you, sir. May I go?" Eduardo asked quietly as he rose to leave.

"Good evening, Eduardo."

Eduardo walked out of the office and returned to the cabin to read. He could not concentrate, although he fought to do so for over an hour before falling to sleep in the chair. Don Edwin had installed a more comfortable stuffed chair in Eduardo's bedroom and another much like it in the mother's room. He had also placed a reading table by Eduardo's chair. Although these were not identified as Christmas presents, Eduardo and his mother both knew that this was what Don Edwin had in mind when he purchased them and had carefully placed them in the rooms. Eduardo was sleeping soundly when his mother checked in on him to say, "Good night." She decided not to bother him but instead simply draped a light blanket over him and went to bed herself.

Lying in her own bed, she thought about the loss of the old man and about how hopeful she had been about the prospect of her son learning that craft, mastering it thoroughly and well, and then settling somewhere nearby. She wondered if the years in the university had changed Eduardo more than she realized. She was not concerned about frivolous pursuits.

She was worried about a much more unsettling prospect: the possibility that education would lead him far away from her. The patrón's suggestion that Eduardo join him in the mining business could give Eduardo opportunity not only to remain but to become wealthy beyond anything she or he could have imagined. But there was something about that which bothered her to no end. She was not certain what exactly it was that bothered her. But it would not go away. Eduardo was a kind, simple boy, a loving person. To be truly successful in business, he would have to learn to become a different sort of person. That prospect worried her more than any other. More than wanting him nearby—where he could care for her in her old age—she wanted him to be the fine, honest, loving man that he had shown so much potential of becoming all through his childhood. A teacher. He should be a teacher.

✳ ✳ ✳

The funeral was short and simple, for a man whose life had been long and lonely. Several members of the small congregation attended Mass. The priest, who had grown to know and love the old man, shed tears during the service. Eduardo and his mother sat quietly, paying homage to the gentleman who had come to matter greatly to each of them.

A young lady unfamiliar to Eduardo sat on the front pew just to the right of the center aisle, as if she were family. The funeral service came to a close and the crowd attended the brief burial in the church graveyard next to the chapel. As the final prayer was said and people began filtering away, the young woman dropped a rose bud into the grave on top of the casket.

Eduardo approached her, his mother hanging back to visit with the priest.

"Good morning. My name is Eduardo. I was very fond of Don Alberto. How did you know him?"

She looked up. Clear-eyed, pale, with deep brown eyes and radiant skin, she smiled softly with a distant look in her eye. "Good morning. My name is Felicia. Don Alberto was my uncle, the brother of my mother."

"I see. He had not mentioned family."

"He and my mother did not communicate for many years. She died long ago. It's very possible that he may have wanted to forget. He had never seen me."

"Excuse me for asking, but how did you know he had died?"

"The priest. Tío Alberto had given his family information to the priest long ago. It was all still recorded and the priest tried to contact my mother and ended up finding me instead. I live not so far from this village. I understand that my uncle was a good craftsman and a good man," she added looking into Eduardo's eyes hoping to learn whether this was true.

"Your uncle was a highly skilled gem cutter. His work was much admired far away from here. He preferred to live where he had always lived. And, yes, he was a very good man."

She smiled more warmly. "It's good of you to say so.'

"It was my great pleasure to serve as an apprentice to your uncle for a short time."

"Why only a short time?"

"I began to study in a university instead of being apprenticed to Don Alberto."

"Have you been happy with that choice?"

He laughed. "It's too early to tell. I've enjoyed very much my studies in Puerto Lindo. I'm almost finished." Smiling politely, she said, "Well, it was good to meet you. I should be going."

The more she spoke and the more opportunity he had to observe her, the more he wanted to get to know her better. "You said you live not far away. Where, if I could ask?"

"In Camponuela, a small village between here and Bogotá." She began to walk away while trying not to turn away from Eduardo. He walked alongside her, persisting with his questions and attention.

"What do you do there?"

"I'm a seamstress and I cook. I was not lucky enough to have a chance to study in a university. My mother was a cook at a large estate. My father died when I was very young as well. I'm proud of the work I do sewing." And she added, showing that pride in her expression, "I'm very good at it."

"If you're as good at that as your uncle was at his craft, then you are very talented indeed."

Continuing to walk, she touched his arm gently and said almost pleadingly, "I have to go now. It was good to meet you."

Too loudly, almost aggressively, he said, "I'd like to see you again." He allowed her to continue walking.

Turning her head back only slightly, she answered, "I would enjoy that." Then she stopped and turned around. "Would you like to walk with me to the place where the bus stops?"

Grinning broadly now, he stepped briskly toward her and walked alongside her down the road, each sharing more and more information with the other until, having arrived at the point where the bus would pass by, they stood saying nothing, each at a loss for words. Felicia had bothered to come to the funeral not because she felt close to her uncle but because she felt alone. She wanted to feel some sort of family connection. She felt drawn to this village where he had spent so many years alone. She sensed one thing in common with the uncle she had never known. She knew what it meant to be alone, to have no family nearby, to have no one to love. She worked long, arduous days with her needle and thread, putting as much of herself into meticulous work as she would have wanted to put into something larger, such as loving someone, anyone... a mother no longer alive, a father she had never known. A husband? No, that was something she no longer bothered thinking about. She had known men, or rather they had known her, but she had not known love with any one man. She was still young. She had her health. She knew from the reaction of men that she was still attractive enough to draw attention to herself even without fine clothes, without having her hair done as neatly and well as the lady of the estate where she worked.

She knew from experience that she could attract men. She knew that the master of the estate where she worked was attracted enough to her to take her by force more than once. She hated him for that. She hated the mistress of the house for pretending not to know. She hated her for being the despicable employer that she could be at times.

Yes, Felicia had come to think less of herself through the years. Her looks counted for little. Her mind was untaught but active and strong. She knew that her mind had the potential of becoming useful. No family. No child. So why would education matter anyway?

The one thing about all this that did hurt was having no child to love and care for. To focus on the raising of a miniature replica of herself. Boy or girl? No matter. Just a child... an extension of herself... and of him... whoever her husband might be.

Eduardo for some reason felt awkward. But he wanted to keep her from leaving if he could. He found himself wanting to grab her and say, "Don't go!"

"And now I must leave," she said smiling, breaking the silence. The bus had arrived. The time had flown by so quickly that she almost lost all sense of time and of why she had come here today. The grief she tried to feel in relation to the old man seemed false or imagined—a fabricated sense of loss. But she had felt drawn here today and now had met someone who might possibly become...no, probably not.

"Miss, are you going with us today?" asked the driver.

"I must go. I *must* leave," she said softly to Eduardo.

And touching her waist, he leaned forward and kissed her gently on the forehead. She blushed and got onto the bus. Eduardo, while watching the bus pull away, committed to finding some way to be with her again. She wondered what exactly had happened. But she felt certain that she would be back someday to be with him. She knew it. It would happen...somehow.

The time to return to the university drew closer. Eduardo's mother had encouraged him to visit the small school he had attended as a boy. She knew that the new teacher was not well thought of by the priest or by others...a young woman hired for that year only. Not as well prepared as she had seemed. Impatient, uncaring. His mother knew that the priest had the administrative authority to hire and fire the instructor at the small school sponsored partly by the Church and partly by donations from O'Connor and others.

This morning, Eduardo had decided to do as his mother asked. He came to the small school and introduced himself to the young woman and explained who he was. Not expecting the visit, she looked uncomfortable as she greeted him and asked him to sit in the back of the class, introducing him to the students and then continuing her instruction. At one point, she asked him to read a story to the class. He read in an animated way, giving life to the characters in a story that was intended for very young children. This one-room school had students of various ages. The older children for the most part looked bored. After completing the story and seeing delight in the eyes of the youngest children, Eduardo felt frustrated at not having been able to intrigue the three or four older students.

He asked the teacher if he might speak for a very few minutes about his experience in this school and about how wonderful it can be to learn about the world outside the small village. Not wanting to seem uncooperative and clearly relieved at having someone to assist, she answered "Of course," and sat down.

Eduardo spoke about how fondly he remembered his days in this school, about the excitement he had felt when he first learned to read and write and how each and every new skill came to him as a welcome addition to his life, making life so much more interesting. He told of the wonderful stories he remembered reading, introducing him to fascinating characters and situations in fiction and to the equally fascinating real-life characters and situations he had encountered in the study of history. His love of learning and his enthusiasm were infectious.

Realizing that he was taking too much time, he wrapped up his remarks and mentioned how important it is for each student to learn as much as possible and to try to find ways to continue learning after finishing school. He sat down again in the back of the classroom and watched, disappointed as the young teacher then returned to her schedule, seeming bored by her work and unable to hide it. Mistaken in grammar and occasionally in facts, she made a very poor impression on Eduardo, who had been fortunate enough to have had a fine teacher throughout the time he had studied here. It made him realize how fortunate he had been.

He sat and listened through much of the morning, assisting the teacher at one point, as the children worked on individual assignments, separated by age group. Then he politely excused himself and left, thinking all the way back to the estate about what it might be like to be in charge of the education of children. To be able to share not only knowledge but a love of learning in general. He had never seriously considered this. He could not picture himself doing it. He knew it would be difficult to survive on as little income as a small school teacher would earn, and feared that it would not allow him to continue to grow, to develop his mind.

He had been offered an opportunity in business that could lead to great wealth. He pulled out the gold watch that Don Edwin had given him. He carried it with him every day. Admiring its beauty, he recalled the patrón's comments: that only so much time is allowed in order to accomplish great things. It was obvious that Don Edwin considered the accumulation of wealth as the greatest of endeavors, the product of talent and hard work.

Eduardo enjoyed his years away in school. He enjoyed nice clothes. He had eaten well and lived in a simple but clean room. He'd had the opportunity to associate with interesting people and to learn much during these years.

And yet, at no point in his life had he felt so confused. He had to admit there was something exciting about the prospect of coming home to learn Don Edwin's business. Part of that would involve being back in Puerto Lindo often. Not that Eduardo found the city itself so rewarding. But it would place him back near the university. And, having learned the business well, having earned enough to prosper, he would be better able to take care of himself and his mother. Don Edwin suggested that there could be the possibility of Eduardo progressing beyond status as an employee toward becoming the owner. Could that be? Why on earth would this man suggest such a thing? Was he so desperate about not having a son?

There seemed to be no point to wondering about things such as this. Eduardo did not understand the man. He did understand that the opportunity already afforded him had opened up choices that should never exist for the son of a maid.

To be a teacher? Why had his mother suggested this? She did not try to conceal that she wanted her son close by. This was not difficult to understand. She had no husband to take care of her as she aged. She had no savings. But aside from self-interest, she truly loved Eduardo and deserved attention and care in return for all the love and attention she had invested in her son.

Was it possible that she understood something about her son that he himself had not yet grasped? It seemed intriguing—the challenge of having a small school and devoting years to the cultivation of young minds. On the other hand, he wondered what it would be like to spend day after day, year after year, covering the same subjects in the same routine with different faces as the only changeable factor.

And this young woman at the funeral? What could possibly have produced her today out of nowhere? Those eyes, too distracting. So much else to think about. All at once. Slow down. Take a breath. One step at a time. Still a few months before graduation. Let it rest at least for now. And back to work.

✳ ✳ ✳

Packed and ready to return to the university the following morning, Eduardo sat reading in the early evening of his final day of holidays. He heard a loud knock on the door of the cabin. Startled, he was not accustomed to anyone approaching the cabin except for his mother, and she never knocked.

"Yes?" he called out loudly, rising from the comfortable chair. He walked to the door, listening. He was puzzled to see Don Edwin standing alone. O'Connor said simply, "Eduardo, I need to speak with you about something. Come with me."

Without waiting for a reply, he then turned and walked straight back to the main house. Although O'Connor had not waited for a reply, Eduardo said clearly, his voice raised so as to be heard, "Yes, sir," and then pulled the door shut behind him.

Following Don Edwin up the steps to the house, across the wide porch and into the patrón's office, Eduardo stood awkwardly once inside waiting for further instructions. Judging by the situation, he felt certain that he had not been summoned here for good news and felt apprehensive about what it might be that he had done wrong.

Don Edwin walked to the area behind his desk, sat and invited the boy to sit in the straight-backed chair facing him. "Eduardo, I'm afraid I have bad news." The boy's mind raced.

"I've had an extraordinary setback financially this month at the same time that I remain committed to an investment elsewhere. It will not be at all convenient for me to pay your tuition and other costs at the university this term."

Stunned and suddenly nauseated, Eduardo could not believe what he was hearing. He considered the possibility that Don Edwin might be joking, but knew that O'Connor was not a joking man. "But Don Edwin, I have only the one semester remaining."

"Yes, I know. I realize that. And that's truly a shame. Perhaps you can pick up where you left off at some later time."

"But, sir, what...?"

"Eduardo, I'm very sorry. There's nothing more to say about this. I've only just learned about it myself today. The cash that would go for your expenses must now go elsewhere and right away. You'll need to make other arrangements for the coming months."

Not knowing what to say or to do, Eduardo could not help himself from asking "Would I be able to work in your business instead?"

"Not right at this time. No." O'Connor rose, signaling that the meeting had ended, but said as warmly as possible considering how uncomfortable he himself felt in having to deliver such bad news, "I'm truly sorry my boy. Now I must go back to work. Good evening."

With that, he sat down again and turned his attention immediately to the papers on his desk.

Eduardo, aware that there was no point in saying anything else, stepped quietly out of the office. Instead of leaving the house, he turned at the doorway to the office in the opposite direction and headed toward the kitchen, entering it to find his mother preparing dinner, already looking tired although there was still much left to do this day.

"My son, what luck! Can you help me?"

Distracted, lost in thought, he wondered how she would take the news about his "good luck." She would probably be thrilled to have her son at home with her a few more months. He answered, trying not to show concern, "Of course. How can I help?"

"Peel these please, my educated young assistant."

He took the small paring knife and began peeling potatoes in the same manner he had learned as a child. "Mother, Don Edwin will not be able to pay my expenses for this last term of school."

She stopped what she was doing and looked up. "¿Cómo? How's that?" she asked in disbelief. "How could he suddenly have so little funds after helping you for so long?"

"He says he's suffered a great financial loss somehow."

By now, her cheeks red with anger, she said bitterly but almost beneath her breath, "He cannot do this!"

The intensity of the outburst surprised him almost as much as the bad news itself had.

She stood fuming and thinking out loud. "I must speak to him."

"No! Mother, please! It was perfectly clear that there is nothing to discuss about this. He has done so much for me already. I have to consider what to do next."

Stopping her work entirely and resting for a second on a stool nearby, she said, "Well, you are right in one way. But there's nothing to consider. You must return to school. You must finish what you've started before the opportunity slips away altogether."

"I've upset you. I should not have told you like this. Please, let's finish preparing dinner and then we can talk about this later." He tugged at her arm gently and pulled her back to the cabinet where she had been working.

She did as he asked. Nothing further was discussed during the evening. Eduardo worked alongside her and then ate in the kitchen silently. They cleaned up afterward and he waited to walk her back to their cabin.

Once there, she reached into her wooden armoire and pulled out a small cloth sack from the top shelf and said, "There is enough here to pay for your transport to and from the school and for some of your expenses in the first weeks. Go. Speak to them and see if anyone can find a way to help you. You have worked hard. You deserve this opportunity."

"I can't accept this," he said handing the small purse back to her. "This is everything you've saved through the years. Here." He tried to give it back to her. She shook her head and refused.

She took both her hands and surrounded his hands with the purse inside. "Make a point of coming up with whatever might be required. Find a way. Do not fail at this, son. You have not worked so hard for so long for nothing."

Listening to her, seeing the determination in her face and hearing it in her voice, he realized that he had no acceptable alternative. He took the purse in one hand and gave her a hug. Fighting back tears, he said only, "I will not fail. I'll make it work somehow. And I will repay you."

Pushing him away, she said, "You must rest now. Go to bed. You must get up early to arrive there tomorrow."

Nodding in agreement, he kissed her on the forehead and said only "Good night." As he stepped into his own room, before closing the door, he turned and said "Thank you," deeply worried about whether being determined to succeed would be sufficient. He couldn't know. Unfortunately he had no choice but to step forward into uncertainty.

Having slept little the night of his arrival back at school, Eduardo got up early and prepared for the day. He spent little of the cash given to him by his mother for the trip back to the campus in the port city. He knew that he would have to budget the remainder very carefully. Although tall and strong, Eduardo felt like a small child abandoned to his own resources and could not lose the flutter in his stomach that he always felt whenever afraid. As she had given him the small cloth purse full of money, his mother sounded reassuring, confident that Eduardo would find some way to make it all work out well for himself if only given this chance. The thought of her having worked so hard for so long and having so little to show for it caused him great pain. It was pathetic and, of course, profoundly unfair for her to have almost nothing after having already given so much.

It was disturbing to think that he could be holding her entire life's savings in his hands in cold hard cash. Concern about the possibility of someone stealing money from him worried him this morning. Where should he put it? Should he go to a bank? No. What if something happened to it there or if he needed parts of it and the bank would not be open or for some reason would not want to give it to him? Hide it in his room? There wasn't much else he could do. And so he carefully made a place for it in the farthest back corner of the highest shelf of his closet, after taking out just enough for food for the first two or three days.

What if he were not able to find a way to pay for his tuition and other costs of study here? What had made his mother so confident that he would find a way? There was something in her voice, in her manner, something deep within her being at that moment that told him there was absolutely no doubt in her mind that this money would be a good investment; that she was completely certain that her boy was going to be successful at whatever he chose to do if he could just get over this one hurdle. There was something very reassuring to him about her confidence. She seemed to have more confidence in him than he knew he had in himself. Perhaps she was right.

The thought of the calm touch of her hand on his arm as she gave him the purse, of the comforting sound of her voice as she said, "You'll find a way," all came together this morning to make him feel less concern. But it could not remove all worries. He wondered what there might be that he could do. Oh well, as she had always taught him, and as her voice continued ringing in his ears ever when she was not there—"one step at a time".

First, he would get through this initial day. He had to register for his final classes. He needed to visit the dean in order to let him know the new situation and to see what could be done. That would be the first order of the day.

But, as he prepared to go for a simple breakfast of a hard roll and tea, he thought about the amulet and wondered whether this was a dire enough situation to merit trying to use it. Trying to picture how a visit with the dean might go, and not being able to see anything good coming out of that visit, he decided that this was exactly one of those desperate times when any sort of help was called for. Why had the amulet been made available to him if not to be used? His mother had always advised him how important it would be to use it only in matters of life and death.

As he considered this, he thought about how ridiculous it was for an educated young man, a university student, to be wasting time thinking about such an absurd piece of rubbish. How silly it was to be so ready to believe in age-old superstitions, basically in magic even though he had no idea at all how to explain what he had already witnessed in relation to the amulet before.

The amulet should only be used in matters of life and death and it should always be remembered that his life might be long if the use of the amulet were carefully rationed out throughout the course of that life-time. But then, after all, why should he assume his life was intended to last so long anyway? How could anyone know? And how silly it would be to forego opportunities to take advantage of any benefit that might come from its use and then to die anyway, having wasted it for years, always waiting from one year to the next for a more important situation to arrive.

What could possibly be more important than this situation now? Having invested so much time and effort and being so close to completion of his degree, how could he possibly allow the situation to float? Would it be the end of his life not to graduate? No. But he would have to go to work immediately and would most probably become involved in work and life to the point where he would never return to school. There was no reason to assume that Don Edwin would be any more committed to helping him financially at a later date than he had been at this critically important juncture now.

Tentatively, Eduardo looked for the amulet among his things, and prepared to hide it away in the precise spot where he had placed the money purse. As he held it, he realized that he could feel no warmth in it; could see no glow. He thought little of that. At this particular moment, he was not concentrating on taking advantage of its power. He wondered if there could be any special significance to the fact that the emerald did not seem to respond to his touch at all. Shrugging off this reaction, he placed it back where it needed to be and carefully tucked it away.

He went to register for his classes. He was told to go first to the dean's office, although given no explanation. Since he had intended to go there anyway, he walked across the small campus to the administration building and approached the door to the dean's office. There was no receptionist in front of his office. The dean used the services of the same secretary used by the handful of other administrators and her desk was elsewhere. He stood at the closed door, hesitating at first, feeling an intense recurrence of that same flutter in his stomach. He told himself to grow up and to be a man and courageously knocked on the door firmly and three times.

"Come in," he heard from the other side.

He opened the door, stepped into the office, and said without any effort at pleasantries or small talk, "Sir, you had asked me to come?"

"Yes. Yes I did, young man. Eduardo, come in and sit down please. I only have to finish the very last of this letter."

Eduardo did as he was told and sat in the same sort of wooden, straight-backed chair in front of the dean's desk as Don Edwin kept in place in front of his very similar heavy wood desk. As he glanced about the office, he saw the shelves of books behind the dean and along one wall, and then noticed all the various credentials of one sort or another and also of various types of recognition. He sat patiently and quietly as the dean completed the letter .

Finally putting down his pen and looking up, the dean leaned slightly forward, indicating that Eduardo now had his undivided attention. "Eduardo, I've heard from your patrón, Don Edwin O'Connor that he will not be paying your expenses this semester. And yet here you are, ready to enroll again. What exactly do you have in mind?"

"Sir, with all due respect, I intend to complete my studies this semester. I am so close to finishing my degree."

"I see. Well, that's admirable. But one thing I don't understand is how exactly you intend to pay. Do you know?"

Eduardo, noticing small beads of sweat spilling down the side of his face, hesitated for a second, felt the color drain from his face and feared that the dean would hear the loud heartbeat that he could hear within his own body. "No. "

The dean laughed slightly and picked up a pencil nearby and began tapping it on the desk, pursing his lips, appearing to consider what he had just heard. "Young man, does it not seem just a bit arrogant for you to assume that you would be able to study here without any financial support and without any plan as to how to obtain it?"

Not knowing exactly how to reply to that question, Eduardo decided to say the first thing that popped into his head which was "Yes."

Choosing not to laugh this time, the Dean simply took the pencil in both hands and sat back in his chair. "You can't register for classes today. You have a room and already moved back into it. Correct?"

"Yes."

"Well, stay there today. You may spend time in the library if you want. But it was wrong of you to assume that we would allow you to attend for free."

At this point, Eduardo recovered enough presence of mind to sit up straighter and to become more engaged in the conversation. "Sir, I had no such idea. But I knew if I was going to complete everything this term, I could not do it by staying at home and giving up. My mother gave me what little money she had, basically all the money that she has and told me to see if I could find a way to make it work. That's why I'm here. I love this school and I love learning. I want to finish my degree. I'll work at anything to earn my way. Please don't send me home."

The dean sat quietly listening to this passionate statement of intent and said nothing. After a moment of considering the young man and the situation, he said, "Go now. But come back tomorrow morning to my office."

Not knowing whether he should feel relieved or not, Eduardo could not help seeing cause for hope. The dean was, after all, not throwing him into the street. It was possible that the distinguished gentleman was trying to determine if there might be some way to help. On the other hand, it was also possible that Eduardo would be allowed to hang around for an additional day and would actually be thrown out for lack of funds. All he could do at this point was to wait.

He left the dean's office feeling depressed and worried about what he would do next if no solution could be found. He waited in the library as had been suggested to him. He tried to read but could not even for a moment manage to concentrate sufficiently to follow what he was reading.

The day seemed to drag on interminably. He took a few minutes to go to the edge of the campus and to get a coffee and small bowl of soup for lunch and then returned to the library—to what had already become his sanctuary, his refuge, the place where he was most comfortable, the place where he felt completely at home.

As his mind raced from possibility to possibility, he could not help dwelling on negative thoughts about Don Edwin for having put him into this situation so abruptly. He felt enormous resentment toward his patrón. He had already begun to resent the emerald amulet and the primitive superstition that it represented. He began to resent God himself for having either put him into this situation or having allowed it to happen.

Although he had managed for three and a half years to avoid resentment of wealth and power that he had heard among the faculty and among a handful of the students, he could not help now hearing echoes of bother-some statements about the unfairness of life and the unjust control over lives that wealth and power wielded in the world. He could not help—given what he'd observed—resenting the wealth of Don Edwin and resenting the power over his life and the life of his mother that this man had always wielded. Eduardo had heard much at the university about the evils of foreign influence in business as well as in politics. Although he had resisted buying into this hatred of all things foreign, the more he considered it the more he began to see Edwin O'Connor and his Irishness as representative of the sort of evil domination of Colombian interests that certain faculty members had discussed and condemned.

Rational enough to be able to weigh the validity of his own thoughts, he tried to persuade himself to remember all the good things O'Connor had provided Eduardo, his mother, and others. Somehow that seemed more difficult to do today than on any other day. He sat, book in hand, unable to absorb a single thought from a single page, mechanically turning the pages.

Eduardo had never, up until this moment, felt such a tremendous sense of frustration or helplessness. He had been encouraged to think that he was in charge of his own destiny while a student. Was he? Obviously not. And, if not, then who was in charge—a foreigner who had abandoned his mother and left her to raise a boy by herself—another foreigner, Don Edwin, controlling her life and the life of her son?

As evening approached, he got up from his seat in the library, tired of attempting for hours to focus on his book He felt exhausted. He felt no hunger. Instead of going in the evening to find something to eat, he decided simply to return to his room and to go straight to bed.

As he entered the building and then his room, more tired and hungry than he fully realized, he began to feel desperation setting in. Before going to bed, he reached up into the hidden spot high in his closet and pulled out the emerald amulet and held it gently. Disgusted with himself for being so helpless that he would lend any credence at all to something like this, he at the same time remembered the extraordinary circumstances surrounding his acquisition of this very special piece of jewelry.

He held it and then placed the chain around his neck. He grasped the emerald and held it tightly in his right hand, closed his eyes and concentrated, asking for any assistance he could get from it. After a minute or so of standing there, he noticed nothing. No warmth, no glow. No miracle. He let go of it and, more disappointed than angry, slipped it over his head and replaced it back to its place in the closet. Enough. He could not handle one thing more this day. He went to bed.

✡ ✡ ✡

He slept restlessly all night. As he awoke early the following morning, he remembered most of the details of what had seemed like a very long dream—a dream involving being at home, his mother in good health and working on her own, and with him in charge of the small school, proud of the progress of the small children under his care and teaching. In his dream, it felt good to be useful, felt good to mold young minds. Not easy by any means. Somewhat like the difficulty of the emerald cut, so important to shaping the delicately precious raw emerald into a beautifully multi-faceted finished stone.

There seemed to be one special child within the class who would do especially well. And, each time that child would perform well, Eduardo felt enormous pride. Throughout the dream, though, he could never see clearly the child's face, although the faces of others were clearly identifiable.

He had often waked feeling scared or slightly unsteady after a dream disturbing but only half-remembered. As he stretched and tried to awaken this morning, he felt inexplicably well and rested, and found himself wanting to return to the dream. As his eyes opened more fully and the day came to life, the same concerns of the prior day crept into his thoughts and brought back the same sense of dry desperation from before. That thought made him want even more to return to the pleasant life, however imaginary, that he had just lived in the dream.

But the day had to be confronted. As much as he preferred to remain safe and comfortable in bed, he got up and dressed and tried to summon enough courage to be able to face the challenge of determining how to stay in school. With absolutely no solution in mind, this task seemed impossible to accomplish.

It was time to return to the dean's office. He walked slowly across campus and entered the same building where he had visited with the dean. He knocked less forcefully than before and heard a warm "Come in" from inside. He opened the door and this time found the dean sitting, leaning back in his chair, pipe in hand, filling it with tobacco. "Come in, please. Sit down."

Eduardo, walking as if in another world, exhausted from hours of worry and close to feeling at the edge of a precipice and a never-ending tumble downward, sat up as straight as he could—unfeeling, unthinking, waiting to hear what would come next.

"You look ill at ease, Eduardo. Please do relax." The dean, tobacco tamped down into the pipe, held it to his mouth with his left hand and lit it with the match in his right and took several long draws, enjoying each puff. He sat forward and held the pipe to the side and came to the point. "Young man, I've visited with the faculty and with two other administrators and have heard nothing but good things about you. You seem to be a budding young scholar."

Eduardo, not knowing what to say, spoke anyway if only to seem polite, and answered, "Thank you, sir. I do what I can. Studying isn't work to me. It's enjoyable."

"Hmm…so I hear. And I understand it isn't a matter of empty effort. You seem to produce very fine results indeed. Have you given serious thought to what you will do after you complete your degree?"

"Well, yes. But it is not at all clear that I'm going to be able to finish."

"Tell me what you're thinking."

Wondering what the point was to this line of conversation, Eduardo focused on trying to reply as respectfully as possible. "I've thought a great deal about it, sir. But I have to admit that I'm still confused and uncertain."

"Well, there's nothing original about that in a young man."

"I've been offered employment in a business. I have also considered the possibility of becoming a teacher."

"Really? And which way are you leaning now?

"That's just the point. I'm not clearly leaning one way or the other yet and have not thought about it at all since learning about my financial situation. I think about nothing now other than finding a way to complete my studies."

The dean leaned back a bit and said, studying his pipe, "Well, for a moment, let's suppose that paying for your remaining studies is no longer something you need to worry about."

Eduardo, who had had difficulty looking straight at the dean until now, seemed startled by this and looked him straight in the eye as the educator smiled, taking a moment to appreciate the look on the young man's face as he received good news. "We're going to forgive entirely your tuition cost for this final semester, and we're going to cover the remainder of your expenses through a grant based on a commitment from you to teach part-time in the small academy alongside the university. What do you think of that?"

Eduardo, speechless, felt tears welling up in his eyes, swallowed hard and took a deep breath, closing his eyes for a second, then reaching up to wipe them with his sleeve. At first beginning to speak, he had to clear his throat and try again. "I don't know what to say, sir."

Still grinning, except now much more widely, the dean answered, "A simple "Thank you" would be sufficient."

"Oh, words can't begin to express how much I appreciate this. Thank you so much!"

"With a prospect like you, Eduardo, this is considered an investment and a good one at that, depending upon what you make of yourself."

"I wish I could know what to promise in return for this, but I don't know what to think."

"Don't worry about that. Only continue to do the good work you've been doing and then become the gentleman and possibly even the scholar that it appears you were naturally born to be. In other words, keep up the good work and don't worry about the rest. Now you'd best go. Go register for your classes and then get to work right away. Put concerns about finances out of your mind for this final semester and focus on more important things. Go."

Eduardo rose and for the first time approached the dean's desk, reaching out his hand and asked, "Might I shake your hand?"

The dean reached across and took the boy's hand. "Congratulations. Again, you've earned this vote of confidence. Now don't disappoint us."

Shaking the older man's hand vigorously, he said "I'll do my best." He let go and walked out briskly, head held higher than before.

After Eduardo had left, the dean sat for a moment considering what this young man might accomplish some day and whether this could possibly end up having been a critical moment in his life. He had experience enough to know that it would probably never be seen as significant to anyone other than to Eduardo as he would grow older. And, as far as the dean was concerned, that would be quite enough as long as the student turned into as fine a man as it appeared he was going to be.

Eduardo, unwilling to dwell on how dismal the future had appeared to be or on how close he had come to what he considered a bleak outcome, instead focused on getting started with his work. He managed to put aside all worries and put all his energy as of that moment into what he would learn during these last few months, knowing that it was more important than ever for him to consider along the way what he would do with the rest of his life following graduation.

At the end of the semester, as Eduardo sat among the thirty or so other graduates, he listened to the comments of the various speakers. The ceremony was brief, except for the four persons who droned on at length about how profoundly significant this accomplishment was for each student obtaining his diploma. There was a primary speaker. But each of the three secondary speakers chose to speak as if in fact the guest of honor.

Finally, the principal speaker offered words of encouragement to the graduates, especially in terms of the difficult choices that would now have to be made concerning careers and other more mundane subjects in the weeks and months to follow. He was surprisingly brief with his remarks. And then, suddenly, the moment arrived.

The dean called the students forward one by one. Eduardo, when his name was called, walked up and accepted his diploma. He shook hands with the dean. The dean winked and whispered, "And a special congratulations to you young man." Eduardo smiled, exited the platform and returned to his seat.

As he approached the chairs lined up for the graduates, he happened to see Don Edwin standing in the back of the room. Eduardo began to lift his hand to wave and then, nudged forward by the graduate behind him, took the two or three more steps to his seat and sat down. He wondered why a man as important as Edwin O'Connor would bother to attend this ceremony. Eduardo had certainly accomplished this last bit of his education as a result of his own determination, but not with his own resources. He had received considerable assistance from the dean of the university. Eduardo had managed quite well at the very end of these past four years without the continued help of the great "gentleman" Edwin O'Connor.

At first glad to see a familiar face, and happy to think that someone who had watched him grow up had bothered to come to this small ceremony, Eduardo also thought about how desperately he resented O'Connor's coldness in leaving him high and dry on the eve of his final semester of study, not seeming to care whether the boy completed his studies or not. Eduardo recalled the resentment he had felt toward this foreigner who owned so much, who controlled so much, including Eduardo's mother's life and well-being.

He considered all this and yet smiled slightly, thinking that perhaps now, with this new credential, he would be able to be independent from O'Connor's patronage. The smile faded quickly as Eduardo remembered that he still did not have a specific position secured, aside from the offer extended by his patrón.

Over the months of his final semester, Eduardo had considered at length what he should do after completing his studies and his degree. He had continued feeling torn between the possibility of working in business, of learning that business thoroughly, of living well in the meantime, and of being able to provide for his mother's care and well-being along the way, possibly becoming wealthy as an heir to the fortune of Edwin O'Connor. He still could not believe how extraordinary that offer had been. He could not reconcile this generosity with the coldness of the news from O'Connor just a few months earlier. But the potential wealth and comfort associated with following that route was extremely appealing.

Eduardo had to be honest. He had always admired, even envied O'Connor's wealth, his fine clothes, elegant cravats, his status (although he had not fully appreciated the extent of O'Connor's reputation as an accomplished mine owner and exporter until having arrived at the university). No matter how long O'Connor had lived in Colombia, he had been and always would remain a foreigner.

Although he had not completely absorbed every resentful detail within the typical professor's rant about the evils of foreign control of assets, of wealth and resources, Eduardo had heard enough of this during his four years in the university to have acquired some of this anti-foreign sentiment.

But at this particular moment on this particular day, Eduardo felt so enormously proud of himself that there simply was no room in his heart for hatred or distrust or resentment toward anyone, even toward the great foreigner Edwin O'Connor who had left him for dead, so to speak, only a short time before. By the time he looked back to see if Don Edwin remained in the room, O'Connor had left. Anyhow, he had been there. Whatever the reason, it was good to see someone interested. Of course, no one could have been more interested in being there than Eduardo's mother. Yet she could not come to the ceremony. She, of course, did not approach Don Edwin asking for funds to make the trip. And it never occurred to O'Connor to volunteer it.

It seemed anticlimactic: the process of stripping his room and of packing to return home after graduation. It was over. Deep melancholy crept into him as he realized that the most fulfilling part of his life up to this point had come to an end. It was difficult to imagine anything else being so rewarding, so full of challenge and enjoyment. He packed up what little he owned and departed, riding home on the bus, looking out the window the entire way instead of reading. There was so much on his mind now that had not occupied it before.

He almost dreaded his first meeting with Don Edwin, which he knew would happen soon, whether Eduardo wanted it to or not. In spite of his backing away at the last minute, the patrón had spent a great deal of money on Eduardo's education and had shown more than a passing interest in the boy's progress. He had seemed genuinely interested in the idea of Eduardo working alongside him in the emerald mining and export business. Even if Eduardo tried to avoid the subject for as much as a day, with Don Edwin at home, the subject would come up anyway. This would be one topic concerning Eduardo and his future that Don Edwin would not allow to lie unconsidered.

Seeing her boy arrive home, Eduardo's mother at first said nothing. Tears in her eyes, she simply stretched out her arms to receive him and embraced him as tightly as ever, rocking gently from side to side. Then she said softly, "My son, my son. Oh my God, how proud I am of you today."

Almost overcome himself, Eduardo pulled away and said proudly, "We did it! See this!" And he pulled out the diploma to show her how it looked with his name written in fancy script. "See. And this as well," he said, pulling out the small purse with all of her money in it, including the money he had spent in traveling to the campus at the beginning of the final semester. They forgave my tuition. They gave me funds for housing and food and allowed me to work teaching. My earnings from teaching went to my expenses. But I was able to save enough of it to replace every penny of what you gave me. You can count it if you want."

Too overcome to speak, she shook her head and clutched the purse to her heart and then hugged him again and looked up and said as if to the sky, "Thank you, God, for taking such good care of my son." Eduardo wondered whether if it had been God or the amulet saving his semester. She then looked at him in the face and told him simply and directly in a quiet voice, "It's good to have you home. I know you must be hungry?"

"Not really. But it's good to be home. Let me put my things away."

"Get comfortable and come to eat whenever you are ready. I'll fix you something. "

Eduardo let her go back to work. As he walked back to the cabin to unpack, he heard that familiar male voice behind him on the porch. "Eduardo! Welcome home." O'Connor was walking out of the house and for the first time that Eduardo could remember was going out of his way to approach him. The patrón stepped briskly off the porch and into the yard. He came up to Eduardo, who had put down his bag. He offered his hand and said again, "Welcome home. Congratulations. I'm proud of you for having been so determined to get your diploma no matter what. Well done. Well done indeed."

Eduardo, thinking how ironic it seemed for Don Edwin to be so warm and congratulatory so soon after having left a young man stuck without resources for his final term. It seemed false somehow. And yet there seemed to be something quite genuine in the tone of O'Connor's voice and in his manner. At least on the surface, he did in fact seem proud of what Eduardo had accomplished. Anyhow, all Eduardo could manage in reply was a respectful, "Thank you very much, sir."

O'Connor sensing a certain amount of coolness in Eduardo's response, chose to ignore this and hesitated for a second. And then as if to change the subject, he patted Eduardo on the side of his shoulder and said as brusquely as always, "Come with me to my office." With that, he turned immediately and began walking back toward the house.

For the first time that Eduardo could recall, he resented being instructed as to what to do. Somehow the situation had changed enough that he thought he should be afforded more respect. He stood in place, not moving.

O'Connor, not surprised to see a newfound resistance in the young man before him, understandingly turned back once he realized Eduardo was not following him. *"Please,* would you follow me? I'd like to visit in my office." Eduardo picked up his bag and asked, "Could I drop off my bag in the cabin and then join you?"

"Of course, of course. I'll be waiting." And O'Connor proceeded to his study.

Eduardo, placing his suitcase on his bed, decided not to open it at all but instead looked in the mirror on the wall, straightened his collar and wondered to himself what the man wanted to talk about. Standing in the doorway of the office, instead of knocking, he simply announced his presence by saying softly, "Sir? You wanted me?"

This time, O'Connor got up and moved toward a leather stuffed chair and invited Eduardo to sit in the companion chair next to and in front of it.

He looked Eduardo in the eye and said, "I want to apologize for my having to complicate your situation at the beginning of this semester. I am sorry for that. Unfortunately, though, as I explained, that could not be avoided."

Eduardo politely said, "I understand," although he did not understand at all and was still most definitely not over the insult and injury.

"I sincerely hope that's behind us. I'm enormously proud of you for being so determined to go back and for finding a way to make it happen without my assistance. That showed tremendous character and commitment: the sort of character that helps a man succeed in business. Have you given thought to what we'd discussed earlier?"

"You mean concerning my future plans?"

"Yes, yes, concerning that."

"I have. A great deal of thought."

"Good! And are you interested in joining me as an employee, basically as my apprentice?"

"No, sir. I have to admit that I am not. That isn't precisely true. I am interested in the opportunity to learn about business. I must admit the idea of eventually having a good income is attractive, as I think it would be to anyone."

"But you hesitate. Why?" And O'Connor smiled sardonically, "Have you learned to distrust wealth? I certainly hope not."

Eduardo chose not to be too honest on this point. "No. But I have thought much about what I need to be doing next—about what would give me the most satisfaction in the long run—about how I could make the greatest contribution in life ."

"Successful businessmen contribute as well. You do understand that, don't you? In creating employment for many, in providing opportunity for many."

"Of course, that's important. The question is whether I'm personally meant for that sort of career. And it's very difficult to know, with no experience."

O'Connor glanced down, visibly disappointed.

Eduardo took advantage of this to ask a question that had been on his mind for months. "Sir, if I could be so bold as to ask, why exactly is it that you'd like me to be involved in your business? Why should I deserve such an honor?"

O'Connor's face brightened considerably at this. "It is in fact intended to be just that, Eduardo: an honor and one I think of as well deserved. You would require time to learn. I would pay you through this time, fairly well I might add, even though you would be too inexperienced to be productive at first. So the situation would be much to your advantage, I think."

"I can understand that. But then that makes it even more difficult for me to understand the whole proposition."

"Speaking truthfully, Eduardo, it is much as I had suggested earlier. I have no son to follow in my footsteps. He's gone. You were a good friend to him. Your mother has served me well and faithfully throughout the years. And I've watched you grow and mature and have noticed more than once that you have qualities that any man would be proud of in a son. I would very much enjoy having the chance to train you and to bring you along. I think you could learn not only business but how to be a gentleman and to live the life of one."

Eduardo shifted uncomfortably in his seat. "Quite honestly, sir, I don't know what to say."

"Well, you don't have to say anything except to agree, as I hope you will."

"It is flattering to know that you think I merit this sort of opportunity. But I hope you will not feel insulted if I say that what I want to do is to teach."

"Teach?! Teach what, to whom?"

"Teach children, sir. I've worked part of the time as a teacher in a small grammar school by the university as a way to pay for part of my expenses this past semester. I enjoyed it. I enjoy the idea of being able to share a love of learning with young people. I think that may be a very good way to invest time and talent."

"Eduardo! Please reconsider. Do you realize how poorly schoolmasters are paid? Do you realize what it may be like to teach an ordinary group of children in a small school year after year? The small school by the university would not be at all typical of schools in the countryside such as here."

"I've considered that as well. And actually I think I'd prefer to be here or very near here rather than anywhere else. I'd like to think that I could begin here and someday build a better school. I think it would be gratifying to see a generation of students growing and learning, with some of them going on to the university themselves because of the beginning I had given them."

O'Connor said with a slightly sarcastic tone, "How romantic." Realizing by now that there was probably little point in continuing this conversation and keeping in mind the youth and inexperience of this young man and the fact that it appeared that he had already made up his mind, O'Connor sat back, resigning himself to defeat. "Where would you begin? You have to have a position in order to start. And there is not one available here."

"That is a problem. I would rather be nearby while…" He stopped, not wanting to state out loud what was going through his mind.

"While your mother is alive and well?"

Rather than speaking in reply, Eduardo simply nodded in agreement.

"Well, that's more noble to my way of thinking than the proposition taken as a whole. Very well then," he said, slapping his hands on the tops of his legs as if to put a period at the end of a sentence. "We're done. Let me see if there's anything at all that I can do to help you with this poor choice that you've made. I'll do whatever I can. Go along then. Good day." And he rose and went back to sit behind his desk.

Eduardo, having grown accustomed to being treated with uncommon warmth and respect at the university, felt dropped again as O'Connor, clearly disappointed if not frustrated, returned to his usual tone and manner as soon as he realized he was not going to get what he wanted. Eduardo got up and left, choosing not to say anything further, afraid that one more word could make the situation uncomfortable.

That evening, dining with his mother in the kitchen, Eduardo told her about his visit with Don Edwin. But first he spoke to her about his semester.

"I was able to study courses of interest to me. So the classes were easy. The time went by so quickly. I knew how little time was left. The one thing that surprised me was how much I enjoyed teaching children."

He had mentioned all this in letters. But this was the first opportunity he had had to tell her about it all in person. "I was always interested in reading and study and in the more difficult courses in literature and history. But these children were more fun than I expected," and he smiled.

Very busy with her work while he sat eating and talking, she was listening although not well. "I'm glad you enjoyed it so much. And I'm so proud of you for being so successful." Then almost as an afterthought, she asked, "Do you know what you will do next?" She asked this with her back to him, hoping he would not notice her concern.

"Not exactly. But I know now what I would like to do. Let me tell you about my visit with Don Edwin."

"I noticed him congratulating you outside."

"He wants me to join him in the business, working as his employee, as his apprentice."

"He had mentioned that before. But I thought he would forget about it. So he still wants that. And are you interested?" she asked, trying not to show in her voice her concern that Eduardo would become too excited about this possibility. She was completely convinced that working with Don Edwin would change her son dramatically and would not make him happy (although she knew it could someday make him wealthy). More importantly she was concerned that the work would take him far away from her.

"It is very flattering that he would consider such an offer. I don't understand it. I cannot imagine why he would do such a thing, or why it seems to be of such interest to him. But I have to admit that the idea of being able to afford nice things seems very attractive."

She said nothing but continued working.

"What I ended up telling him was that I appreciated the offer but would prefer to teach children."

Stunned by this statement, she turned and looked to see if he was being serious. Seeing on his face that he was, she asked, "Are you sure?" And then, "How did he react?"

"He seemed extremely disappointed. But he took it well. And yes, I am as sure as I can be right now about anything."

"You would not live so well. You do understand that?"

"Of course. But I think I could make a living at it."

As she stood with her back to him, she was smiling as she realized how much this increased the chances of his living somewhere nearby. "I must finish up here. And you must be tired."

"Of course, Mamá. I should leave you alone. Good night." And he went over and kissed her temple as she turned slightly toward him.

In his bed, he lay awake for hours. Thinking about how long ago he had lain in this same bed awake, worrying about the trip to the university for his first year, concerned about whether he would be able to perform as expected, about what it would be like being away from home; concerned about his mother and how she would get along without him. The past four years had brought so much change. He was not only more knowledgeable (if no more wise), but he had matured and his thoughts were more focused on the future now. He had conquered the university, especially in this final term. He had learned much. Now, his worries centered not only on the next week or the next month or six months, but on the rest of his life.

What could it be like to be a "gentleman," if that were truly possible? He tried to picture himself as a gentleman and had difficulty seeing himself in that position. He had an easier time imagining himself as a college professor, although he knew that the required doctorate would be completely unattainable.

No. What he had already accomplished was astonishing. He knew it. And he felt deeply an appreciation for having been given the opportunity he had already been given. He was ready to plan how he could give back. And, aside from any noble sentiments about giving of himself to others, he had been surprised to learn that he enjoyed the small children in the school this past semester. He would miss them. He found himself looking forward to having new ones to teach, to nurture or cultivate. But enough for now. His mother had been right. He was exhausted. He had not realized how tired he had become in recent weeks. Finally, he drifted off to sleep feeling enormously satisfied. There was so much in his life already. Yet there was something missing. He could not decide exactly what. But he felt it. He knew it. Whatever was missing seemed vague, uncertain, undefined. And yet what he had already was unmistakably real. And, for now, he would settle for that.

The next morning Eduardo went to the parish priest. His mother said that the priest had asked to speak with him. Eduardo walked to the village and knocked on the door of the small hut beside the church. The priest answered and greeted him warmly. "Eduardo! Welcome back. Come in, please, come in."

He walked into the austere hut and sat down with the priest in one of the only two chairs available. "My mother said you wanted to see me about something."

"Yes, yes, I did. Did you enjoy the university?"

"Very much. I could not have been luckier."

"The work was yours, my boy. The opportunity was given to you by God. But you had to take advantage of it, and you did just that."

Eduardo felt the need to clarify. "It was Edwin O'Connor who paid most of the bills."

The priest smiled. "Believe me, my son, whatever Don Edwin has was made available to him by God."

Eduardo, although a believer, felt slightly annoyed by this unquestioning version of belief. Instead of arguing, he said only, "Hmm...."

The priest walked to a small desk and picked up a paper. "When Don Alberto Gonzalez died, we did not find any papers at first. Later this was found. It speaks about a niece of his who lives not far from here."

"Really? Well, yes I met a young woman who claimed to be his niece."

"Exactly. I met her as well. It seems that the old man, without family, had managed to save quite a bit of money through the years and left this simple will and testament bequeathing all his savings to her. Could you take it to her and advise her in person?...unless you are about to be occupied with work somewhere. I would do it myself but cannot leave my parish for something this time-consuming."

"No, not yet. I'm home and do not have a situation yet."

"That's perfect. Then you have the time to do this for me, don't you."

Eduardo smiled and acquiesced, knowing there was no point to arguing with this priest once he had made up his mind. "I'll do it. Do you know how to reach her?"

"Yes, here is her address and full name. She is employed at the estate of Don Diego Sanchez, a banker in the town of Montillo. But his estate is closer to Camponuela. Here is a map."

Eduardo accepted the handwritten document along with the letter from the priest certifying the validity of the document and then got up to leave. "Is this all I can help you with?"

"There is one other thing. The schoolmistress at the local school has been dismissed. Would you consider taking the position for the coming year?"

Flinching at the suddenness of this announcement, Eduardo asked, "Why? Why would she be dismissed so abruptly?"

"I'm not at liberty to say. But she is already gone. I am assisting with the last days of class myself. Are you interested or not?"

Eduardo surprising himself by hesitating for a moment wondered if Don Edwin had been involved in this decision. Deciding that it mattered little whether he had been or not, especially since Eduardo himself had seen how dismally incompetent and uncaring the young teacher had been, he finally smiled and answered, "Of course I'm interested. This particular school is small. But I have to begin somewhere. And where better to begin teaching than in the same school where I began my studies?"

The priest clapped his hands together loudly and exclaimed, "Stupendous! Marvelous! Now that's one less thing for me to worry about. You've helped me a great deal today, young man, and it's much appreciated."

"Actually, you've helped me even more. Thank you. I hope you have a good day."

"Oh, I almost forgot. Here's some money for the trip to Montillo. Enough for the bus and meals for the day. I think Señor Sanchez will have a place for you to stay overnight. The trip's not long. And I do appreciate your seeing about this. Good day now."

✡ ✡ ✡

As he got off the bus, he asked the driver for directions for the remainder of this trip on foot. The road was clear, another dirt path, but one with plenty of roadway from side to side. He walked about one kilometer to the estate of Señor Sanchez and arrived at the front gate, finding it open. Above the gate was written in iron the words "Reposo del León" or Resting Place of the Lion.

Eduardo could not help grinning as he considered how this banker must view himself. Even so, no matter how exaggerated his impression of himself, the conspicuous display of wealth in the grounds and in the primary house was impossible to overlook. This was most assuredly a man to be reckoned with.

Eduardo had not arrived to deal with the great banker himself. He had come only to deliver news to the young employee, arriving as an emissary sent by a lowly priest. He walked up to the front of the house, greeted by three large dogs probably intended for security purposes, even though disappointing as guard dogs. Each wagged its tail in greeting and approached as if only to say "Hello," not questioning in the least the credentials of this stranger. The dogs barked at first but stopped as if recognizing the visitor.

Standing at the front door, he knocked firmly on the door facing and waited. A maid, stony-faced, came to greet him. Her coolness stood in stark contrast to the warm greeting he had received from the dogs. "Yes. Who are you?" she barked rudely.

"I'm here to speak with Señorita Felicia Dominguez. Is she here?"

Walking up behind the maid, Felicia answered on her own behalf, "I'm here." And seeing who it was, she smiled. "It's you once again. Thank you, Alicia. I know this young man."

"Humph," the older maid said, not making it clear whether she disapproved more of him or of the girl. Alicia left and went back to her work. Felicia stepped outside onto the porch. "You would normally be expected to go to the back door, you know."

"I'm sorry. At the estate where my mother and I live we have always had free access through the front door. You look well today, exceptionally well."

Although appreciating the compliment, she did not acknowledge it. She was attractive and knew it, but she placed far less importance on her own looks than did most men. "What is it that you want?"

Having forgotten how beautiful she was, he did not know exactly how to respond. At this particular moment, what he wanted most was to be able to get to know her and to be able to spend time with her. Fortunately he knew better than to say exactly what was on his mind. Instead, he answered matter-of-factly "I need to discuss something with you. Is there a place where we can sit and talk?"

Felicia had forgotten how distractingly handsome this young man was. She had not forgotten him—far from it. He had been on her mind for months. And she had wondered how she would find a way to get closer to him—respectably close, but close nonetheless. She also found her mind dwelling too much on appearance. She had learned long before to look at the person within, and yet for some reason with this particular young man felt distracted, unsettled. "There is a gazebo behind the house. We can sit there. But I don't have much time to visit. Follow me."

Eduardo had come only because he had promised the priest that he would do so. But here now alongside her, he realized that he was glad that he had come. There was something extraordinarily captivating about her eyes and her expression—something he had not noticed in anyone before. He had had entirely too much on his mind when he first met her. But now he noticed so much more detail. He wished desperately that there could be more time to spend with her.

"Come on. I do not have all day," she said turning to encourage him to catch up with her pace.

As they reached the gazebo, he gestured to her to sit. "Please, I think we should sit to visit about this. May I stay with you for a moment?"

"Don't be ridiculous. Of course you may sit. Now what is it that you want?"

"*I want you. That's what I want,*" is what he thought to himself. The words that actually came out of his mouth however were, "I have some news to share with you."

"Go on," she said impatiently when he failed to speak quickly enough.

"When your uncle died, at first no will was found. But later one was discovered." He pulled out the original letter with her uncle's handwriting. From the other pocket, he pulled out the handwritten note from the priest certifying the validity of the will. "He left you all his savings, the entirety of his estate. To look at him and the way he always dressed and to see his modest studio, all of us assumed that he had nothing at all. But then the priest realized that there was a significant sum deposited in a bank in Bogotá. And Don Alberto left this to you. You only have to go to the city to claim it and it will be yours."

In a state of total disbelief, she stared at the documents. "How much?"

"I don't know exactly. But the priest said it was enough to merit claiming."

She said nothing, trying to let the news sink in.

"Well, that's it. That's what I came for. It was good to see you again. A pleasure. I should leave now. But the bus doesn't come by until tomorrow morning. Would there by any chance be a spot here on the estate where I could stay tonight?"

"Of course. There's a shed with a cot in it. You can spend the night there. I'll ask first. But I'm sure it would be all right"

"You're pleased, are you not? About the news?"

"I married very young, when I was fifteen. My husband was killed in an accident in the mines before we could have a child. It has been *very* difficult for me. I may not be rich with this sum. But yes it will make a great difference. I'm very pleased."

He started to get up to leave. She pulled him back, and touched his arm. "Sit, please. Sanchez is not here today. I want to hear about you. Did you finish your studies?"

He sat back down and relaxed, glad to see that she seemed as interested in learning more about him as he knew he was about her. "I did. That also was difficult."

"And what will you do now? Go away to work in Puerto Lindo?"

"No. I loved the university. I loved my studies. But I did not like the city at all. I'm going to teach in the small school at home."

"Really? That surprises me. I would think a young man would want to get away."

"Get away from what?"

"I don't know. To go someplace better, more interesting, more exciting."

"Is that what you want?"

She laughed. "No. Not at all. But young men always seem to think that way."

"One thing I did learn while at school was that I'm not much like other young men. That may be why I ended up spending most of my time alone."

She looked at him, studying his face, his hair. She smiled. "No, I think maybe you are different." She sat quietly for a moment. Eduardo seemed to have run out of conversation. Finally, she broke the silence. "Do you have a girl?"

"Excuse me?"

"A girlfriend? A promised one?"

"No. Why do you ask?"

She looked down, then looked back up, shaking her head softly. "No reason. Only curious. That's all. You know, I do have to get some work done."

"I can sit here and read. I brought a book."

"We can visit more over dinner. You can eat in the kitchen with me once my work is done for today."

"Until then. Meanwhile, I'll enjoy it here."

She began walking away but then turned, walking backwards a step or two saying, "I'm very glad that you came." Then she turned and continued walking.

Eduardo sat for an hour or so, unable to concentrate on his book, eventually getting up to walk about the estate. There was much to notice about this young woman. He had never felt exactly the same way. It was confusing. Even more puzzling was the fact that she seemed to be more interested in him than anyone he had ever met. There was something unsettling about this. Enough to keep his mind completely occupied and to make the afternoon hours pass quickly.

In early evening, she came out of the house and walked to where he sat.

"Do you do anything but read?" she asked jokingly.

"It's a habit after so much study for the past four years. I've always loved books. They're my connection with other places and times."

She sat beside him. "Tell me about the place where you live."

"Well, you saw the small village. That's where the school is. Edwin O'Connor is the man who has employed my mother for decades, for all of my life. He is... he was Irish. He has been Colombian for decades, and owns emerald mines. He's a good man, wealthy, successful. He has much. But he has always seemed lonely."

"Successful how?"

"I don't understand."

"You said he's very successful. And yet he lives alone, for decades with no wife, no children. How is he successful?"

"At business, of course."

She just shrugged this off, dismissing it as unimportant.

Eduardo realized what she was getting at and asked, "Do you feel lonely with your husband gone?"

"He is dead. It's as if he never existed."

Surprised by her coldness, he asked, "Did you not love him?"

"I did, when he was with me. But that seems long ago."

Deciding to change the subject slightly, he said, "I've been too busy these last years to feel lonely. I'm looking forward to beginning a new job. I wonder what it will be like living in the same quiet environment, the same place where I grew up."

"Are you hungry? It's much too early for dinner? But Don Diego is accustomed to afternoon tea. And there are always sandwiches, cookies, cake or toast. It's set every day for teatime whether he's here or not. We've all become accustomed to it."

"Sure. Just show me where."

They walked together into the house. "Tea" was set up in the kitchen. Although the owner of the estate was away on business, none of the servants were presumptuous enough to set up tea for themselves on the dining room table. But there was nothing wrong with setting everything in the kitchen. She ushered him into the kitchen and had him sit on a high stool. She stood and sipped her tea and ate cake, as he did.

The principal cook began preparing dinner. Felicia excused herself and walked outside with Eduardo. Standing at the back door, she let him go. "I will not see you tomorrow. I have to walk to meet the bus very early," he said, wondering if he should say the rest of what was on his mind. Saved from having to make that choice, he heard her answer, "I am glad that you came today. Would you mind if I were to visit you sometime soon?" Eduardo smiled, relieved that he had not had to decide whether to invite her or not. "I'd like that very much." He extended his right hand to shake hers. She hesitated and then took it. Feeling awkward and at a loss for words, he said simply, " Good night." As he walked away, she said not too loudly, "We'll see each other again soon."

Eduardo had greater difficulty sleeping that night than he could remember. He felt more off balance than ever. He felt anxious about whether he was doing the right thing in deciding to teach children. He wondered what it would be like living so far away from the university. And then there was the persistent image of Felicia's face, her smile, and the way she sat listening so intently to everything he said—something he was not accustomed to—the subtle scent and the lingering memory of her presence after she had gone. He felt concern about what it was going to be like to focus on everyday life while thinking about her each day. He hoped that that would not be the case, at least not as much as this night.

The next morning, he walked to where the bus would stop. Away from the Sanchez estate and down the road he walked, realizing that nothing had changed after hours of sleep. The image of Felicia relentlessly lingered in his thoughts. What disturbed him most was the realization that he enjoyed having the constant presence of her with him, even when she wasn't physically beside him. It was truly unsettling in a way that nothing had been before.

✵ ✵ ✵

Three months passed quickly for Eduardo. He continued living with his mother and worked at the mine to produce income. He enjoyed the routine of physical work during the day and then coming home exhausted, cleaning up, and reading all evening. His dinner visits with his mother were brief. He still felt comfortable with her and enjoyed being at home, but he found less and less to talk about with her. It was not that he considered himself better than her in any way now than before. It was simply that there was so much going through his mind now that he could not share without making her even more self-conscious than she already was about her lack of education. Life seemed very different now. The difference had nothing to do with his mother. Eduardo himself had changed. Somehow the closeness to and dependence on her—which had been even greater as a result of the lack of another parent in his life—had lessened as he matured. What gnawed at him even more was the perplexing feeling that something was missing in his life—something significant. And that feeling would not go away.

Still, he loved his mother deeply. His appreciation of all she had done for him continued. He struggled to find something to visit with her about in the evenings, usually while eating dinner in the kitchen of the big house and with her finishing up preparations for Don Edwin's dinner. O'Connor traveled less now.

Eduardo thought that he might be imagining this, but could not help thinking that O'Connor seemed lonelier than ever. Now, no longer a boy, Eduardo realized that it was possible that Edwin might sometimes—or possibly always—have been away from his estate in order to be close to someone in particular and that that particular someone might no longer be in his life. More than once Eduardo allowed his thoughts to follow this trail, each time fighting to drop it and to remember that he was probably being too imaginative or at least too inquisitive.

Even so, it was unmistakable, this fact that O'Connor was home more and more and yet seemed less happy than before. In spite of the fact that O'Connor's life and the lives of Eduardo and his mother seemed closely intertwined, that was not the actual situation at all. Their lives now were worlds apart, even while living on the same estate for many years. No matter how close he seemed, O'Connor was the great patrón, the lord of the manor, the founder of the feast. He was most definitely the employer and Eduardo's mother clearly the employee. Although O'Connor had shown extraordinary interest in young Eduardo's life and progress, Eduardo was after all nothing more than the son of a maid, an incidental occupant, a son of a servant. He was simply there.

Despite the restlessness within him that he could not deny, Eduardo at the same time appreciated the safety and security of having a comfortable, familiar place to sleep and eat, and of having honest work to do each day, without pressure or worries. This period of adjustment in between completing his studies and beginning a career did in fact feel comforting and safe. He might be a young man needing to prove himself. He might have an active mind needing exercise. He might need to be out on his own, more independent. But he had to admit that it felt great to live within the confines of the estate of the patrón and within the protective oversight of the one woman who had occupied his life up to this time.

He would have to speak to the priest within days about taking over control of the small school house, ensuring that everything was clean and ready, that books and supplies were in place. He would have to gather his thoughts about how to plan his teaching of the various age groups. It was a very small school. He would have to keep each age involved in separate levels of study and would have to do this within the limited space of one large room.

He could do it. He knew he could. It would not be easy. It would certainly not pay well. But he tried, each time he considered it, to remember the opportunity he had been given to continue his education. He thought how wonderful if might be to give, over the course of several years, an even better beginning to the education of his group of students, preparing them so that they could find ways to further their education. Not a bad way to pay back the gift given to him earlier.

But meanwhile, much had to be done each day, each month, each term. And it was time to begin.

One day, having advised his supervisor at the mine that it was time to end his temporary employment and to collect his final pay, he counted his wages. He went that next day to the priest and discussed the funds that would be needed to acquire the material he would need: new books, writing materials, etc. The priest, not convinced that all new supplies were really needed, nevertheless did not want to discourage the young man in his enthusiasm and so agreed to do everything he could to collect through the parish the required funds. He visited the schoolhouse along with Eduardo and offered to find help in cleaning it up for the first day of school. He shook Eduardo's hand as he left, wishing him well and thanking him profusely for making the sacrifice of doing this, of giving up much in order to contribute much. Eduardo appreciated the vote of confidence. But then he wondered how much of a sacrifice it was that he was making. Better not to dwell on that. As he began the work of cleaning—unwilling to wait for help—he spent two or three hours arranging, cleaning, and preparing the school.

Toward the end of the afternoon, he heard a voice at the door. A very familiar voice. A voice he had no idea he would hear so soon or so unexpectedly.

"Good afternoon. And how are you?" the young woman asked quietly, trying not to startle him as she stood in the opened doorway.

He turned. "Felicia! What a wonderful surprise. Why are you here?"

"You have to ask?"

Embarrassed by this reply, he explained, "I only meant that I had not expected you. I thought I would hear something from you before you arrived."

"There was no need for that. I left the Sanchez family. I live here now. Would you like to walk?"

He dropped what he was doing and followed her. This time, instead of offering a hand to shake, he could not resist giving her a hug as he came to her. He was for a second overwhelmed by the warmth of the embrace and by the gentle fragrance of her hair. He let go and stood back. "You look so well."

"You, too."

They walked together slowly, with no particular place in mind, simply strolling down the path into the village itself."

"Why did you leave?"

"When you came to give me the news of my inheritance from Tío Alberto, I mentioned that it could make a difference in my life even if it did not make me rich. It already has. I went to Bogotá and dealt with my uncle's bank. They did not hesitate to distribute the funds. It was more than I had ever dreamed that I might have. My uncle may have lived simply, but he saved much through all those years. I began to walk out of the bank with a suitcase full of money and then realized how vulnerable I was. I decided to turn back and to take only a small part of it with me. I deposited the rest in an account of my own at that bank. I thought about how terrified I would be carrying it all for the entire trip back home. And then what would I do with it? The bank in the village would be small and vulnerable compared to this larger bank in Bogotá. I carried with me more than enough to do what I had in mind."

"Had in mind? You have a plan already?"

"I have had a plan in mind for quite some time now. I did not have the means to make it happen." Then she remained silent for a moment.

Eduardo could not stand it any longer and raised his voice slightly as he asked, "And so what was it? Tell me."

"To come here…to have my own shop…to be my own boss and to be a seamstress on my own. Part of what my uncle left me was the studio and apartment. I own it. Now I live in it. Would you like to see it?"

"Of course! How wonderful for you." Eduardo began to say *How wonderful for us!* but held back. He could not help himself, though, from showing how excited he was as he said, "And you'll be closer."

She smiled and said, "Yes."

✳ ✳ ✳

IV.

Eduardo usually completed each teaching day at school by midafternoon. Then he would stay for an hour or more straightening up the mess and preparing for the following day's work, sometimes grading papers and sometimes staying late to tutor a particular student. He would make the brief walk to the other side of the village to the small cottage where Felicia lived.

With her own sewing shop, she now produced enough money to begin saving. Along the way, Eduardo found himself enjoying as much time as possible with her during what was left of each evening. He worked through that first academic year teaching and learning firsthand what all the challenges were in relation to handling his small school. Meanwhile, he continued living on the O'Connor estate in the same cabin with his mother.

In the evenings and during weekends, he found time to visit Felicia. It took very little for him to discover that he felt a closeness to her that he had never experienced with a girl. Felicia wanted Eduardo to fall as much in love with her as she had been with him from the start.

The courting process took longer than Felicia had hoped that it might. Eduardo enjoyed her company and yet persisted in remaining completely focused on his teaching and, in his spare time, on his studies. He continued reading literature and history as if he were still in the university. During his time in school his approach to his own education centered around personal goals each day, each week. He complied with requirements established by his professors. To his way of thinking these requirements were incidental to, but fell far short of, his own goals. As far as he had been concerned during that time, he was pursuing his own education and coincidentally happened to be doing that within a community of "scholars." He spent his four years in the university having a great deal more in common with his professors than with his fellow students. Snobbishness did not cause the distance between his peers and him. He was simply bored by the other students' lack of concentration, by the easy way in which they were distracted by uninteresting endeavors such as drinking, gambling, and womanizing off-campus. There had been moments when he felt lonely, partly as a result of this distinction between their priorities and his. But he never at any point thought that the solution to this should involve adapting himself to try to fit in more easily with these people.

He did not know what the solution might be. He did know that he found certain girls attractive. But the physical attraction he could not help feeling—even to the sort of women the other boys preferred… women who could not carry on a decent conversation—was something he distrusted within himself. This sort of relationship seemed to lead nowhere, offering nothing. He left the university, having managed to complete all four years of study and his degree, without ever having established a relationship with a woman. This did not in any way seem extraordinary to him, since he had no reference point against which to measure his own situation.

No one could have enjoyed four years in a university more than Eduardo did. No one could have appreciated an opportunity more than he appreciated his. And yet, without realizing it, he had gone through the entire process without learning anything at all about women or about anything else concerning human relationships.

He had always been happy on the O'Connor estate, protected by and lovingly cared for by his mother. True, he regretted the absence of a father in his life. Without knowing exactly what it would have been like to have a father around, he could not help feeling a gap that he thought might have been filled by the love between father and son .

He passed through a period of uncertainty as he completed his studies, not so much because he sensed a need for greener pastures elsewhere, but because he was not sure what he might miss by deciding to remain in the place where he had been born. He had always been keenly aware of the lovely things that Don Edwin possessed, and had from time to time felt a slight envy concerning these material possessions. Nevertheless, as he began to mature, he realized that he had no need for material things, but instead valued Don Edwin's kindness.

There had been no father figure in Eduardo's young life aside from Edwin O'Connor. Despite the formal distance that Don Edwin always maintained between himself and Eduardo and Eduardo's mother, he had done much more for them than Eduardo later learned was typically done by men of similar accomplishment and stature toward servants and servants' families. Eduardo had not sought out information concerning other "lords of manors," but he did manage to overhear comments during his four years in school—comments indicating that it was not acceptable to keep anything other than total emotional distance between employer and employee or between property owner and servants. He gathered, not so much from his professors or fellow students as from his own reading about the concept that much of the evils of the country's history related to one extent or another to the undue influence of foreigners. O'Connor was foreign-born. Even though O'Connor had lived in Colombia long enough to consider himself anything but foreign, he fit the stereotype of someone coming from Europe and taking over, of conquering all that was native to the adopted country.

Eduardo kept this in mind, although it faded, along with many other ideas that diminished as the university years faded into memory. As he heard peers comment about the importance of keeping apart from employees, from servants, Eduardo found this snobbish concept far more foreign than anything he had experienced relative to Edwin O'Connor. O'Connor treated his servants as employees and kept them at arms' length. True enough. But, on the other hand, he treated them with dignity and respect and even compassion.

As each year passed, Eduardo came to appreciate more and more all that Don Edwin had done for him. There was, in Eduardo's mind, more to admire about Don Edwin than to resent, despite what others might think.

Felicia, on the other hand, disliked and distrusted O'Connor from the moment she first met him. She instinctively understood Eduardo just as quickly, and observed within Eduardo, despite any comments to the contrary that he might make from time to time, that Eduardo greatly admired and respected O'Connor and that there was something more emotional than rational about this profound degree of respect. Eduardo was quick to defend O'Connor the first time Felicia made critical remarks about him and about his foreign heritage. Eduardo reminded her at that moment that there was also "something foreign" about himself in his own heritage. Rather than to argue with him, she discreetly determined not to bring up the subject again. But her attitude toward O'Connor never changed. She had had too many bad experiences with "Europeans" before.

As the end of that first teaching year approached, Eduardo realized that he was attracted to Felicia and that he needed and wanted to be with her all the time. Although he had no earlier experience to judge by, he decided that he must have fallen in love with her. The attraction was overwhelming by this time and he knew it was time to ask her to marry him. Once he screwed up the courage to declare his love and to propose marriage, she accepted as soon as asked.

They discussed it with his mother, who was thrilled to see her son finally growing into manhood. Eduardo's mother had certain misgivings about this young woman but admitted to herself that she had been given no reason to distrust her. The girl, extremely practical, appeared to love Eduardo, and seemed healthy and capable of taking good care of him and of bearing strong children. So, understanding much better than Eduardo realized that she was aging rapidly now, his mother was glad to see that her son would have someone to take care of him, to love him, and possibly to provide him with family. She put aside her concerns and welcomed the prospect of her son taking a wife.

The small wedding ceremony took place in the village chapel. Felicia had no family attending. Eduardo's mother sat quietly along with a few other members of the parish congregation. And although Don Edwin was on one of his business trips on this date, he gave them as a wedding present a brand-new mechanical sewing machine that he had imported from the United States. He understood that Felicia had a small business and knew that her work would be a key part of their income through the years. On the one hand, Felicia deeply appreciated the generosity of this gift—something that would make her work easier. On the other hand, something within her made her want to cringe at the idea of accepting such an extravagant gift from someone she did not and could not feel comfortable around. The benefits she would reap, however, from accepting the gift far outweighed any resentment she might feel toward the giver.

Prior to marrying her, Eduardo escorted Felicia to the spot where she could board a bus and travel to Bogota. She had withdrawn considerably more of her money from the bank in Bogota than she had initially taken out. Returning to the village the following morning, she deposited this money in the small bank there, holding out enough to settle the purchase of a small cottage. The owner of the small home had died and his heirs, not wanting this small building and needing the cash, decided to sell. Knowing that it would be more comfortable to live in this lovely but simple cottage than to live in the apartment attached to the studio, Felicia gladly invested the funds needed for the purchase and envisioned a long, happy life with Eduardo and any children that might come along someday.

With a cottage available for them, and now properly wed, they began their married life together. The village had grown noticeably in the years prior to this. In addition to employment increasing at the nearby mine, there was employment now related to a rock quarry opened by another investor. And the process was underway of cutting trees in the beautiful forest for sale of timber. With new development, more and more families had settled in the small village.

Along with the village, Eduardo's small school also grew. Donations made it possible for him to earn considerably more than had ever been possible in this position in earlier years. Life was good. He loved the children he taught. He had down to a fine art the juggling of time and space within the school. The youngest children had to be taught their numbers and how to read and write. The eldest had to be pulled forward in their studies and learning, keeping them busy with projects during the day and at night. The different ages in between also had to be kept busy with schoolwork appropriate for their ages. It was not easy.

The little school proved not to be boring at all. If anything, it was almost more than he could handle. But he did love the children very much, was enormously patient, and learned quickly that he had an intuitive talent for knowing how to juggle all the conflicting demands on his time and his talent. He knew how to keep the children busy and learning and interested in coming to school. He also kept the parents happy. And this became one reason for families to settle in this small village rather than settling in two nearby villages.

Life indeed was good.

As Eduardo had spent his entire childhood with his mother every day, and then after finishing at the university had lived with her every day, he had not noticed how much her work had aged her, and how much more quickly it was aging her now. Seeing her sometimes now no more often than once a week, he began to notice how much she was slowing down.

One weekend, he walked to see about her and found her sick in bed. She had a bad cough and seemed to have a fever. Getting her hot soup and tea, he visited only briefly before returning home. The next morning, worried about her, he went back and found her up and about, without fever now but still with a nagging cough. He made a point of checking on her each day for the following week, although his absence each evening clearly irritated his new wife. His mother improved enough the second week for him to carry on a normal work schedule.

After that, he visited twice a week to check on her and realized over the coming month that her cough was not going away. Whether the cough itself was gradually exhausting her or whether its persistence was merely a symptom was difficult to determine. The one thing that became painfully obvious to him was the fact that his mother's health was rapidly declining.

One evening, he returned home to Felicia after seeing about his mother. He found Felicia in an unusually good mood. It had worn him down over the prior month, having to spend as much energy on his teaching as he knew he had to spend, having to worry about his mother's health, and then having to deal with occasional bouts of irritability and short temper from his wife. It was good to arrive home to a hot meal and a friendly, welcoming temperament this particular evening.

"How is she?"

"Not well. She gets through the days, but whatever this is wears more heavily on her all the time. She does seem improved, though."

Felicia smiled and said cheerfully, "Maybe she's turned the corner and will get better now."

He looked up from his steaming bowl of soup at her face, wondering what the cheerfulness could be about. It stood in too stark contrast to what he had encountered most evenings. "I hope so too."

"Maybe some good news would make her improve tremendously."

"Well, it might. What exactly did you have in mind?
"Concerning us. For example…I don't know…maybe news that she is going to be a grandmother?"

Dropping his spoon, he stared in disbelief. "Pardon?"

"I'm going to have a baby."

"That's wonderful!" exclaimed Eduardo, jumping up from his seat and grabbing her, hugging her tightly before letting go. "Oh, maybe I should be more careful with you."

"I'm all right. I think it will go very well."

"Are you sure?"

"I'm positive. I have waited until I was absolutely certain before mentioning it to you. I've known that you had enough on your mind. But this is such marvelous news that I couldn't wait any longer."

He sat down. "A child," he said wistfully. A faint look of panic spread across his face as he looked up at her. "I have no idea how to be a father."

"Apparently you do."

"No, no I mean that I don't know how a father's supposed to behave toward a child once it's born. I don't…"

"You'll do very well. As much as you care about your children in the school and as patient as you are with them, you'll do perfectly well with your own. I've watched you from the day I first met you. One reason I chose you was because I felt certain you would be not only a good husband but a wonderful father." Touched by her vote of confidence but still not persuaded, he looked down at the floor and changed the subject. "Maybe you're right. Maybe we should share this news with my mother now and see if she improves. She must improve."

✵ ✵ ✵

When Eduardo and Felicia shared with his mother the good news, his mother was thrilled of course. And she did perk up during the week immediately following that announcement, appearing noticeably more positive in outlook each time he visited her.

But the cough persisted nonetheless. Her loss of weight and appetite did not improve. And although her eyes sparkled once again, her color did not return. Eventually, after a couple of weeks, she became ill again, having to remain in bed unable to work. The situation was worsening despite her hopes now for a future of seeing her son have a family and of seeing a grandchild, and then someday to see it grow and develop into a delightful person.

Eduardo tried to keep up his own spirits as much as possible during this time. Instead of staying after the end of school each day, he began neglecting preparation for the following day and instead walked the route from school to the O'Connor estate to see about his mother in the late afternoons each and every day. He would then walk the distance back toward the village to his own cottage to spend the remainder of each evening with Felicia. As the weeks passed, he himself became increasingly tired and worn down by exertion but even more so by stress, worrying constantly about the one person who had been the anchor of his life for as long as he could remember.

Spending as many evenings as possible with his wife, he tried to give her his undivided attention each evening and on the weekends. He was watching his mother die and he knew it. He could not accept this, although he realized that there was absolutely nothing that could be done about it.

O'Connor noticed the change for the worse and brought a doctor from Puerto Lindo, purportedly for a visit overnight at his estate, pretending that they were nothing more than good friends. But he made a point of having the physician spend time with her "only to see if anything could be done about that pesky cough."

The doctor handled it discreetly, sustaining a cheerful attitude throughout, examining her informally in O'Connor's study, and pretending during the process to be distracted by continuing a conversation with Don Edwin all the time. Meanwhile, he managed to check all her vital signs, heard her uneven heartbeat and managed to hear clearly the sounds of a disturbing condition in her lungs. Breezily wrapping up his "examination," he patted her hand and said she would live another forty years. He pulled out of his bag a very small bottle of syrup, and said, "Take this at night to help you sleep. You need rest. You'll be fine."

Once he had left the room, the doctor as softly as possible said to Don Edwin that her condition was indeed serious and that, in his opinion, she had very little time left to live. O'Connor, visibly taken aback, blanched at this news. The doctor said nothing further, although he could not help wondering why O'Connor would be so deeply concerned about the health and well-being of a maid. He had known Edwin well enough though to know him to be a good man, a compassionate employer and decided not to attach any great importance to it.

"Should I take her to Puerto Lindo to a hospital?"

"No. There would be greater risk of her infecting other patients than there would be hope of her recovery. With that in mind Edwin, you need to keep her out of the kitchen. Have her work at something else around the house, something lighter. She will not feel up to working much longer at any rate. More than anything, she needs rest and isolation. And I would take care of this immediately. Get yourself away from the house and don't settle back in until you have someone else in the kitchen."

"My God. I knew she was not well. But I had no idea..."

The doctor was near the end of his visit anyway and excused himself to go to bed. O'Connor was going to return with him early the following morning and would contract a second cook while in the city. He said little during the trip back to Puerto Lindo.

Eduardo was notified by another of Don Edwin's servants that another cook/maid was being retained to "take a load of work" off of his mother and to allow her to do lighter work as her health might permit. He did not, in his message, convey the brunt of the story, choosing instead to wait to tell Eduardo in person.

Even without the diagnosis and bleak prognosis, Eduardo could see that his mother was in a rapid period of decline. His obsession with the situation increased day by day and finally, one Saturday morning, without mentioning anything to Felicia except to say that he was going to walk in the woods that morning, he headed in the direction of the estate and then beyond it and onto the path into the forest that he had taken as a small boy. He had not been able to purge his mind of a sense of complete help-lessness here in recent weeks. He could not make his mother the strong young woman she had once been. He could not restore her health. His religious faith, which she had taught him, remained and he tried prayer but sensed that even that might not produce her recovery.

In desperation, he thought to himself what he could possibly do. Nothing came to mind, except for the one thing that seemed to apply only to him. And he began to wonder whether it might apply to anyone else.

He knew it seemed blasphemous to consider almost worshiping an object, worshiping or even honoring unduly anything or anyone other than God himself. But, still... What else was there? He realized that God would answer every prayer, even if only to say firmly and with-out explanation or apology *"No."* Well, and this was what frightened Eduardo even more, that sort of answer was definitely not going to be acceptable. Something had to be done.

For the first time in years, he spent time here in the same familiar for-est, in the midst of lush vegetation, listening to the sounds of birds and monkeys high above within the canopy. Engaged again with the world he had known as a boy, he walked along that same path, noticing with great admiration the way the late day's rays of sunlight played on the ground below as he walked, as if each ray of light were shooting down through the canopy, piercing through the limbs one at a time, making a special show just for him.

As he walked farther away from the estate, he decided to continue toward the cave. At this moment, there was as little on his mind as he could remember since his childhood. The one thing that did occur to him was the same childish curiosity that had led him and his small friend into that cave so long ago. He could not keep from wondering if the cave still looked the same and if there might be once again that same old woman deep within the network of tunnels or possibly some-one else.

He stood in the entrance, thinking, "What is there about this place that is so fascinating? It's old, filthy and dark. Undoubtedly one of the most dangerous places anywhere around." And then, *years of experience clearly having taught him nothing*, he entered the cave, this time having to duck down to keep from bumping his head.

As if drawn along a rope guiding him straight toward the spot where he and his friend Sean O'Connor had last seen her, Eduardo walked without hesitation knowing instinctively how to proceed. Even without a light, he knew by heart how to feel his way forward. Somehow, neither profound darkness, nor the dank disgusting smell of the place, nor the feel of a spider's web brushing against his hair and shoulder could dissuade him from walking forward.

As he turned one final turn, he hesitated and saw a glimmer of light dimly penetrating the darkness. He stepped forward more cautiously and saw the shadows playing upon the wall of the tunnel up ahead, as light slipped out the entrance to the same inner chamber where he had found the old woman before.

Up to this point, he had ignored the inner voice telling him ever so faintly to turn back, to grow up and to give up on what had very likely been nothing more than an experience dreamed up by the collection imaginations of two highly creative boys. Now he felt the need to listen to that voice, to run, to escape, as he stood listening to sounds of someone stirring within the inner chamber. A man now, having acquired an ability to sense imminent danger, Eduardo began to turn to leave. And then he heard a voice.

"Oh come now. You've walked this far. You might as well continue," said the old woman in a feeble, familiar voice.

The old woman whom he and Sean had encountered earlier had already been old years before. She would have to be by now.... She must be dead by this time. She could not possibly sound the same, be just as alive or look the same as she had so many years before. Again, mature young male or not, he felt the same adventurous tug of curiosity pulling him forward as he had felt while a boy; as he stepped toward the entrance to the chamber. And there she was, knitting this time in a rocking chair. She looked up, smiled and greeted him cordially.

"How nice to see you again! Come in. Come in." She continued rocking in the old pine rocker, a candle burning brightly next to her in a tall stand, and with other candles around the chamber. "Sit down, young man," she said as she gestured with her elbow toward a three-legged stool near her, as if she had known someone were coming. As if she had known specifically that he was coming?

He stepped toward the stool, more sceptical than ever, yet willing to watch and to listen and to take it all in—whether the experience was real or imagined. It would be difficult to imagine the smells, the sounds of the candles dripping wax on the earthen floor, the sight of the flickering light and of the earthy aroma of the old woman.

There was something curiously comforting about this person, this apparition. "You're troubled about something and have a question for me? Yes?"

"How did you know?"

"How did I know what?"

"Well, first of all, how did you know that I was coming?"

"And what's second of all?"

"How could you possibly know that I was drawn here to ask a question?" "My young friend, an old man once asked me, "Have *you ever noticed how the Irish always answer a question with a question?*" and I answered *"Do they now?"* She spoke with a delicately lilting Irish brogue, an accent he had not noticed during the first encounter.

"If you are a ghost, then you may disappear as quickly as you arrived. So I'll ask my question now. The amulet. You said there are three times in a life when it can help protect. Could one of those times be used to save someone else?"

"Of course, with luck."

"What do mean?"

"Well, not precisely because of luck. But if you wish it sincerely enough, deeply enough, to benefit someone you love in your place; then yes, it would work."

"Sincerely enough?"

"Yes, but only you can know how deeply you want to spend that one time on saving someone else."

"Who are you? And what is this about? I have to admit that I cannot believe this has happened to me."

"Well, the better question would be *"Who are you?"* And you won't really know that yourself until it's all over."

"You make so little sense," he said disgustedly. "But you do seem to know what there is to know about the amulet."

"Oh, I know much more than that. *I* know who you are, even if you do not."

He peered at her intensely. "What are you talking about?"

"I'm not the one to tell you. Not now."

She put down her knitting and got up. "You must go. I have to move on and cannot waste time."

Remaining unmoved, he said somewhat defiantly with a nervous chuckle, "And what if I don't leave?"

She laughed. "Then you'll be sitting here on the floor in the dark, deep within a lonely cave. I cannot say that I recommend that." And then her tone darkened and she said more firmly, "Now go. You're too old now to play the part of defiant little boy." And she turned her back, and said more firmly still, "Go. Leave, and do not come here again."

He thought back over all he had experienced in relation to this cave, this old woman or spirit or whatever she was, and in relation to the unexplained amulet. He decided it was best to do as she said without arguing. It seemed that he had obtained the information he needed, even though he found it impossible to believe. Without saying anything further, he turned and walked out, stepping quickly out of the chamber and backtracing his steps. As he exited the cave and stepped into the daylight, he realized that the sun was still high. It was mid-day or early afternoon. Only the morning had passed. He needed to walk directly home so that his wife would not worry. He also needed time to absorb what he had seen and heard and what he had learned this morning.

✲ ✲ ✲

He returned to his cottage where Felicia was waiting with his early afternoon lunch. They visited. He half listened. She thought little of his behavior, since she had already become accustomed to his absent-mindedness recently.

The afternoon passed quickly as she puttered about the cottage and as he pretended to read. By late afternoon, he excused himself to walk to his mother's cabin. Felicia knew by this time that whatever it was that concerned him was more serious than usual. But she reassured herself by assuming that it had to do with general moodiness or worry about losing his mother. She did not look forward by any means to having to support him emotionally once his mother was gone, since she understood all too well how close mother and son had always been.

Arriving at the cabin, he found his mother sitting up in bed. She had slightly better color but still had the same nagging cough and looked exhausted. She greeted him cheerfully. That helped. He had still not grown used to the sight of her being sick in bed. He pulled up a chair and sat close to her and touched her hand.

"How do you feel?"

"Very well. I don't have the stamina to work. But I feel better today than I have." She smiled. But then she saw in his face that he was not doing well. "What's wrong?" she asked.

He attempted to force a smile and answered not too convincingly, "I'm all right."

She took his hand in hers. "What's wrong?"

"I don't deal well with the idea of your being so ill. It's difficult for me. I've never had anyone but you to talk with about anything."

"Son, you have a wife now. Lean on her. She seems to be a strong woman."

"I know that. And I do depend on her. But there's something I can't discuss with her."

"What?"

"The amulet. She would think me crazy if I were to tell her about it."

"Then don't tell her." She watched him and realized that there was more.

He looked up at his mother and looked into her eyes, unable to hide the redness in his own. "I know now that the amulet can be used by me to save someone dear to me."

She looked away and breathed deeply, triggering another round of coughing. Once she was able to stop, she said, "I've always known that, son."

"How?"

"Long ago, I embraced the Church. But my mother was never a Christian and her father had been a shaman within our tribe. The reality of spirits and of unexplainable events was something I was raised to believe in. The miracles talked about by the Church were small by comparison with miraculous powers believed in by my people through the centuries."

"I saw her again."

"Who?" she asked, wondering if he meant who she thought he meant.

"The same old woman in the cave."

"What were you doing there? It's no safer for an adult than it is for a child."

"I wanted very much for her to be there so that I could ask a question. I wanted to know if the amulet can be used to protect someone other than its owner. And she told me that it can be. But she also said something that confused me. She spoke about the importance of my knowing who I am. When I asked her what she was talking about, she only said that it was not her place to tell me."

His mother's eyes became wet and she kept silent for a long moment. "You seem very worried about my not being here for you to talk to. It's important for you to know that you will not be alone. You have a wife who seems to love you very much. You will have at least one child." And she stopped to take a deep breath.

"There's something you're not telling me. Isn't there?"

"Son, I lied to you when I told you about your father. Your father was not English and he isn't dead. Your father was...is...Irish. Edwin O'Connor is your father."

Eduardo, stunned, hesitated trying to absorb this news and then said angrily, "And you would tell me something this important now after I've spent my life thinking something else?" He pulled away his hand.

"Son, when he and I were together, we were very young. He was extremely handsome. He did not take me by force. He was charming but married. His wife would never have allowed me to remain here if she had known. He did not want to take advantage of me. He never approached me again in that way. But he did want me to be near enough for him to know that I was taken care of and also that you would be safe and well cared for. He continued to employ me on the estate."

"When you were born, instead of feeling embarrassed and hateful and sending us away, he kept me nearby, and eventually placed you and me in this comfortable cabin. He always saw to it that you and I were perfectly well cared for. I have no complaints about him at all. I was no longer in love with him. But I had no reason to hate him. He has always been kind to me...and especially kind toward you. I want you to know who you are."

"So I became his heir, once Sean died."

"Not exactly. You were born illegitimately. To Edwin's credit, he did try to provide you with everything he might provide a son: a full education and opportunity to take over his business eventually, not by right of inheritance but as an opportunity to be earned. He could not offer you the name of O'Connor."

And Eduardo, his head lowered now, said almost to himself, "And by refusing the offer to work with him, I made it more difficult for him to help me."

"That's not true. He's helped you get what you want. Instead of insisting on his own idea, he paved the way for you for teaching, which was entirely your idea. I know him well enough to know that he will not abandon you if you really need him."

"I must talk to him."

"Not about this! Please! No. You must not do that. He's spent too many years maintaining this situation, retaining his dignity, and he's far too set in his ways to feel comfortable being confronted in that way. Believe me, I know him well. Besides, he made me swear never to tell you. Although I've betrayed him now, I would not want to make it worse by letting him know that I've betrayed his confidence."

Eduardo tried to change the subject back to what he had originally had on his mind. "I want to use the amulet to save you, Mother. I needed to know if that was possible. That's why I risked going into the cave again."

"Oh don't be silly. I've lived my life. It's true that I would have enjoyed watching your children grow. But that wasn't meant to be. I've been blessed with a wonderful gift in having a son and being able to watch him live comfortably and well, growing into a fine young man. That's more than enough for me."

Eduardo knew that this was her final word on this subject.

"You are young, Eduardo. There will be many challenges during your life. You will find yourself wishing that you had more than one chance to benefit from the amulet. Choose that moment wisely. Keep your mind on what is important in life and use the amulet at a moment when there is absolutely no other way." She stopped and adjusted her position in bed, trying to sit up straighter. "I know too much about the beliefs of my ancestors to ignore the power of something like this, even though I know it is directly against my faith. My faith in God is strong. Who knows? Maybe the miracle of the amulet was brought about by God, maybe by his enemy. Who can know? Either way, you and I know that the miracle itself is real. It doesn't matter what the source of its power is. Does it?"

Did the news of his heritage change anything? Not really. He could now observe Don Edwin and might begin to appreciate more fully the link between them. He might be able to notice things in common beyond the obvious such as his own "unexplainable" green eyes. His thoughts flew back through all the moments of his life when he had interacted with "Señor" O'Connor. He thought back to moments during his first days at the university, moments when other students would learn that he was being sent by the great Don Edwin O'Connor. He remembered the look on each face as the person indicated not only recognition of the fame associated with the name but admiration for the accomplishment of this gentleman. Was it a shame that Eduardo could not possess the O'Connor name? It hurt to know that the tie had always been there but might never be fully acknowledged before the law and in the eyes of the Church.

"Mother, do you not resent the fact that I came along and that you ended up never having a true husband?"

She wilted visibly from exhaustion during the conversation. But she smiled and her eyes glistened in a way Eduardo hadn't seen in months. "I've had you as a son. And that has been plenty."

Then she coughed almost uncontrollably for a few minutes. He handed her a glass of water from the table by her bed. The coughing stopped. And she said, "You must go home to your wife. You've spent enough time with me."

He leaned over and gave her a kiss on her temple. "Are you hungry?"

"Not at all. Thank you. I need to sleep. I love you, son, and I'm very proud of you. Now go."

Wanting more than ever to be able to stay with her this night, no farther away than his old room next to hers, he knew that she was right. He must leave. His place now was with his wife in his own home. And so he left. "Sleep well," he said as he stood in the doorway before shutting the door behind him. "Good night, Eduardo," she said almost cheerfully as she settled into bed to sleep.

He did not rush home, but instead walked more slowly than usual, thoughts crisscrossing randomly back and forth in a jumbled confusion. O'Connor's foreign heritage suddenly did not seem so foreign after all. It could not, now that Eduardo realized that he himself was an extension of O'Connor.

Meanwhile, efforts to deal with this new realization became interwoven with thoughts concerning the emerald amulet and its potential for good; the impossible choices required in the use of it; and concerns about the conflict between his religious faith, which had grown stronger as he had matured, and the possibility that the amulet and its power could somehow represent direct opposition to that faith.

Too much to deal with all in one day. And he was tired. Tired of the burden of having to weigh so carefully the factors involved in deciding when to use the amulet and when to save it.

Finally, he arrived at his cottage and went in, finding his wife reading by candlelight. "How was she?"

"Worn out. I hope she sleeps well tonight."

"Perhaps she will," she answered, more focused on her book than on the exchange with her husband.

V.

A decade passed after the death of Eduardo's mother. He mourned terribly for her the first year. The intense pain and sense of loss faded slightly in second year, then diminishing further in the third and so on until he was left only with pleasant memories about time spent under her care and love.

Meanwhile, his relationship with Felicia grew stronger through the years while he learned to accommodate differences in outlook and approach to life. A child was born—a boy.

This child quickly became the center of Eduardo's life. Eduardo did, as Felicia had foreseen, grow and mature into a patient, loving father. The love he felt toward his students seemed to grow greater each year.

Years passed quickly. Felicia had great success with her shop. She worked long, hard hours, although now working for herself and for the benefit of her family. The small school continued to grow along with the village. As soon as Eduardo took control of the program and began making his mark, people in the surrounding areas learned about the quality of the school and wanted their children to attend. The Church increased its support, proud of the work accomplished by Eduardo in this small parish school. Like an oasis in the middle of a wilderness, in spite of the ignorance and lack of civilization of the countryside, this little academy produced well-educated young citizens capable of holding demanding jobs. They would mature into thinking adults, questioning citizens demanding opportunities for themselves and their families—or so Eduardo hoped.

The Church and other donors were thrilled about the quality of work being done, ecstatic about the apparent return on investment—and all because of one man: one well-prepared, dedicated educator. Nobody was more proud of Eduardo than his father Don Edwin. Edwin had very much hoped that this young man would come into the mining business. But he respected the young man's own priorities.

All had gone well through the decade after the death of Eduardo's mother. Eduardo was still young enough to have many years ahead of him. He began to dream about what could be accomplished in developing a small college locally, giving his students the option of living near home while continuing to pursue the higher education that he had so well prepared them for.

He was now settled into a comfortable life with his wife and boy. He no longer thought about what it might have been like to have joined O'Connor in the mining business—about what it would have been like to have a larger house, finer clothes, more things.

Eduardo and Felicia lived comfortably with the money he earned teaching and with her income from her small business. He lost all sense of restlessness and felt completely content.

Felicia made up her mind upon first meeting Eduardo that he was the man for her. Fortunately for him, she turned out to be exactly what he needed in a wife—a faithful companion, good mother and frugal manager of money. She presented him with no problems whatsoever. They took good care of each other.

The relationship worked so well that Eduardo began occasionally to worry about whether it was all too good to be true. But whenever he found his mind wandering into this line of thinking he decided that it was not possible to imagine life without Felicia. He could not live without her.

He began to consider himself a wealthy man. This does not mean that he lacked ambition. His interest in the establishment of a small college nearby was beyond ordinary and was about as ambitious a dream as anyone could conjure up, especially within the context of this environment in such simple surroundings involving such uncomplicated people.

Eduardo had come to believe deeply that any person could be developed into a knowledgeable, informed, reasoning citizen, who is curious about the world and able to reason through questions no matter how complex or profound. He had faith in humanity and in an ordinary person's potential to benefit from education. He had, after all, seen with his own eyes the products of his efforts.

✵ ✵ ✵

Don Edwin went through a period of time after the death of Eduardo's mother when he newly discovered penitence and devout faith, attending Mass each week in the small chapel and even conversing occasionally with the priest—never going so far as to offer confession—but listening to the young priest's thoughts about various questions of increasing interest to an aging man.

This period of time was brief. Within a year he tired of the platitudes offered each week during the poorly reasoned and badly communicated homilies. Edwin was an educated man, a thinking person and would have appreciated interaction with a better educated cleric. But, after all, the priest was doing the best he could; he was truly earnest in what he felt, thought and said and was absolutely unbending in his belief in God and in the unquestionable authority of the Church.

Don Edwin had always been too flexible in his views about religion to accept unquestioning obedience to the authority of any particular institution. He had no problem imposing his will on his own employees within the context of a business and brooked no opposition within that setting. The problem was that, throughout most of his life, Edwin found religion too "fuzzy." He often considered the Church's responses to legitimate questions excessively simplistic and self-serving.

O'Connor had grown up in Ireland in a culture rich not only in Catholicism but at the same time equally rich in belief in the supernatural—in the reality of "the little people" and belief in a world of screaming banshees in the dark of night and a uniquely Irish sense both of melancholy and appreciation of another world slightly beyond the reach of our five senses.

This background left him open-minded about the miracle-influenced religion of Catholicism. It also prepared him to be open to the possibility of an "other world" here around us that might have little or nothing to do with the Church's religion.

Eduardo, even as a boy exposed only slightly to Don Edwin's thoughts, noticed O'Connor's Irish melancholy and love of poetry. He also noticed more than once Don Edwin's openness to otherworldly phenomena.

One Saturday morning, Eduardo sat reading in his cottage, unable to concentrate on his book. Felicia sat across the room from him, hand-sewing a shirt for their son Albertito, who by this time was nine years old. Albertito, named after Felicia's Uncle Alberto, the gem cutter, played noisily outside with a friend. He had been a strong, healthy, active child and was growing quickly.

Eduardo had become increasingly disturbed about the fact that he had never actually sat down to speak with Don Edwin about the family connection. He honored his mother's wishes in terms of not discussing it openly. But the sharp sense of obligation toward that promise dulled through the years. And now, as the father watched his son grow and progress, he realized it might be important someday to have an open discussion with his biological father about their relationship. This sort of discussion had been avoided long enough. It had bothered him more and more through these past weeks. Finally, this morning he put the book down. He walked across the room and bent over to kiss Felicia gently on the head. "I'm going to Don Edwin's estate to visit with him."

She looked at Eduardo. She already knew that her husband had been preoccupied about something in recent months. "Visit about what? Is everything all right?"

"Of course. He's been gone. And I want to visit with him. It's nothing to be concerned about."

She chose to drop the subject for now but could not help worrying.

Eduardo walked briskly from the cottage through the village toward the O'Connor estate. As he approached the property, he thought about how little the estate had changed throughout his life. O'Connor had not considered it good use of his money to enlarge his home or to improve it. But he kept the outside of it painted, so that it always looked presentable. He maintained the roof and did not allow anything around the estate to continue in disrepair. He invested only enough each year to keep it all the same, to maintain some semblance of normalcy and continuity.

O'Connor's wealth had increased tremendously. His first two mines continued being productive. He had acquired a third mine, and now with these three he controlled a major part of the emerald mining capacity of the region and of the country as a whole. Eduardo knew this much, even though he had never immersed himself in details concerning the businesses. It was not difficult to know the extent of wealth and power that Don Edwin O'Connor had accumulated over the course of a lifetime.

Don Edwin, not impressed with himself or by his own wealth, was self-aware enough to have become leery of those seeking his attention. Seldom did anyone approach him without either directly or indirectly asking for money. He had never been a gregarious man. He had tolerated social events as long as he could enjoy (or perhaps hide behind) the company of his wife. But after her death, he made no effort to accept social invitations. He had no friends by this time. Puerto Lindo was a place where he could do business, could visit and have a change of scenery. But it was not home. It could never be the same.

Had he become a hermit? Not really. Not in the sense of being an enormously eccentric person, unattractive, withdrawn, and uninteresting. No. It was not practical to attempt social events at the O'Connor estate considering the distances to be traveled by the class of people that he would be expected to associate with. His life had simplified itself. He was quite comfortable with it as it was. He simply did not expect, nor particularly enjoy, visits.

Knowing this, Eduardo felt reluctant to initiate contact with his patrón. The one thing that had changed was that the large iron gate that had always been left open was now generally kept closed and could only be opened by a servant. A bell rung by hand by any visitor standing at the gate would bring forward the servant charged with identifying guests.

Eduardo stood at the gate, considering for two or three minutes whether this was the right time, or for that matter whether any time would be the right time to sit down with Don Edwin to discuss openly what each knew to be of great importance. They had up to this time always had a cordial relationship although from the proper distance.

Eduardo was happy with his wife, his son, his job. But after his mother's death, he had increasingly felt a need for connection with at least one parent, a need for open communication with Don Edwin. He did not know how to bring up the subject. It was entirely possible, considering how old Don Edwin had become and how peculiar he had always been, that O'Connor would not take it well. It was possible that it could be a disastrous conversation, ending what had been a reasonably comfortable relationship.

But here he stood outside the gate, both figuratively and literally outside looking in. He reached up tentatively, grabbed hold of the bell cord and pulled it two or three times. The bell rang loudly. The normal background noises of birds, insects, frogs and other creatures that had always enveloped this area within a blanket of familiarity seemed to have disappeared. They had not, but Eduardo was so completely lost in his own thoughts that he blocked out all sound except for the penetratingly loud, resonant clanging of the bell. He waited patiently. Finally, a servant he had not met approached the gate.

"May I help you?"

"I'd like to know if Don Edwin is in today. I assume that he is."

"Could I ask your name?"

Irritated by the combination of having to ring a bell to gain entrance and then by having to defend himself by giving some sort of explanation as to who he was, Eduardo answered with uncharacteristic coolness, "Tell him it's Eduardo...*his* Eduardo." He felt the need to say it exactly this way and yet immediately regretted this indiscretion.

"Please excuse me for the moment," the servant said formally as he turned and walked back into the large house, across the same porch that Eduardo had crossed so many times before. Eduardo waited patiently. For the first time that he could remember, he felt keen resentment at being made to feel as if he were an outsider. He reminded himself that this situation with the gate, with the new and uninformed servant was not something aimed at him personally. And yet the circumstances of the moment produced within him the first deep feelings of resentment that he had experienced concerning his relationship to this man, to this estate owner, to his patrón, the first such feelings he had felt in a very long time.

Eduardo stood and waited—reason struggling with emotion. He breathed deeply and began to notice sounds again of birds, frogs and all the sounds of the forest.

The servant approached young Eduardo. He walked more quickly this time than he had when he had first approached the gate and the unknown visitor. He stepped up to the gate, unlocked it, apologizing as he turned the key in the lock, "I'm very sorry, sir. I know now who you are. Señor O'Connor is at home and would like very much to receive you. Please come in. And please forgive me for treating you so distantly."

Eduardo said, "Don't worry." Eduardo realized this poor man was merely doing his job and needed employment badly enough to care deeply about not offending either his employer or anyone of importance to his employer. Eduardo remembered his mother being in exactly the same situation and yet always maintaining her own sense of dignity.

Eduardo proceeded through the gate, head held high, in the same posture he had observed among the faculty of the university. He tried to appear outwardly confident even though unsettled by the prospect of sitting in front of Don Edwin and of confronting him with the knowledge of who he was. He had that taste of fear as he walked across the porch, free again to enter through the front door of the great house, as he had been free to do so often before, but now entering into unfamiliar territory.

He approached the door of the study and saw Don Edwin, completely focused on papers in front of him, pen in hand, lost in his own world as

Eduardo remembered him being so often in the past. Edwin looked up. "Eduardo! Hello. What a pleasant surprise." He rose and gestured with his right hand to the chair in front of the desk. "Please, have a seat. What do you have on your mind?" And O'Connor sat back down, waiting to hear Eduardo's response. He was clearly glad to see the young man. He had never been warmer upon seeing Eduardo enter a room. Eduardo felt his chest tighten with anxiety as he sat down uncomfortably, forcing a smile.

"I hope you are well, Don Edwin."

"I am. I am. Very well, thank you for asking. Much older now, as must be all too obvious. But still alive and well." As he spoke, he rearranged papers, placing most of them to the side, clearing the area immediately in front of him and leaning forward slightly, arms on the desk, fingers comfortably intertwined, ready to listen. Sensing that Eduardo was at a loss for words, he asked further, "Your lovely wife and boy? Are they all right?"

"They're very well, thank you. I cannot believe how quickly Albertito is growing. Very active mind. Active boy." Then he stopped. He had hoped that the words would flow naturally and that it would all come out smoothly and well. He could not at this moment produce any words at all. He knew what was on his mind but could not spit it out.

Don Edwin continued smiling but by now realized that Eduardo was having difficulty bringing up whatever was on his mind. Instead of seeming impatient, he tried to help. "You seem to have something in particular on your mind, young man. What is it? You can say whatever it is to me. Go ahead."

Although Eduardo did not believe this literally, he could not help reacting to the expression on the patrón's face. It was one of complete openness, patience and understanding. It was the expression a father might have as he watched a son struggling to find words for some important conversation. And then the words came out on their own. Eduardo finally opened up.

"Don Edwin, before she died, my mother spoke to me about several things. She promised you that she would not share some important news with me and kept that promise throughout most of her life. But as she realized she had little time left, she also realized that she could not leave without telling me something." He hesitated. "I think you know what I'm referring to."

By this time, the smile on Don Edwin's face had faded. Surprising Eduardo by his reaction, O'Connor did not turn red with anger. He did not explode in emotion. He just sat quietly, his expression revealing more sadness than anything else. It was his turn to be at a loss for words now. He sat, releasing his hands and rubbing his palms together slowly, studying them as if somehow in this process he would see how to react, how to approach a moment that he had hoped would never come.

Braver now and sensing that O'Connor had become disturbed by the subject, Eduardo began to speak more frankly. "She told me that you are my real father. She spoke well of you, with great respect and understanding. She spoke of you in much the same way as if she had loved you all those years."

By this time, Edwin found it difficult to look at Eduardo and rapped one set of knuckles lightly on his desk. He kept his face down hoping that the wetness of his eyes would not show.

"The reason she shared this with me then was that it was terribly important to her that I know who I am—not so that I would have any specific claim on anything, or anyone—but only so that I would understand my real identity and heritage. She had always lied to me telling me that my father was English and had died long before. But she did not want to go to her own grave with her only son believing such a lie."

"I tried to treat her well." Edwin said now looking up at Eduardo, hoping for some indication of forgiveness.

"She had no complaints, I tell you. She was well cared for. She understood your situation while your wife was alive. She, I think, would have been very happy to have become your wife after that. But she never appeared to resent her life. She focused all her love and attention on me. I couldn't have been better protected or loved. And when she spoke to me about this she mentioned several times that our comfortable life would not have been possible if it had not been for you."

"What else could I do?" Don Edwin asked out loud, more to himself than to Eduardo.

Without stopping to think before speaking, Eduardo said, "You could have married her after the death of your wife."

O'Connor frowned at first but looked down again. "Yes, you're right."

"But you must understand that there was not the slightest sign of resentment toward you, no sign of malice toward you at all in her voice, in what she said. She had been very content with her life and was especially proud of me. At the same time, she wanted me to understand that I could never have had the opportunity for education if it had not been for your interest in me."

Don Edwin got up and walked to the window and stood with his back to Eduardo. "I'm an old man now, Eduardo, with many regrets. But the biggest regret by far is the way I remained obsessed with my business, passing up the chance to marry your mother. Your mother was a fine person, intelligent and with character far beyond what anyone could reasonably expect from someone with her background. No education. No fine family. And yet..." He turned and sat back down at his desk. " I've done well for myself in this country. My family had nothing in Ireland. Señora O'Connor was a good woman from a distinguished Colombian family. But she became pregnant while unmarried. The man who fathered Sean ran away and never returned. I had already fallen in love with her and married her. Then Sean was born, very close to the time you were born. I had for many years thought I would never marry or have children. Then suddenly I was married and had two...one with my name although not my real son...and then one truly mine who could not have my name."

Eduardo sat listening, surprised by the way Don Edwin was reacting. Eduardo's anxiety vanished. Now all that remained were feelings of discomfort in discussing something so delicate and intensely personal with someone he had spent his entire life keeping at a distance exactly as the older man had always kept him.

"I'm glad that she told you. You should know that I've watched you with great pride as you've grown and progressed. You're right that I should have gone the extra step and made you my son in name."

Eduardo chose to remain silent and waited to see what else his father might volunteer. Instead, Don Edwin seemed lost in thought for minutes.

Eduardo said, to break the silence, "I did not know whether I should do this. But I could not keep it inside me any longer."

Edwin smiled again. "Son, why did you wait so long to mention it?"

"I had become accustomed to the idea of your being nothing other than my mother's employer. You treated me well. I was afraid your attitude would change too drastically. I did not want to lose you as well as my mother by bringing up a subject you wanted to avoid."

"I understand. To be honest, I've had a hard time hiding the fact that I needed a son. It might have been better to bring it out in the open, at least between you and me." He got up, approached Eduardo and put his hand on his back. "Thank you for being the fine young man you have become."

Eduardo, filled with emotion, could say nothing else and excused himself. "I must go. I need to return to my family." He walked out of the study, with Don Edwin alongside him.

"Of course, of course. Stay close to them. Appreciate them as much as you can. Hold nothing back." Eduardo could not help thinking that this would have been excellent advice for Edwin to have followed. At the same time, Eduardo knew that it was sincere advice offered by father to son and based upon years of experience and regrets about lost opportunities.

They shook hands. "Come more often."

Eduardo nodded and left the house, heading back toward his cottage. It had never occurred to him that Don Edwin would take this so well. He had worried for years about how he might alienate Don Edwin by too openly confronting him with knowledge of the truth. What a tremendous waste of years.

Eduardo realized that if he had had the courage to approach O'Connor sooner, he might have been able to enjoy a closer relationship with his father. During the walk home Eduardo felt more than anything a sense of loss of time and opportunity.

Once more he thought about how hard it would still be to feel completely comfortable with Don Edwin, given the fact that he had passed his entire life up to now thinking of him as lord of the manor, a benevolent but distant benefactor.

How different life would have have been if Eduardo's mother had become the second Señora O'Connor. She had no idea about social graces involved in entertaining guests. She would have felt out of place at receptions or social events in the city, accompanying Don Edwin. She was intelligent and literate, although not formally educated.

His mother had always seemed perfectly content. Maybe she preferred it the way it played out. She was safe from harm, safe from starvation. Her child was being raised in a positive environment and in some ways was treated as if a member of the family, especially after the death of Sean O'Connor.

Maybe there was nothing to regret. Maybe the only real loss was the lack of a good family name for Eduardo, a name carrying with it stature and also access to a great deal of material wealth. It would be nice for Albertito to be able to have the name he deserved.

Eduardo pulled out the gold pocket watch that Don Edwin had given him so long before. He had carried it with him throughout the years, until now having forgotten the reminder from Don Edwin that the gold signified material wealth and that the timekeeping aspect served as a reminder about the shortness of life. He smiled as he held the watch in his hand and remembered that moment—the moment the gift had been lovingly handed to him. He was not as interested in material wealth as Don Edwin had always been. Now, after this morning's visit, he wondered if Don Edwin himself had always been so intensely interested only in wealth. Edwin seemed lonelier than ever. His money seemed to give no comfort.

Eduardo did not regret his decision to avoid a career in business. As he walked home, though, he wondered if he should regret it. Wouldn't it be nice, he thought, to have beautiful clothes and to be able to provide them for his wife and child, to have a large, splendid house with servants, to have interesting objects of art scattered about the home... not only lovely to look at but also giving evidence of extensive travels worldwide by the lord and lady of the manor? Wouldn't it be convenient to have a fine, good-looking automobile allowing them to travel for hours without having to depend on a bus or train? He ended up arriving at the same conclusion he had always reached before. Yes, all these things would be wonderful to have, but he could not picture himself having them. He could not see himself spending days, weeks, or years working hard at making money while accomplishing nothing of any real value to anyone. Don Edwin had been about as successful as any man could be. Yet where had that gotten him?

It appeared, based on what Eduardo had observed through the years and had heard this morning, that O'Connor might have loved Eduardo's mother, although not enough to marry her after the death of his wife. He would not have had to admit publicly to having fathered Eduardo. He could have adopted him, claiming this to be an act of generosity, adopting the son of his new wife in order to create a family unit and to show commitment to the woman he had married. He chose not to do any of this. He, in so many ways, showed not only compassion and concern toward her and her boy, but went much further and ensured that the boy had every opportunity that a son might have had—except for a family name and sense of heritage.

O'Connor was now closer to the end of his life than to its beginning. He welcomed Eduardo's awareness of the true situation. He seemed relieved to be able to speak about it openly. He did in fact seem to regret some of the choices that he had made.

Eduardo had a great deal to feel thankful for. He had made the correct choice for himself, and realized that he felt sorry for Don Edwin. Edwin O'Connor had made his own choices and had remained committed to them. But Edwin seemed now to need a sense of family. This was much to assume based on one morning's conversation. But Eduardo admitted to himself, as he approached his own doorstep, that here he felt completely at home, totally at ease, content in the life that he had chosen.

As he entered the door, Felicia greeted him with a gently scolding tone, "Where *were* you?! You were gone longer than I expected."

He sat at the small dining table and invited her to sit with him. "I went to visit Don Edwin." He turned to young Alberto and said, "Albertito, please go outside and play for a while. But stay close to the house where we can see and hear you." The boy did as he was told. He had been kept indoors against his will by his mother encouraging him to study. He was glad to be set free.

"And?" she asked, sensing by Eduardo's manner that there had been something out of the ordinary about this particular visit.

"There was something I needed to discuss with him, something very important. I had never talked with him about it. I've never spoken to you about it." He stopped for a second, wondering exactly how to ease into this and could not find the perfect words. Instead, he said it outright. "Before my mother died, she decided it was necessary for me to know something that I had never been told. The story I had always gotten from her was that my father was English and had died tragically before my growing up to the point of being able to remember him. I accepted that as the truth. I had no reason not to. She kept to this story throughout my childhood and years at the university, but she could not end her life without telling me that it was not true."

"I don't understand why you needed to speak about this with Don Edwin."

"Because it has very much to do with him personally. What she went on to tell me was that Don Edwin is my father. He was married to Señora O'Connor when I was born. After his wife died, he chose not to suggest marriage to my mother. She saw nothing unusual about this and went along with it without mentioning it to anyone. He continued to employ her, kept her in a comfortable situation, and also saw to it that I had everything I needed. And that was that."

"This explains much, doesn't it," she said.

"A great deal, but not everything."

"It explains why he was so willing to subsidize your education."

"That's true. But there's much about it that I still don't understand. Possibly because I don't really know him. I can't know his mind."

She said, "Why could he not have married your mother and adopted you? He seems otherwise to be a good man. But this..."

"Don Edwin *is* a good man. It would have been even more difficult to understand his losing his wife and then marrying one of his maids and adopting her son. It would not have looked good either for my mother or for him."

"Would not have looked good to whom? He had—he has no family. He only associates with businessmen and has always been that way. He could have done it."

"Perhaps. But my mother never seemed to resent it at all. She was content to live with a roof over her head, to have plenty to eat, adequate clothing, and with her son alongside her. She was happy, and I was as well. And now as I look back, I realize that Don Edwin must have felt better knowing that we were both nearby where he could be certain that each of us was well cared for."

"What a peculiar man!"

"I suppose. But he was good to us. And he is getting older quickly. He travels less. He's there by himself more and more and is lonely. I feel sorry for him."

"Sorry for him!? Do you have any idea how wealthy that man is?"

"No one knows that better than I. But he seems sad nevertheless, and profoundly alone."

She shook her head. "You are entitled to his wealth once he is gone."

Eduardo squirmed in his seat slightly and looked away for a second. "I don't want his money."

Now thoroughly irritated, she exclaimed, "You know that you are his only surviving son and yet you don't want what he acquired throughout his life? Are you completely crazy or only a fool?"

"I'm not crazy. I may be a fool. But even as a fool, I'm very blessed with what I have. I couldn't be happier."

More calmly now, she answered, "I'm happy too, Eduardo. You're a good husband and a good father. All I ask is this. Don't close the door completely on any inheritance that Don Edwin might want to leave you. I'm not thinking of myself. I'm thinking of how it might help Albertito during his life."

"Of course. I understand. But that isn't for me to decide. I will not press in any way at all. Money is not why I went to him today. I think he knows that. And I will not say or do anything to make it appear otherwise." He stopped for a second, and Felicia allowed the silence to linger. "It would be wonderful just to be able to speak more freely with him, if not as father and son then at least as friend to friend."

Deciding that it was not wise to pursue this further, and noticing fatigue in Eduardo's face and in the way he sat, she let the subject drop. "I'm glad that you went. And I'm glad you shared this with me." She reached over and placed her hand on his and added, "You'll have time to get to know him now. Relax. Let's think about other things."

Agreeing with her and smiling weakly, Eduardo got up and went about the remainder of his day, paying special attention to Albertito in the evening after supper. Lying in bed that night, Eduardo could not let go of thoughts about what it might have been like to have a father all those years; all those years that he spent dreaming about what his English father might have been like and meanwhile having his real father in front of him. He lay awake wishing that he could turn back time. And yet he looked forward to the possibility of finally being able to get to know his real father and to allow him, if he proved to be interested, to spend time with the grandchild. The more he considered this, the more relaxed he became before slipping off into one of the deepest sleeps he had managed in weeks. But not before considering the fact that there was still one major truth in his life that had not been openly discussed with Don Edwin or with Felicia. He could not picture himself being able to discuss it with either of them without being thought of as crazy.

His mother had not only known but had understood and accepted unquestioningly the miracle of the emerald amulet's existence and its power to protect. She gave wise counsel about its use and about the importance of refraining from using it casually. But she was no longer around. Eduardo was now the only person aware of the amulet's existence and power. He had shown it to Felicia and had said that it was a precious gift from his mother. He had not shared the whole truth about it. But now, with the equally troublesome truth openly discussed—the truth about his own origin and his potential inheritance—perhaps the time would present itself for him to share knowledge about the amulet with the adults he now felt closest to. Perhaps.

✲ ✲ ✲

Eduardo continued in his work during the days. His and Felicia's life continued with their caring for and raising young Alberto. The primary difference was that now Don Edwin had become a greater part of their lives. He would occasionally arrive in his car to visit them on Saturdays for no more than a few hours at a time, never overstaying his welcome. Felicia grew to feel quite at ease around him. Edwin seemed to enjoy watching the boy play and treated Albertito with attention and grandfatherly affection. He invited them to spend Sunday afternoons with him each and every week. And Eduardo and Felicia frequently accepted this standing invitation.

Don Edwin hired a senior manager to oversee all the operations of his mines and then retired, continuing to see about the investments which served as the anchor of his holdings. He settled into the life of a country gentleman and began to look healthier and happier, taking on a better color, putting on a little weight, looking less haggard than before.

With O'Connor at home almost all the time now, he was available for Eduardo on those increasingly frequent occasions when Eduardo would come to visit, often to walk about the estate with his father. Eduardo looked forward with anticipation to these walks two or three times a week after finishing responsibilities at school and before being home in the evening with his wife and child.

O'Connor became noticeably warmer and more openly affectionate. The careful distance he had maintained throughout the years seemed inappropriate now. A big hug and a hearty welcome greeted Eduardo each time that he came to visit. It took Eduardo time to adjust to this. He had, throughout his life, felt comfortable with considerable distance between himself and the great patrón. But now he realized he no longer considered Don Edwin as "the Patrón." He could not at first bring himself to refer to him as "papá" but relented, which seemed to please Don Edwin greatly.

On the other hand, O'Connor adjusted quickly—once given the opportunity to do so—to the idea of Eduardo being his acknowledged son. He referred to him either as Eduardo or often as "hijo," as "son." It was as if he had been starved for years, kept away from a great feast of relationship and then, suddenly with the feast laid out before him, began to enjoy it.

Spending more time with his father gave Eduardo more glimpses into who his father really was. Had the old man changed? Possibly, with age, with greater maturity. Possibly more because of experience, because of wisdom acquired over the years and a realization about what mattered most. Or it might be that he had not changed all that much. Eduardo had never been able to spend time with Edwin and, having no special reason to do so, had never noticed as many details about him. The more he got to know him, the more puzzling it seemed that Edwin was so introverted relative to people outside of his business dealings or outside of his immediate community—a community which had always been limited primarily to the grounds and personnel of his estate. Edwin O'Connor was in fact a peculiar man. Felicia had been correct about that. But as Eduardo got to know him more and more, Eduardo did not think of O'Connor as peculiar but instead saw him as a welcome addition to life, even if a bit late.

One day, while walking around the perimeter of the estate with Don Edwin, Eduardo suggested that they venture into the forest. He led the old gentleman along the path leading toward the cave. The path did not involve steep climbs and the distance between the estate and the cave was not great. It had only seemed a great distance to small boys venturing out to a place where they should not have been.

As they neared the area where the cave entrance would be, Edwin stopped, realizing that they had wandered out farther than he would have on his own. "You know, we should turn back. We've gone quite far enough."

"Just a little farther. There's a clearing up here where we can sit before returning."

"All right," Don Edwin replied compliantly.

They sat on logs around the edge of the small clearing. Eduardo decided that there might not be a better time to bring up the subject than now and so decided to push ahead. "Don Edwin?"

Don Edwin interrupted gently. "Eduardo, you should learn to feel comfortable calling me "father" or "papá" or whatever seems best to you. It's foolish to keep such distance now."

"Thank you, father, I will." After hesitating for a second, he continued, "This is a significant spot for me, although no one but my mother ever knew why."

Looking playfully intrigued, O'Connor asked simply, "Really? How's that?"

"Well, how do I say this?" Looking for words as he so often found himself doing when something mattered to him greatly, Eduardo then said the first things that came to mind. "When I was a boy—when

Sean and I were boys—we wandered outside the estate and into this forest one morning." He gestured to the entrance to the cave. "This cave seemed to beckon us. We knew we should not go into it. Or at least I knew. Sean wanted very much to go inside and teased me for hesitating. I was afraid not only of the cave but of the trouble we were likely to find if it were discovered that we had been in it. We wandered into it and used our lights to find our way down a path, almost a corridor, exploring, curious, not trying to find anything in particular. As we walked farther, we began to hear familiar sounds and then saw light coming from a chamber just off to the side." Stopping, Eduardo wondered how a grown man could possibly tell the rest of this tale to another fully grown man without one of them laughing or, worse, without being considered a lunatic. "If I go on, you must promise not to laugh at me."

Don Edwin grinned. He agreed to restrain himself. He wanted very much to hear the rest of this short story, whether true or not. "I promise."

Eduardo hesitated and then decided that there was no way to share this without sounding ridiculous. Accepting this inevitability, he continued. "We walked to the entrance to the side chamber. The light grew brighter as we approached. Flickering candlelight removed the darkness that had been the most intimidating part of venturing inside the cave. The lighted chamber seemed warm and inviting. As we stepped inside, there was an old woman, white haired and small. As she turned and noticed us, she invited us in. She seemed to know that we were going to arrive. How could she? But she did know. And during the visit she fed us and made us even more comfortable, showing us a beautiful piece of jewelry—an amulet made from an emerald."

Don Edwin, up to this point had sat, genially smiling, listening well, clearly interested in anything his son might tell him. At this point in the story, however, his expression changed subtly. The smile faded. His expression melted into a more serious one, eyes focused more intently on Eduardo, as if the story had somehow entered into an a subject area not only believable but faintly disturbing.

"She gave it to Sean, not to me. She called him by name, as if she already knew him, and she explained that it could offer protection to its rightful owner throughout a lifetime. She recited a charming rhyme in English that made it clear that the amulet could protect the owner only…"

"...three times and three times only," Don Edwin quietly interjected, speaking almost beneath his breath.

Eduardo stopped and glared at his father, astonished that he had not laughed. Very much like a little boy, Eduardo asked his father in disbelief, "Papá! _How_ do you know this?"

Don Edwin straightened his back and moved his shoulders as if to look for a way to appear more in control. "Never mind that right now. Go on."

At first unable to proceed with his story, Eduardo saw in his father's face an intensity that indicated he was truly interested in hearing more detail. He carried on with the telling of his tale. _"He who holds this, less malice or vice, is protected completely, but so only thrice."_ "That's how it went."

"Yes, go on. What happened next?"

His father looked away into the distance, distracted. Eduardo, watching his father's face intently, continued. "Sean took the amulet. We left the woman and walked back to the estate. Sean was bitten by a snake when we stopped for a brief rest. We tried the amulet right away. It did nothing. He mentioned that it felt cold to the touch. There was no glow emanating from it. You know the rest of that story up through the loss of Sean, except for one thing."

Edwin looked straight into Eduardo's eyes and asked directly, "Where has it been all these years?"

Perplexed by his father's knowledge of something so extraordinary, and also caught off-guard by the sharp tone in his father's voice, Eduardo hesitated to answer and instead—showing his Irish heritage—answered a question with a question. "Why do you ask, Papá? And more importantly how could you possibly know about the amulet in the first place?"

"Where is it?" Eduardo's father persisted.

"It's safe. Please answer my question."

Don Edwin relaxed, or at least appeared to do so, realizing that he had made his son extremely uncomfortable and considering how it must appear to Eduardo. Edwin sat up, took a deep breath, gathered his thoughts and began, "You have probably often thought that you dreamed the entire experience—that there is something unreal about the woman in the cave and the power of the amulet. It is all very real, but not to be discussed with anyone outside our family."

Eduardo sat, listening, transfixed by something he would never have expected and still scarcely could believe.

"My father, back in Ireland, had a similar experience when he was a boy there. Wandering aimlessly about the hills one day, he ventured into a small cave and came across an old woman exactly as you described. He kept that secret to himself once he had the amulet. He said it felt warm in his hands. It glowed delicately the first time he held it. He used it to save his own life three times before trying to give it to me. One day he took me aside and told me the entire story. At first, I assumed he was lying. He was fond of telling tall tales and took special delight in watching gullible listeners. But I realized as I listened to him that morning that he was not lying. There was something profoundly honest in his eyes and expression.

"I don't want it," he told me to my astonishment. "I'm afraid of such things. I'm afraid that God himself would strike me down if I were to grow attached to it. He handed me the amulet and said nothing as he watched me take it. But both he and I noticed that it did not glow in my hands. I felt no warmth.

"You see? I think it's a trick or a curse. I don't trust it. I don't want anything to do with it. You do with it what you will, my son." He walked away and never mentioned it again.

The first time I tried to use it for my own benefit, it did nothing but remained as cold and unresponsive as a stone. Thoroughly disgusted, I took it back to the cave where he said he had gotten it, and I left it inside the entrance, afraid to venture inside. I was angry that the amulet would ignore me, and hurt that I could not simply inherit from my father something so special. I put it out of my mind and never returned to that cave. I never had the courage to speak to anyone about it as you have this morning with me."

Don Edwin stopped, breathing deeply again and looking away. As he turned back his head, Eduardo could see a tear streaming down his father's cheek. "So my boy, Sean, my dear sweet boy could not benefit from it any more than I could." And he looked at Eduardo. "I have no idea how it followed me and mine here from Ireland. It must be bewitched. But it has helped you?"

Since there seemed to be no resentment in Don Edwin's tone, Eduardo sensed that his father was more deeply puzzled than angry or frustrated. "Yes. Twice now."

Don Edwin looked up and closed his eyes. "Thank God, at least one of my sons can benefit from it." Then thinking through all that he had heard, he looked less relieved than concerned. "Twice already? And you are so young."

Edwin sat with a hand on each knee. Eduardo reached over and placed his own hand on top of his father's hand and said quietly, "Mother knew about this because I told her. She never laughed at or disbelieved me whenever I spoke of it."

"I'm not surprised by that. She had become a devout Catholic, a pillar of her small church. But her people understood the supernatural and she would not have questioned it either."

"I tried to use it to save her at the end. But she would not let me."

Edwin now smiled for the first time since the earliest part of their conversation. Smiled and seemed supremely satisfied. "That most definitely does not surprise me. She cared too deeply for you."

For a time, each man sat quietly. Then Don Edwin reached over with his right hand and patted his son's hand and said more briskly, "We must go. Life goes on. And we need to get back home. Your wife will be worried about you."

They walked slowly back, retracing their steps without speaking. Don Edwin was deeply lost in memories. Eduardo did not want to interrupt him and at the same time also needed a little time to process all that had been thrust upon him this morning.

As they emerged from the forest and stepped into the open area at the edge of Edwin's estate, Edwin stopped and said to his son, "You must be extremely careful about how you use the amulet now. I want you to have a long, healthy, happy life. Any benefit at all that you can gain from the stone is extremely important."

"I know. But there are times when it's difficult to know what choice to make. When to use it and when to wait."

Don Edwin only nodded in agreement. He did not bring up the subject of the amulet again. Before Eduardo left him to return to his cottage, he did ask this, "Eduardo, does your wife know about the amulet? Or your son?"

"Neither."

"Good. For now, keep it to yourself. There may be a time when you will feel that you have to discuss it with her. But not until then."

"I know. Thank you for listening. I'm glad that I told you."

"Until this day, I had never thought about it, and that seems strange even to me. But there is a great deal of my father in your eyes. Not only the same green color, but the same expression and smile. I'm sorry I had never noticed that before." He gave his son a hug and a firm pat on the back and said for the first time Eduardo had ever heard from him, "I love you, son, very much. Now go. Go home to your family."

That evening, after spending time reading and then helping his son with homework from school, Eduardo went in to tuck his boy into bed. Albertito both considered himself and actually was too old for this ritual. But Eduardo especially wanted to say "goodnight" to his only son this evening and was going to do so with or without full approval from the boy.

"I want you to know that I'm proud of you, my boy, and that I love you very much. I don't say that very often. But I do love you." He gently patted the boy's shoulder and then walked out.

Not accustomed to this behavior from his father, Albertito accepted it and settled in feeling safe, protected, and free to drift off to sleep without concerns.

Back in the common room with his wife, Eduardo read again. Sewing a pair of pants and repairing a shirt, she looked up and asked, "What exactly happened today? It seems to have had quite an effect on you. Are you well?"

"Perfectly all right. Maybe that's it. We're all doing so well. I guess I realized I shouldn't take that fact so much for granted." And he looked back at his book, making it obvious that he did not want to continue visiting about this particular day, at least not at this moment. He would choose his moment. Felicia, by now understanding very well the signals her husband could send out when he did not feel comfortable discussing something, discreetly dropped the subject and continued with her sewing. She also knew that, if it were important, the subject would come up again, probably sooner than expected. All that was required was patience. Whatever was on his mind would be discussed eventually. She relaxed and forgot about the subject completely for now.

Many people would have considered Eduardo's family's life exceedingly dull. A quiet village. A small, unassuming cottage. A life for the father as a schoolmaster in a tiny school. Only one child, a boy, and a well-behaved one at that. Eduardo had long since forgotten about what life might be like if other choices had been made.

Felicia—ambitious enough to want desperately to escape from her former situation as an employee at a wealthy banker's estate and certainly determined enough as a young woman to marry Eduardo, no matter how long that process might take—now had all that she wanted. She had a good husband, a comfortable home, a healthy child, her own very small business allowing her to work on her own schedule, giving her independence that many people would envy. Albertito wanted for nothing. None of the three members of this family had anything to complain about. Life was good.

Eduardo knew that many of his fellow students at the university would have been absolutely bored out of their minds with such a life and would have worked to avoid what many might have seen as mind-numbing predictability.

Eduardo always carried the gold watch that had been given to him by Don Edwin so many years before. He would admire it each time he took it out to check the time. But now, given the life Eduardo had chosen, the gold watch no longer served as an association with wealth and the short time any man is allowed to acquire it. He admired the watch now for its inherent value—more than anything else for the fact that it always reminded him of his father. This meant more to him of course through the years. As Don Edwin grew older, he became more and more house-bound and less attached to preoccupations with business. This gave time for a truer father-son relationship to develop and flourish.

Seeing his father at least every other day, Eduardo could not maintain the perspective that would have helped him notice how rapidly Don Edwin was aging. The old man's health was failing steadily. Edwin at first had been strong enough to drive from his estate toward the village and to Eduardo's and Felicia's cottage to visit them and his grandson. Eduardo, so glad to have his father more openly part of his life, refused to acknowledge how rapidly the situation was deteriorating. First the old man became unable to make these small excursions and then became unable even to take his daily walks about the estate.

Only Felicia both noticed and accepted the fact of Don Edwin's visible decline. She understood that her husband was failing to acknowledge this unpleasant development because its acknowledgement would remind him of how little time was left. He relished each day—working, being with and caring for wife and child, and interacting with a "newly found" father.

He would walk to the estate and back two or three late afternoons each week and each Saturday morning. On this particular Saturday morning, as he approached the gate, now generally left open at the times when Don Edwin expected that he might be visited by his son, Eduardo found his father not seated in the study but still in bed.

A tray set to the side gave evidence of a small breakfast having been taken in bed. Don Edwin sat up, pale but alert and obviously looking forward to the possibility of seeing his son.

"Papá! Why are you still in bed? How unlike you."

Edwin grimaced and said sourly, "I know. It's embarrassing. But I did not feel like getting up and dressing this morning. Sit down. I want to speak to you about something."

The dutiful son Eduardo sat in the straight-backed chair by the bed and waited to listen, realizing his father was prepared to say something important. Patiently, respectfully he sat, hands folded in his lap, waiting to hear what his father had to say.

"Son, even if it's not obvious to you, it is obvious to me that I'm growing weaker each year and now each month. I've had a great deal of time alone to think about many things. I've thought about my life and what I might have done differently if given the chance. I have to be honest. There isn't anything concerning my choice of career or my pursuit of success in business that I would have done any differently. I loved it from the time I first began it. I was good at it. And the sort of success that I wanted required all of my time, talent and energy. As success came, my goals ended up being stretched out farther and farther into the future, so that there was never a moment when I could stop and feel completely satisfied with what I had. The demands I made on myself grew greater each year, and because I was good at what I did, I became richer all the time. Now, time and age have pushed me to the point where I'm past the point of growing and building."

"Father, don't..."

"No, no, let me continue. The only life I'd known came to an end and then a new life began: one that has turned out to be far better. It began the day you came to speak openly with me about what your mother had told you. From that point on, I began learning what I had missed. And that's the only regret I have. I should have married your mother and paid less attention to my work. I didn't. Or if I hadn't gone that far, I should at least have spoken openly with her and you so that we could have been closer to each other after Señora O'Connor's death. But that's all past now. It's pointless to dwell on regrets. What I wanted to say to you is how happy it has made me to have you here in my life in these last few years. You've been a good son. You've turned into a fine man. I would like to think that Sean would eventually have grown into his own sort of good person as well. But the one thing I know is how wonderful it has been to have you.

I realize that I don't have much time left. And it would be ridiculous for me to have worked so hard, to have accomplished so much, and to be so fortunate as to have such a fine son remaining alive and not to pass along what I have. My attorney is coming here Monday morning, and I'm going to establish a new will leaving my estate in a trust to be used to help you in any financial emergencies that you or your wife might have during your lifetime and then to help Albertito with his education."

"Father, it really isn't…"

"You made a deliberate choice to live without wealth and I'm convinced that you chose well for yourself. I respect that choice. But I want to know that you will be taken care of and that my grandchild will be as well."

Eduardo looked down, overcome with emotion and mumbled, "I don't know what to say."

"I mentioned once, quite some time ago, the fact that you remind me of my father. And I also see much of you in Albertito. You've convinced me that you understand—far better than I ever did—the fact that money cannot take care of everything, and that it isn't the most important thing in life. That's why I'm making funds available for your care and for the care of your family. I know it won't change you. There is a part of it left specifically for you to use for growing your little school. Use that well and wisely, son. I know that you will."

Eduardo, sitting up straighter, said, "First of all, you are wrong. You have years and years left to be with us. And so this planning is completely out of place."

Don Edwin grinned. "Well, that sounds encouraging. Maybe you're right. In that case, I'll not have to think about this." He could not help chuckling at the fact that Eduardo truly refused to believe that his father was in the process of slipping away, could not see it, would not accept it if he did. "I've enjoyed life very much, Eduardo. But I spent too much of it alone. Don't lose what you already have."

Seeing that his father looked exhausted from the strain of considering in advance what to say and then going through the difficult process of saying it out loud, Eduardo changed the subject and spoke about smaller topics: events of the week, tidbits of information about Alberto's progress in school. Before the morning ended, Edwin looked so drained that Eduardo got out of the chair and said, "You look as if you need to sleep before lunch. I'll go now. I'll be back tomorrow." He grabbed his father's hand and squeezed. Edwin, although not with the grip he had once had, squeezed his boy's hand in reply and smiled before closing his eyes. "I do think that I need to sleep. Take care and remember what I've told you."

"I'll remember. Don't worry."

✫ ✫ ✫

Eduardo continued his visits for weeks, finally acknowledging his father's rapidly worsening health. A number of cases of typhoid were beginning to appear in families in the surrounding area. He became extremely concerned about his father's weakness and vulnerability and began going to see him each and every afternoon. To ease the strain on Eduardo, although the son had specifically asked this not to be done, Don Edwin began sending a servant in his car to pick up Eduardo and to drive him to the estate at the end of the afternoon and then back home again, a gesture Eduardo accepted in order to save time.

Finally, one day when he visited, he realized that his father was not making sense. He touched his forehead and saw that his father had a high fever. He asked the staff to call a doctor. Eduardo decided the following day to move into the house with his father at least for a few days. The priest began keeping school on his behalf while Eduardo attended Don Edwin. The fever refused to break. It was determined that Edwin had in fact contracted the typhoid that Eduardo had feared. Less than a week went by before one afternoon when Edwin, sleeping peacefully, simply stopped breathing.

Eduardo had mourned the loss of his mother intensely. Yet the loss of Don Edwin was more sharply painful than anything Eduardo had ever experienced. Felicia cringed at the sight of her husband sobbing uncontrollably in the privacy of their home. It hurt her deeply to see him suffer so deeply. It puzzled her as to how anyone could so completely lose control. She wondered to herself if she somehow lacked something inside that would allow her to feel love so desperately for anyone that the pain of loss could make her feel inconsolable. It was something she had never experienced. It was difficult to comprehend. She had never wanted in her life so much to be able to ease someone's suffering. And yet there seemed to be absolutely nothing she could say or do that could help Eduardo as he grieved.

Don Edwin was buried on the grounds of his estate, in accordance with his wishes, rather than in the small cemetery by the church as Eduardo (and as Eduardo's mother, undoubtedly) would have preferred. Don Edwin had not been an atheist by any means. But he had never been devout enough to see it as anything but hypocritical to be buried in a church cemetery. His truest devotion had been to reason rather than to faith.

Weeks went by without any noticeable improvement in Eduardo's state of mind. He worked. He managed to concentrate on his students and their needs during the day. He struggled to remain properly focused on his wife and child in the evenings. But Felicia realized that he was completely at a loss late each afternoon and on Saturday mornings, unsure where to go or what to do to keep his mind off of Don Edwin. He would sleep at night, but in a restless and deeply disturbed sleep, frequently waking up to the sound of his own whimpering.

Within a month, drained by overwhelming grief and by inability to feel hunger or ability to rest, Eduardo himself fell ill, coming down with a high fever. Dreading the worst, Felicia sent Albertito for a physician who came to examine Eduardo. The doctor gave her the bad news that her husband had contracted typhoid fever. The doctor said, "He is so thin and weak and his resistance so low that he was bound to become sick with something."

She spent each day and night caring for her husband, even at times finding herself praying for his recovery, although she could not remember resorting to prayer before—something she had always seen as far too similar to the superstitions of the Indians. She believed in the supernatural, as everyone in her family before her had believed. But neither Christian faith nor Indian traditions seemed to her to be sufficient as ways to obtain results apart from her own efforts.

Within days, Albertito was feeling ill and came down with the same fever. She felt a deep sense of panic pervading every corner of her being. Could she lose them both?

On the second day of Albertito's sickness, Eduardo recovered sufficient presence of mind to realize what was happening both to him and to his son. Weak, unable to eat and uninterested in drinking anything other than lukewarm tea, Eduardo could not sit up in bed but could think and speak clearly enough to know that he must do the only thing he was capable of doing at this point.

"Felicia. Felicia," he called to her, bringing her in from Alberto's bedside to his room. She came quickly to him, glad to see him no longer delirious from the fever and lucid enough to call for her.

"How can I help you, my love?"

He gestured toward his closet. "There. Please look there, in the back, on the highest shelf."

She did as he asked and emerged from the large armoire holding the emerald amulet in her right hand. "This! Is this what you want?"

He nodded and said with a sigh, "Yes. Please bring it here."

As she walked toward his bed with the amulet held in her hand, she asked with a puzzled tone, "But why would you need this?"

She gave it to him and he held it. She could not help exclaiming quietly almost to herself as she saw it in his hand, "It's glowing." She reached down to touch it lightly with one finger and said, "It's warm now." She reached over to feel his forehead, mainly trying to decide if his fever were so high that it could have produced this phenomenon simply by his holding the stone in his hot hand. His fever seemed slightly lower, however. She said simply, "I don't understand."

Realizing that the amulet's power still existed, Eduardo looked enormously relieved and let it go immediately. Laying it down on the bed, he told her, "Bring Albertito to me."

"What do you mean? Eduardo, he's very ill. He needs to stay in bed."

"My love, please do what I say. He's bigger now. But you can still carry him. Bring him to me and lay him beside me."

Completely at a loss for words, but unwilling to argue with her husband, she did as he asked, went into the boy's bedroom, pulled back the covers and reached down, picking him up in her arms and carrying the boy, still groggy with sleep to her husband's bed. She lay him down beside Eduardo. Eduardo struggled to sit up as much as he could, making room for his son. He took the amulet and placed it around his own neck and then embraced his son as completely, as tightly as he could manage, leaning his head against his son's, enveloping the boy within the embrace not only of his love but of the protective power of the amulet. Eduardo said nothing but closed his eyes, thinking of the advice he had been given both by his mother, by the old woman in the cave, and by his father...to make choices wisely and with great care.

This choice was not difficult to make. He decided without hesitation.

He kept the boy in his arms for what seemed like an eternity to Felicia. Watching the emerald glow and seeing both her husband and her son so comfortable, so much at peace, she remained silent and waited, trusting that whether her husband was in fact lucid and knew what he was doing or not—that he appeared to be so and deserved this time with his son.

Eduardo released his hold and relaxed, leaning back. He took off the amulet and returned it to Felicia. "You may put this back now. And you may take him back to his bed. Make him comfortable. He will sleep now. And he will be better when he wakes up."

Too tired herself to question him, she returned the amulet, noticing that it felt cold to her touch and no longer glowed once in her hands. She returned Albertito to his bed, tucking him in and arranging his pillow. She noticed tiny beads of sweat forming on his forehead and running down his cheeks. She placed her hand gently on his forehead and realized that his fever was already breaking. He seemed to be soundly, peacefully asleep now, breathing more normally as he would during any healthy night's restful sleep for a healthy child.

When she returned to Eduardo, she saw him with his eyes still open but darker now. He was burning up with fever. She sat by him and waited for him to volunteer an explanation. When he said nothing, she prompted him gently, "Eduardo, speak to me. What was this about?"

Although exhausted, he managed the strength to tell her the entire story. She listened patiently. She had no problem at all believing. Toward the end of his story about the amulet and its role in his life and the first two times he had used it for his own protection, he commented that the one thing that had puzzled him even more than the power of the stone itself was how easily his mother and also his father, from such different backgrounds, had accepted the story and had believed it, focusing only on how best to use the power of the stone during the course of their son's lifetime.

"And you, Felicia, must do this now for our son. This was my third and last use of the stone. And it was an easy decision for me to use it for my son and for his protection. I want the amulet to be his now, and hope that it can help him as it has helped me. But you must guide him carefully in its use. Keep him headed in the right direction and encourage him to make the right choices. Find other ways to protect or to save him if you must."

The only moment when she questioned him was when she asked, "How can you believe in this and then believe in God too?"

"How can I know that God did not give us the amulet in the first place? I only know that it's real. I don't have to understand it." And he grabbed her hand and looked directly at her. "Take care of him. Don't depend too easily upon the amulet. It won't be enough by itself for a lifetime."

"I will. Now you hush. You need to rest, too. You both do. I'll be here all night. Don't worry."

Unable to go on, he nodded in agreement and took a deep breath and closed his eyes. She slipped away from his bed and into her son's room and sat watching and waiting. Little Alberto's color returned to normal even as he slept. He was resting quietly. She reached down and took the boy's hand and held it loosely in her own. She remained in the rocking chair by the boy's bed for hours, watching over him, prepared to protect him not only now but for as long as needed.

Made in the USA
Lexington, KY
25 February 2012